Lights, Camera, BABY!

MORGANA BEVAN

<u>Tropes:</u>

Accidental pregnancy, one night stand gone wrong, fish out of water, opposites attract, forced proximity, Hollywood romance

<u>Content Warnings:</u>

Unplanned pregnancy, family trauma, abandonment issues, body image issues, breeding kink.

<u>British English</u>

To all my American readers, I'm a **British** author and this book is written in **British English**. There are variations in the language between the US and British English. That means some words are spelt differently. Hell, we speak differently.

Happy Reading!

Morgana x

Lights, Camera, BABY!

MORGANA BEVAN

CHAPTER ONE

EMMA

"*J*ust a few hundred more to go." I wiped the sweat from my brow, cursing under my breath as I fumbled with yet another string of lights. The banquet hall buzzed with activity, but I felt oddly alone.

My arms ached, and my fingers were stiff from handling the delicate glass bulbs. But I couldn't stop now. Abi wanted a picture-perfect backdrop for her wedding photos, and I'd give it to her.

If I pulled this off, it could catapult my business to the next level. No pressure, right?

At least you're still breathing.

I grimaced, both saddened and grateful for the reality check.

Life had rewarded my parents for their hard work with an early death. I'd been only nine and barely aware of what death meant. If my mother's American sister hadn't agreed to take me in, I would have ended up in foster care in the UK.

Aunt Ginny had moved me across the pond and committed

to raising me. But she had also torn me away from my friends and the only home I'd ever known. Then she'd all but abandoned me to deal with the culture shock.

I tried not to shit on my aunt, but the older I got the harder it became to ignore the bitterness. The last thing she'd wanted was to be responsible for a nine-year-old.

I shook my head, dispelling the gloomy thoughts. This was nothing compared to that time of my life. I could handle a few measly light bulbs. I could handle my assistant quitting. I could pull off a wedding that had a guest list overloaded with Hollywood royalty all by myself.

I closed my eyes for a moment, taking a deep breath. The faint scent of fresh flowers mingled with the crisp, freshly laundered linen tablecloths, reminding me of the beauty I was working to create.

While I strung the lights through the wire frame for Abi's photo op station, I ran through my mental checklist, ticking off backup plans for every possible disaster. It calmed me, knowing I'd prepared for the worst.

"Watch it!" a waiter yelped.

"Sorry, sorry," a male voice mumbled.

I turned, nearly losing my balance on the ladder. Charlie Delacroix, Finn McCarthy's agent, weaved through the room, his eyes glued to his phone while staff dodged around him. I recognised him instantly from the photo binder I'd compiled of all five hundred guests. It was my job to know everyone, to be prepared for any eventuality. What I hadn't prepared for was how devastatingly handsome he'd be in person.

His dark hair was artfully tousled, and his jawline could cut glass. The fitted suit he wore did nothing to hide his athletic build. But it was his eyes that caught me off guard – a gorgeous hazel that seemed to see right through me. I became extremely aware of my sweaty, dishevelled state.

His phone rang and he answered it with a hard jab. "No,

absolutely not," he barked, drawing curious glances from the staff bustling around him.

He seemed oblivious to the chaos he was creating — a chair scraped loudly as he bumped it with his hip, a flower arrangement wobbled when he brushed past it. It was like watching a bull in a china shop, if the bull was wearing an expensive suit and completely engrossed in a heated phone conversation.

He made it next to impossible for me not to eavesdrop. Somehow I continued to string up lights, but my curiosity had definitely gotten the better of me. Less than half my attention remained on the display.

"Tell Vanessa she needs to issue a statement now, before this gets out of hand." He ran a hand through his hair.

I admired the way his rolled-up sleeves revealed tanned, muscular forearms. My eyes trailed down his body, taking in the broad shoulders that tapered to a trim waist. The way he moved exuded confidence, every gesture purposeful and commanding.

What would it be like to have those strong hands on me, to be the focus of that intense gaze? I shivered at the idea of it.

It's clearly been too long since you've gotten laid if bare forearms are making you hot and bothered.

I forced my attention back to the task at hand, trying to ignore the way his presence seemed to electrify the air around him.

"I don't care if she's in the middle of a shoot," Charlie continued, his voice rising. "If we don't get ahead of this story, it'll be all over the tabloids by morning."

Another pause and my blood pressure rose almost in sympathy.

"Look, just get her on the phone. Tell her it's about the photos. She'll know what I'm talking about." He sighed. "And for the love of god, make sure she doesn't post anything on social media until we've crafted a proper response."

"Alright, call me back as soon as you've spoken to her," Charlie said, his tone softening slightly. "And hey, thanks for handling this. I know it's early."

He ended his call but in his distraction, he backed right into my champagne-flute pyramid. It teetered for a heart-stopping moment before crashing to the ground in a cacophony of shattering glass.

"Shit!" He spun around, his eyes wide with horror as he took in the destruction at his feet.

"Are you kidding me?" I scrambled down the ladder. "Do you have any idea how long that took to set up?"

His shock gave way to contrition as he met my gaze. "I'm so sorry. I was completely distracted. I didn't even see the display there."

"Clearly," I muttered, surveying the damage. Shards of crystal glittered on the floor, reflecting the light from the bulbs I'd just hung. It was almost beautiful, in a disastrous sort of way.

A waiter appeared with a dustpan and brush, but Charlie intercepted him, taking the cleaning supplies. "Let me help you fix this." He knelt to sweep up the broken glass.

"No, it's fine." I tried to take the brush from him, but he dodged me. "I can handle it."

He flashed me a smile that made my knees weak, despite my irritation. "Come on, it's just as much my problem as yours. Besides," his voice dropped to a conspiratorial whisper, "I'm guessing you've got about a million other things to do before the guests start arriving tonight. You shouldn't have to deal with my clumsiness on top of everything else."

I hesitated, torn between my need for control and the unexpected allure of his offer.

In the end, I relented with a sigh. "Fine. But be careful with the unbroken glasses. We'll need every single one we can salvage."

He nodded. "You got it. I really am sorry about this." He

gestured at the mess around us with an apologetic smile. "I promise I'm not usually such a bull in a china shop."

Despite my irritation, the corner of my mouth twitched upward. "Well, I suppose accidents happen." I knelt down to begin sweeping up the smaller shards. "Even to Hollywood hotshots like yourself."

Charlie chuckled, the sound surprisingly warm and genuine. "Hollywood hotshot? Is that how you see me, Ms Sullivan?"

"Emma, please." I glanced up at him almost against my will. There was something magnetic about this man, it made me helpless to resist.

"Emma." His lips quirked and I almost sighed at the sight.

"I'm just calling it like I see it. Big-time agent, wandering aimlessly without looking where he's going and barking orders into his phone? Seems pretty hotshot to me."

Like someone used to cleaning up other people's messes while his assistants cleaned up his.

He had the grace to look slightly embarrassed. "I promise I'm not always on the phone dealing with crises. Just most of the time."

I raised an eyebrow, carefully placing a larger piece of crystal into the pan. "Sounds thrilling. Is that why you decided to liven things up by destroying my champagne tower?"

Charlie laughed outright at that. "You caught me. I just couldn't resist your impeccably stacked glassware. It was crying out to be toppled."

Despite myself, a smile tugged at my lips. There was something disarmingly charming about his self-deprecating humour.

"Well, Mr Delacroix." I stood, holding the dustpan full of broken glass between us like a shield. "Next time you feel the urge to destroy wedding decorations, maybe give a girl some warning first? Give me a chance to set up a decoy."

"I'll keep that in mind." He smiled before taking the

dustpan from me to dispose of the broken glass. "And please, call me Charlie."

As he walked away to empty it, I couldn't tear my eyes away from him, a confusing array of emotion swirled inside me. Annoyance at the mess he'd caused, certainly, but also a spark of interest I hadn't felt in far too long.

I shook my head, trying to clear it of these dangerous thoughts. I was here to work, not to get starry-eyed over some handsome Hollywood agent. But as Charlie returned, flashing me another apologetic smile, I had a feeling this evening was about to get a lot more interesting than I'd planned.

The next few hours passed in a blur of final preparations. I positioned myself near the back of the room, clipboard in hand, ready to tackle any last-minute issues. As the space filled with well-dressed guests, their excited chatter rising above the soft background music, I allowed myself a moment of pride. Despite the setbacks, everything was coming together beautifully.

"You've outdone yourself, Em."

I turned at the sound of my name and a familiar voice, coming face to face with a familiar redhead. "Eva! Oh my god, it's been forever!"

Eva pulled me into a tight hug. "I can't believe it! When I introduced you to Abi, I knew you'd do an amazing job, but this is beyond anything I could have imagined."

I grinned, genuinely happy to see a friendly face. "I know I've said it before, but I can't thank you enough." I shook my head, smiling while gratitude flooded me. "I can barely comprehend the opportunities this wedding could bring me and it's all thanks to you."

Eva waved me off with a laugh. "Please, I knew you'd be the best in the business. Abi's lucky to have you."

Our conversation was interrupted by the arrival of more guests. Eva wrapped a stunning pixie-haired brunette in a warm hug. Ros Butler, one of Abi's best friends and second bridesmaid.

Ros took one look at the place and whistled. "Jesus, girl. Did you leave any flowers in the ground?"

"Oh please, if I'd done any less, I'd be failing at my job. But I can't take credit for this colour explosion. The restaurant staff are the real MVPs here."

Eva's jaw dropped as she took in the lush greenery and vibrant blooms. "Wait, you didn't do this yourself? It looks exactly like the sketches you showed Abi!"

"I know, right?" I smirked, unable to keep the pride from my voice. "Gave them the plans last week, ordered the flowers, and they nailed it without me hovering. Though I'd be lying if I said I didn't check everything twice when I got here. Maybe three times."

I'd planned to be here to supervise but with my assistant quitting, I'd been forced to let go.

Ros whistled again, clearly impressed. "Well, if this is what you accomplish without breaking a sweat, I can't wait to see what magic you've worked for tomorrow."

I basked in their praise for a moment.

As we chatted, more guests poured in, filling the room with that pre-wedding buzz of excitement and nerves. I spotted familiar faces from countless planning sessions — Finn's rowdy groomsmen and their partners, his family who had made the long trip from Ireland, various close celebrity friends.

Abi and Eva had also lost their parents at a very young age, one of the reasons Eva and I bonded in the beginning. Their list of invitees might have been the shortest I'd ever handled in my career.

I'd never considered what my wedding guest list would look like, but it would be just as short.

I claimed my spot at a tiny table near the back as dinner

kicked off. Perfect vantage point to spy on — I mean, oversee — everything. The gentle clink of cutlery mingled with warm laughter, creating that perfect ambiance I'd been stressing over for weeks. I allowed myself to relax a fraction.

When speech time rolled around, I had my clipboard at the ready. You never knew when someone might need an emergency tissue or a gentle nudge off stage.

One of Finn's best men, Nathan Logan, started things off with an on set story that had me snorting into my water. Next, Eva delivered a tear-jerker that threatened my perfectly applied mascara.

Then Charlie stood up. I leaned forward in my seat as he cleared his throat.

"For those who don't know me, I'm Charlie Delacroix, Finn's agent and self-proclaimed cupid," he began, earning chuckles from the crowd. "Now, I can't take full credit for the magic that is Finn and Abi, but I will say this — I knew from the moment I signed Finn up for 'Married Blind' that he'd find his perfect match. Or at least some quality entertainment for the rest of us."

Finn's voice cut through the laughter. "Oh, come on. That's not how it happened and you know it!"

Charlie's grin only widened. "Ah, but it is, my friend. Let me paint you all a picture." He turned back to the crowd, his eyes twinkling with mischief. "One where our dear Finn got caught in a compromising position with a certain director's daughter in a very public restroom."

"We talked about this, Charlie!" Finn shouted as the room hooted and laughed. Abi took his hand, holding him down when he tried to stand up.

Unless you lived under a rock, there was no way to miss that scandal and the resulting headlines. Finn had played the field and graced the tabloids frequently before that instance, but he'd never come so close to burning his career before.

"What? I'm not naming names." Charlie cast an innocent

glance around the room, but he couldn't hold back the tiny smirk quirking one corner of his lips. "Anyway, our star's options were either 'Married Blind' or a long, lonely stint in direct-to-streaming purgatory. And boy, did he fight me on it."

Finn groaned, burying his face in his hands as the room erupted in laughter. I laughed along despite my best efforts to maintain professional detachment.

"But here's the thing about fate — sometimes it has a way of sneaking up on you when you least expect it. Finn went into that show expecting to find a gold-digger looking for her fifteen minutes of fame. Instead, he found Abi."

"I did not think that!" Finn interjected, looking horrified.

Abi patted his arm consolingly. "It's okay. I thought you were a self-absorbed pretty boy, so we're even."

More laughter rippled through the room as Charlie nodded sagely. "See? A match made in reality TV heaven. I've known Finn for years, and I've never seen him as blindsided — pun absolutely intended — as he was when he realised he was actually falling for his 'TV wife'."

"That's... actually true." Finn's expression softened as he looked at Abi.

"It just goes to show, sometimes the best things in life come from the most unlikely places." Charlie scanned the room, briefly catching my eye.

For a moment, the rest of the room faded away, and it was just us, sharing a silent acknowledgment of... something.

He winked and then lifted his glass, his eyes gleaming with genuine warmth. "To Finn and Abi — proof that love can bloom even in the harshest of lights. May you always remember that sometimes the best decisions are the ones you're pushed into making. Especially if I'm the one doing the pushing."

Everyone laughed, and Abi finally let Finn up to pull Charlie into one of those obligatory man-hugs.

As the speeches continued, my gaze kept returning to the

dark-haired Canadian, much to my annoyance. The way he laughed wholeheartedly at the jokes, the attentive tilt of his head as he listened to the emotional moments, it all drew me to him. This was a far cry from the distracted bull in a china shop who had decimated my champagne tower earlier.

By the time dinner wound down and guests began to mingle, my perception of Charlie had shifted dramatically.

The brash Hollywood agent had been replaced by a man who clearly valued friendship and love, who took genuine joy in the happiness of others. It was… attractive, in a way I hadn't expected and wasn't entirely comfortable with.

You're not here to ogle the guests, no matter how well they fill out a suit.

I threw all of my attention into last-minute checks and staff coordination. Anything I could possibly do to distract myself.

But I couldn't stop stealing glances at Charlie as he worked the room, mingling with guests, all easy charm and sharing laughs with the happy couple.

At one point, our eyes met again across the crowded space. He flashed me a smile that made my heart skip a beat, and I quickly looked away, cursing the blush burning up my neck.

But as I watched him chat animatedly with Finn's mother, making the woman laugh with delight, I knew I was in trouble. Our brief encounters had left more of an impression than I cared to admit, and despite my best efforts to remain professional, a part of me was looking forward to seeing more of Charlie at tomorrow's wedding.

CHAPTER TWO

CHARLIE

I couldn't pull my mind out of the gutter.

It had been years since anyone had caught my attention. Why did that have to change at Finn McCarthy's wedding? I was meant to be on my best behaviour. And while I was on a whining spree, why did it have to be a woman who lived four thousand fucking kilometres away? The woman lived closer to my mother in Ontario than me, for fuck's sake.

"You alright there?" Finn clapped me on the shoulder, startling me. "No matter how talented you think you are, you can't turn whiskey into gold, so stop staring at the bleeding glass."

A perpetual grin always claimed his lips these days. Ever since he'd admitted his feelings for Abi. The man's reputation had done a complete one-eighty because of that woman and I'd be eternally grateful.

"I'm fine." I forced a smile. "Just taking a breather from all the schmoozing. How about you? Happy to have finally locked down the girl of your dreams without a million cameras recording every move?"

His gaze drifted across the room to where Abi stood, laughing with a group of guests. Her red hair caught the light, making it look like fire. "Happier than a pig in shite, mate. She's everything I never knew I needed."

"Well, don't go getting all sappy on me now." I clapped him on the back, biting back a wince at the ache of loneliness chewing at my insides. "Just because you've turned over a new leaf — for the better, I might add — doesn't mean the rest of us don't have reputations to uphold. Can't have people thinking I represent lovesick fools."

Finn snorted. "Too late for that. Now come on, stop being such a wet blanket and enjoy the party. It's not every day your best client gets hitched."

I opened my mouth to argue — he had in fact gotten hitched nine months ago — but movement across the room caught my eye. Emma stepped through the door, clipboard in hand, looking like a vision in a deep blue dress that hugged every curve. Her dark hair was swept into an elegant updo, a few tendrils escaping to frame her face. The need to drag my fingers through it gripped me.

Fuck me sideways. The woman got more beautiful every time I saw her.

Before I knew what I was doing, I was making my way across the room. Finn called after me, but his voice faded into the background noise of the reception. Emma glanced up as I approached, her expression guarded. Those eyes that had haunted me all damn day were even more striking up close — a warm brown flecked with gold.

"Mr Delacroix. Come to destroy any more of my hard work?"

I winced, remembering the champagne tower fiasco from yesterday. "About that... I wanted to apologise again. Properly this time, without the distraction of shattered glass everywhere."

Her brow arched, but I couldn't miss the hint of a smile tugging at the corner of her lips. "I'm listening."

"I'm sorry for being a complete klutz and ruining your display," I said, meeting her gaze. "And for being distracted and not watching where I was going. The wedding is absolutely beautiful. You've done an incredible job."

Emma tucked a strand of hair behind her ear. "Thank you. That's... actually very sweet of you to say."

"Sweet? Me?" I placed a hand over my heart in mock offence. "I'll have you know I'm a ruthless Hollywood hotshot. We don't do sweet."

She laughed, and the sound did funny things to my insides. "Well, in that case, I suppose we'll have to start over. Emma Sullivan, Abi and Finn's wedding planner."

Which I'd known all along, of course. It was my job to know. "Charlie Delacroix, agent and occasional bull in a china shop." I took her offered hand. Her skin was soft against mine. The need to hold on and never let go struck me. "But please, call me Charlie."

She stared at me, her teeth teasing her lower lip for a moment while she considered me. If it were possible for my heart to stop beating, it would have.

"Alright," she finally said, her voice carrying a hint of amusement. "I suppose I can give you a second chance."

"You won't regret it, I promise. Can I buy you a drink to seal the deal?"

Emma glanced at her clipboard, then back at me. "I really shouldn't. I'm working, after all."

"Come on, one drink." It surprised me how much I wanted her to say yes. "I'm sure the bride and groom would insist their hardworking planner take a moment to enjoy the fruits of her labour."

She hesitated, and I held my breath. What was wrong with me? I never got this worked up over a woman, especially one

I'd just met. But something about her had me off-balance in the best possible way.

"Oh, alright." She set her clipboard down on a table tucked into an alcove and smiled at me. "But just one."

I beamed, feeling ridiculously victorious. "Excellent choice. What's your poison?"

"Surprise me."

I led her to the bar, hyper-aware of her presence beside me. "Two gin and tonics, please. With a twist of lime."

Emma raised an eyebrow. "Gin and tonic, huh? Trying to impress me with your sophisticated tastes?"

Instead, I laughed. "Nah, just figured you'd appreciate a classic. Plus, it's clear — less chance of ruining that gorgeous dress if I have another clumsy moment."

A blush crept up her cheeks, and pure satisfaction rushed through me.

"What's the craziest request you've ever gotten from a client?" I asked after we collected our drinks.

I'd expected her to say the champagne centrepiece. Something I could hold over Finn's head at a later date. Instead, she told me about a bride who wanted doves released at the exact moment of her first kiss. As ridiculous as it was, I never wanted her to stop talking about those bloody birds. She could have read the dictionary to me and I would have hung on her every word. Absorbed in the way her eyes lit up as she spoke, her hands moving animatedly. Captivated.

Before I knew it, half an hour had passed. Our glasses were long gone and the waitstaff had started to file into the banquet hall.

"Oh god." Emma glanced at her watch. "I can't believe I've been neglecting my duties for so long. I should really get back to work."

Before I could stop her, she rushed away, slipping through my fingers in more ways than one.

*A*s guests took their seats for dinner, I made my way to my assigned table. My heart did a little flip when I spotted Emma already seated, looking slightly flustered as she eyed me and arranged her napkin on her lap.

"Well, well," I said as I slid into the chair next to her. "Fancy meeting you here."

She rolled her eyes, but I caught the smile she tried to hide. "You know, for someone who claims to be ruthless, you're not very good at playing it cool."

I clutched my chest in mock pain. "Hit a man where it hurts, why don't you?"

"Charlie!" a familiar voice called out before she could respond. "It's been too long."

Aria Campbell — a country singer whose agent also coerced her into joining *Married Blind* last year — stopped at our table with her husband in tow. Showtime.

"Lovely to see you again." I stood and held out my hand to shake hers across the table, being extra careful not to knock over Emma's centrepiece. "How's the new album coming along?"

She beamed, her red painted lips curling up. "It's going wonderfully, thank you for asking. We're hoping to wrap up recording next month."

Her jet black hair hung in waves above her shoulders, shorter than the last time I'd seen her. She wore a gold figure hugging dress that might have drawn my eye before yesterday. Now, no one could compete with Emma in my mind. In any case, Aria looked good tucked into Kyle's side, his six-foot-five frame dwarfing her five-foot-nine. She probably felt short for the first time in her life.

"Fantastic news." I grinned, shaking Kyle's hand. "Good to see you, man. Keeping this one out of trouble?"

He chuckled. "Tack on a 'trying'. You know no one stops Aria when she's on a roll."

"I shouldn't be surprised to see you. Even Nicole is wandering around here somewhere."

"Now that did surprise me." Aria took the seat Kyle pulled out for her and a waiter rushed over to pour her a glass of wine. "As far as I knew, no one heard from her after filming ended, but I'm glad she's here. I hope it means she's healed enough that we don't remind her of bad times."

The three of us glanced towards the blonde sitting three tables away from us with Toronto's newest hockey player and his wife. The man next to her had his hand resting on the back of her chair and she kept throwing him dreamy smiles when he wasn't looking.

"That does look promising."

The rest of our table mates joined us, and we cut the gossip short. Just because we knew the behind-the-scenes details of the legal nightmare *Married Blind* turned into didn't mean others needed to.

Instead, I introduced them all to Emma. She threw me a little smirk that meant who knows what and fell straight into easy conversation with the pink-haired woman next to her, Mona Baines, Shaun Martin's wife and now one of Abi's best friends.

As the conversation flowed around the table, I found myself torn between playing the role of charming agent and wanting to focus solely on Emma. I'd gotten so caught up in the familiar routine of working the room that the first course was served before I could give her all of my attention again.

I leaned in close, keeping my voice low. "Sorry about that. Old habits die hard, I guess."

She quirked a brow at me. "Showing off for the celebrities."

"Never. Although…" I bit my lip as I studied her. "I have to admit, it's kind of fun watching you try not to look impressed."

She rolled her eyes, but I caught the hint of a smile. "Please. I don't look starstruck."

I smirked. "Yes, you do."

"Really?" Her eyes widened at my nod. "Damn. I even practised while I prepared my binder."

"Your binder?"

"Don't make it sound weird. I needed to memorise every guest in case of issues."

One sentence, and I knew everything I needed to know about her work ethic. I shouldn't have been surprised after seeing her in action yesterday and this morning. My assistant did something similar, meticulously preparing fact files of all the important people in Hollywood and updating them every time I had to attend an event.

Wait.

"If you knew what everyone looked like and where they were sitting, why did you look so shocked to find me at your table?"

She blushed. "I, uh... I wasn't actually supposed to be eating." She picked up the napkin and started twisting it almost unconsciously. "There were some missing guests, and Abi insisted I take one of the empty seats. She didn't tell me which table until just before, and she'd stolen my binder. I couldn't remember who was supposed to be here until you turned up."

I laughed; the image of Abi strong-arming her own wedding planner into enjoying the party was just too perfect. And very Abigail McCarthy. The woman had been a force of nature for as long as I'd known her.

I turned in my seat, catching Abi's eye at the head table. She grinned and raised her glass. I lifted mine in return, mouthing a silent 'thank you.'

Turning back to Emma, I smiled. "Well, I for one am glad you're here. It would've been a shame to miss out on your company."

She rolled her eyes, but I caught a hint of her amusement. "Smooth talker."

"I try," I said with a wink. "So, tell me more about wedding planning. I bet you've got some stories that could rival even my craziest Hollywood tales."

She laughed, her eyes lighting up. "Oh, you have no idea. Ever had to wrangle a runaway groom who got cold feet an hour before the ceremony?"

"Getting Finn on *Married Blind* felt that way sometimes, but no." I leaned in, intrigued. "What happened?"

"Let's just say it involved a fire escape, a very determined mother-in-law, and me sprinting three blocks in heels."

We traded stories back and forth, laughing over the absurdities we'd both encountered in our respective industries. I was captivated before, but after an hour listening to her and holding her complete attention, I was an utter goner.

"… and then the best man realised he'd left the rings in the taxi," Emma was saying, her eyes sparkling with mirth.

I shook my head in disbelief. "What did you do?"

"I might have bribed a random stranger on a motorbike to chase down the cab."

"Did it work?"

She grinned triumphantly, her brown eyes sparkling. "Got the rings back with two minutes to spare."

"Impressive." I tapped my glass against hers. "I'll have to remember to call you next time one of my clients has a meltdown before a premiere."

The words hung in the air between us, laden with possibility. Our gazes clashed and the air evaporated, closing in and stealing away the chatter surrounding us. I became hyper-aware of how close we were sitting.

A lump formed in my throat. Nerves? Desire? I reached for the salt shaker, trying to distract myself before I did something that would have Finn teasing me for weeks.

My hand brushed against hers, and I swear electricity

jolted through us. Emma's breath caught, and for a moment, we both froze, trapped in each other's gazes.

The clinking of a glass broke the spell, signalling the start of the speeches. I reluctantly pulled back, but I couldn't shake the feeling that something had shifted between us. I turned my attention to the front of the room, hoping it would lessen the pull and give me a shot of self-control. Of course it would never be that easy. I was acutely aware of her presence beside me, the warmth of her leg pressed against mine under the table.

ten minutes later, a waiter appeared at my elbow, breaking the moment. "Mr Delacroix? There's a call for you at the front desk. They say it's urgent."

I sighed and threw Emma an apologetic smile. It was only half practised. I was sorry to leave her, but as much as I enjoyed her company, any longer and I'd embarrass myself.

"Duty calls, I'm afraid." Standing, I tapped my suit pockets for my phone. "Save me a dance?"

She smiled, a mix of amusement and something else I couldn't quite place in her eyes. "We'll see. I do have a job to do here, you know."

When I finally made it back to the reception, the dance floor was in full swing. The Edison bulbs cast a warm glow over the room, creating an almost dreamlike atmosphere. I scanned the crowd, my heart sinking when I didn't immediately spot Emma.

But then I saw her, clipboard back in hand, directing a group of waiters with the precision of a military commander as they circulated with champagne, her brow furrowed in concentration. I wandered over to her, trying to be casual.

"You know, there's a law against all work and no play at weddings, right?"

Emma jumped slightly, then turned to face me with a wry smile. "Is that so? And let me guess, you're here to enforce it?"

"Well, someone's got to." I held out my hand. "Come on, darling. Five minutes without thinking about work. Doctor's orders."

She hesitated, glancing around at the bustling reception. "I don't know... my assistant quit yesterday, and there's still so much to do..."

"Five minutes won't hurt you." I wiggled my fingers. "The world won't end if you take a little break. Promise."

She sighed, but a smile tugged at her lips as she set down her clipboard. "Fine. But just one dance, and then I really do need to get back to work."

I grinned triumphantly, leading her out onto the dance floor just as a slow song started to play. How's that for perfect timing?

As we swayed to the music, I pulled her closer, my hand resting on the small of her back. She fit against me perfectly, like two puzzle pieces clicking into place. The scent of her perfume enveloped me, and I revelled in the warmth of her body pressed against mine.

I ducked my head, my lips close to her ear. "You know, if I didn't know any better, I'd say you were put on this earth to test my resolve. How am I supposed to focus on anything else when you're around?"

She shivered slightly, and when she pulled back to look at me, her cheeks were flushed. "Smooth. Does that line usually work for you?" Her tone was teasing despite the heat in her gaze. "I must admit, I'm a little disappointed. I thought you'd be more creative."

I laughed, spinning her out and then pulling her back in. "What can I say? You've got me all turned around. I'll have to up my game if I want to impress you, eh?"

"Maybe you already have," Emma said softly, her brown eyes meeting mine with an intensity that took my breath away.

The song ended far too soon, and I reluctantly let her slip back into the crowd with claims of checking on the cake cutting. But throughout the rest of the night, I found my gaze continually drawn to her. The way she moved through the room with effortless grace, the sound of her laughter carrying across the space, the flash of her smile as she caught me looking... it was intoxicating.

Whatever was happening between us, I knew one thing for certain: I didn't want this night to end.

CHAPTER THREE

EMMA

*A*s the last of the guests finally trickled out, I let out a long breath, allowing myself to feel the bone-deep exhaustion that had been threatening to overtake me all evening. I rolled my shoulders, trying to ease the tension that had built up over the course of the day. I glanced around the room, taking in the wilting flowers and the flickering candles. The wedding had been a resounding success, but the magic of the day was fading, leaving behind a bittersweet ache.

Abi and Finn had snuck out hours ago, lost in newlywed bliss. I couldn't blame them — if I had someone looking at me the way Finn looked at Abi, I'd want to be alone with them too.

Hell, only professionalism had stopped me from ducking out myself. With Charlie throwing me suggestive glances all night and making it his mission to get me hot and bothered, I might have self-combusted.

I scanned the room, searching for the determined Canadian. He'd almost stuck to me with more efficiency than my shadow tonight, encouraging me to enjoy the night.

I was just about to start my final walk-through when a warm body stopped behind me and a familiar voice sounded close to my ear.

"Quite the party."

Turning, I almost bumped into Charlie's chest. He took a step back, giving me space, but his intense, hazel gaze never left mine. At some point during the night, he'd loosened his tie and destroyed the careful styling of his hair. It stood on end in some places, almost artful despite the disarray. He looked like he'd just had a good roll in bed, all relaxed charm and smouldering eyes.

Inexplicable jealousy clenched in my gut, hot and angry.

"I thought you'd left with the rest of the guests." I hoped my voice didn't betray the little flip my stomach did at the sight of him.

"And miss the chance to steal more of your time? Not a chance." His lips curved into a slow smile that did far too much for my sex-starved body.

I raised a brow, trying to maintain my composure.

Do not throw yourself at the man.

"Oh? And what makes you think I have any time to spare?"

He chuckled, the sound low and warm. "Considering the bride and groom disappeared hours ago, and the last guest just stumbled out the door, I'd say your official duties are over." He took a step closer, backing me into the wall while his voice dropped to a husky whisper. "Unless, of course, you have some pressing engagement elsewhere?"

My heart rate kicked up a notch. Was he really suggesting what I thought he was? I studied him, taking in the way he carried himself, the breadth of his shoulders under that perfectly tailored suit, the intensity in his dark eyes.

He's gorgeous.

I became acutely aware of how long it had been since I'd been with someone. How long since I'd felt desired, wanted.

I'd been so focused on my career, pouring every ounce of energy into building my business, that dating had fallen by the wayside.

You could have this, a little voice in my head whispered. *Just for tonight.*

I bit my lip, considering. It was crazy, right? I didn't do one-night stands. But Charlie... was looking at me like I was the only woman in the world.

"You're right," I said, surprised by the husky quality of my voice. "My duties are over."

His eyes darkened, and he took another step closer. A few scant inches separated us and his body heat blanketed me. "In that case," he murmured, "how would you feel about extending this evening? Just you and me?"

Meeting his gaze head-on, I asked: "What did you have in mind?"

"Well, if we didn't live four thousand miles apart, I'd suggest dinner and hopefully many more dates to follow." His smile widened, becoming almost predatory. "But I'd be terrible at a long distance relationship. I do happen to have a very nice hotel room not far from here. Room service, king-size bed, spectacular view of the city..." He trailed off, letting the implication hang in the air between us.

I swallowed hard, my mind racing. He was right, if he lived closer, I would have found the time to date him. I'd never experienced such strong chemistry before and the thought of losing this in the morning saddened me.

But could I handle just one night with him?

It was crazy. Reckless. Totally unlike me.

And yet...

"Just tonight?"

Charlie nodded, his demeanour serious despite the heat in his eyes. "One night. No expectations. No tomorrow." He grimaced. "Though I really wish there could be a tomorrow."

Screw it.

I took a deep breath, feeling a mix of excitement and nerves swirling in my stomach.

"Okay."

The word was a barely audible exhale, but it was enough. Charlie's eyes flashed with heat as he took my hand, lacing our fingers together.

His grin was positively wicked as he pulled me from the banquet room.

The lobby was mercifully empty as we crossed it, save for a lone security guard who nodded politely as we passed. I kept expecting someone to stop us, to ask where we were going or why we were going upstairs together. But no one did.

When we reached the elevators, Charlie pressed the call button and the doors slid open immediately. He gestured for me to enter first, his hand coming to rest on the small of my back as he followed me in. The touch, even through the fabric of my dress, sent a jolt of electricity through me.

As soon as the doors closed, he turned to me, his gaze dark with desire, lingering on my face, drifting down to my lips, before locking with mine. My breath caught at the intensity.

"Last chance to back out."

But I didn't want to. For once in my life, I didn't want to overthink or over analyse. I wanted to feel, to experience, to live in the moment. Before I could think better, my fingers curled in his shirt and I tugged him towards me. Instead of answering, I went up on my toes and pressed my lips against his.

He responded instantly, wrapping his arms around me, holding me tight against his chest while his lips devoured me. I might have started it, but he finished it.

His lips were soft but insistent, moving against mine with a hunger that made me pant. I gasped, and he took the opportunity to deepen the kiss, his tongue sliding against mine in a way that made my knees weak.

I wrapped my arms around his neck, pulling him closer as the elevator began its ascent. Each floor that passed was marked by a soft ding, but I barely noticed, lost as I was in the sensation of his mouth on mine, his hands roaming my back, pulling me flush against him.

When we finally broke apart, we were both breathing heavily. Charlie rested his forehead against mine, his eyes closed.

"Jesus," he muttered. "You're perfect."

I couldn't help the little laugh that escaped me. "You hardly know me."

I ran my fingers through the hair at the nape of his neck and he opened his eyes, fixing me with a look that made heat pool in my belly.

"Oh, darling," he said, his voice low and full of promise, "by the time I'm done with you, I'll know you very intimately."

The elevator dinged once more, and the doors slid open. We broke apart, both of us a little dazed. He took my hand, lacing our fingers together, his grip tight, almost as if he expected me to disappear. Heart pounding, I let him guide me through the halls. When we reached his door, he fumbled with the key card for a moment before finally getting it open. He stood back, allowing me to enter first.

The room was beautiful — spacious and elegant, with floor-to-ceiling windows offering the promised breath taking view of the city. But I had seconds to take it in before Charlie pulled me back into his arms.

This kiss was different from the one in the elevator. It was slower, deeper, filled with a promise of things to come. His hands skimmed down my sides, coming to rest on my hips as he backed me into the wall.

"You have no idea," he murmured against my lips, "how hard it's been to keep my hands off you all night."

I smiled, nipping at his lower lip. "Show me."

A low growl escaped him, and his hands were everywhere — in my hair, caressing my face, skimming down my neck. He caught the zipper of my dress and paused, his eyes meeting mine in a silent question.

I nodded, and he slowly lowered the zipper, his fingers trailing down my spine as he did so. The dress pooled at my feet, leaving me in nothing but my lingerie and heels.

Charlie took a step back, his eyes roaming over my body with undisguised appreciation.

I refused to let my insecurities take over. Instead, I reached for him, my fingers working at the buttons of his shirt.

"Your turn," I said, my voice huskier than I'd ever heard it.

He grinned, shrugging out of his jacket and helping me with the buttons. Soon, his shirt joined my dress on the floor, and I took a moment to appreciate the view. He was all lean muscle and tanned skin, with just the right amount of chest hair. I ran my hands over his pecs, revelling in the way his muscles jumped under my touch.

"Like what you see?" he asked, a hint of amusement in his voice.

I looked up at him through my lashes. "Very much."

His eyes darkened, and then he was kissing me again, harder this time, more urgent. His hands found my thighs and he lifted me easily, pressing me back against the wall as I wrapped my legs around his waist.

The feel of his skin against mine was intoxicating. I ran my nails down his back, drawing a low moan from him. In response, he ground his hips against mine, letting me feel just how much he wanted me.

"Bed," I gasped, breaking away from the kiss. "Now."

Charlie didn't need to be told twice. He carried me to the king-size bed, laying me down gently on the edge before dropping to his knees and tugging my thighs open. I stared down at him, his dark eyes locked on mine as his hands started their exploration.

"Were you this wet during the reception?" He brushed his thumb across my damp panties and I jolted. He grinned up at me, the picture of wicked delight.

He did it again and again, circling my clit through the fabric, watching me with eagle eyes for the slightest reaction. My throat closed up and my eyelids began to flutter.

He's barely fucking touched you.

It had been a while, okay?

"Answer me, Emma." He teased the edge of the material, his touch light but my body didn't care. Heat gushed through me.

I swallowed. "Maybe."

"Maybe what?"

"Maybe I was wet." I panted as his fingers dipped into my panties, brushing against my clit before retreating. I let out a soft cry.

He hummed in approval, his gaze fixed on my pussy. "Who made you wet?"

"You did."

"Good girl."

In one swift move, he hooked my panties and dragged them off me. A satisfied light entered his eyes as he stared at my bare pussy, even as his shoulders tensed. His fingers danced along my inner thighs, teasing, tracing, promising, but he shied away from where I desperately needed him with an amused sort of determination.

"Are you trying to drive me crazy?"

"Maybe," he said, his grin growing wider. "Or maybe I just like hearing you gasp."

Then he moved his touch higher, higher, until he brushed against my clit again. I gasped as he wanted, my hips bucking involuntarily. He chuckled, the sound vibrating against my sensitive skin.

"Easy, darling," Charlie murmured, his voice low and full of promise. "We've got all night."

He continued to tease me, his touch light and playful, making me crave more while he traced intricate patterns on my skin. He kissed my inner thighs, his lips soft and warm while the stubble on his jaw scraped deliciously against me

And then, he shifted, his hands moving up to my hips as he leaned in, his breath hot before his mouth replaced his fingers and his tongue flicked out, finding the spot that made me moan.

"Please," I whispered, when he went no further, my voice filled with need.

He chuckled. "Such a polite way to beg."

But he didn't make me wait any longer. He swirled his tongue against my clit, his fingers pressing against my entrance, pleasure winding tighter and tighter inside of me. I gripped the sheets, my body writhing under his skilled touch. He was relentless, his hands and mouth working together, driving me towards the edge.

"You taste incredible." He lapped at me once more before he added, "But I want more."

Two fingers pressed against my entrance, pushing inside in a slow, steady rhythm. He curled them upwards, hitting that magical spot that made my toes curl. I moaned, my hips bucking against his hand as he continued to work me with his mouth and fingers.

The pressure built, waves of sensation crashing over me as he brought me closer and closer to the edge. His fingers moved faster, his tongue more insistent, until I could barely contain myself.

"Fuck," I whispered, my voice filled with need. "I'm close."

Charlie didn't stop, his focus unyielding as his lips clamped down on my clit, suckling hard and forcing me over the edge. My body convulsed with pleasure as I came, the orgasm washing over me and leaving behind a shuddering, gasping mess.

I writhed under him, my body wracked with pleasure as he

continued to lap at me. He drew out the moment, stoking the aftershocks until I begged him to stop.

While I lay there, panting and shaking, he slowly removed his fingers, his tongue tracing one final circle around my clit before he lifted his head. His hazel eyes met mine, filled with a mixture of satisfaction and intense lust.

"You taste amazing." He licked his lips. "I can't wait to do that again."

I grinned, my body still humming with pleasure. "I'm sure we'll find time."

After all, we had hours before sunrise.

Charlie stood, dropped his boxers on the floor and then gathered me in his arms. He moved so fast, I barely got a glance at his thick and hard package.

He repositioned us in the middle of the bed, placing me in the centre, and his fingers instantly returned to tease my pussy. He wasn't done and I couldn't muster the energy to utter so much as a gasp of surprise that he'd lifted me so easily. Still my body thrummed with anticipation and need, taking anything he was willing to give.

Hovering over me, his hard cock brushed against my thigh. I let out a moan, desperate for him to fill me. His fingers disappeared and he shifted, covering my body with his own. His lips found my neck, trailing hot kisses down to my collarbone as his hands explored every inch of me.

I arched into his touch, all thoughts of professionalism and self-control long forgotten. In that moment, there was only Charlie — his hands, his lips, the weight of his body against mine and the desperate, coiling need inside of me to come again. And again.

He unhooked my bra and tossed it aside without removing his lips from my needy body. With a firm grip in his hair, I dragged his face back to mine and revelled in the way he consumed me, owned me.

Meanwhile, it was my turn to do a little exploring. I

dragged my hands up his sides, across his taut pecs and down to his abs, tracing every line I could find while Charlie continued to tease me.

If there was one thing I was starting to learn about this man, it was that he enjoyed working for his pleasure. So instead of sinking into me like I expected, he teased me with the tip of his cock pressed against my swollen lower lips. I let out a moan, desperate for him to fill me.

Before he could, I stopped him. "Do you have a condom?"

He paused, his brow scrunching up in thought.

"I'm clean. I don't really do the sleeping with complete strangers thing," I said, rushing on like he even needed an explanation. "But I'm not comfortable going without one."

"It's okay. I was trying to remember where I put them." He got out of bed and walked over to his suitcase, his taut, toned ass on display. "And for the record, I'm clean too. It's been a while."

My mouth watered at the sight and I barely heard his response. The only way it would get better was for him to turn around and finally give me an eyeful of his cock.

He dug through his suitcase and then grunted when he found what he was looking for. Turning back to me, he held something out. My brain wasn't interested in the thing in his hands, it zeroed in on his rock solid length.

The man obviously took care of himself. With a torso as chiselled as his, he had to. He was a complete contrast to me and my slightly rounded stomach. I hit the gym (*sometimes*) and I ate healthy food (*most of the time*), but working out always fell to the bottom of my to do list when my workload called for it (*nearly every week*).

Besides, I was comfortable in my body, flaws and all. Going by the heat in Charlie's eyes as they roamed my naked form, he liked what he saw. *So what if I have a dessert addiction I'm unwilling to kick?*

"Will these be enough?" he asked, a hint of amusement in his tone.

My gaze shifted to the roll of foil hanging from his hand. "Do you intend for me to be able to walk tomorrow?"

He laughed, his gaze filled with heat. "Absolutely not."

I raised an eyebrow, trying to keep my voice playful. "So, you were planning on leaving New York with a few notches on your belt, huh?"

"I've been too busy for much action lately. But..." he prowled towards me with the absolute confidence of a man who knew he had me, hook, line and sinker. At least for tonight. He sat beside me and leaned in, his voice dropping to a low, intimate whisper while his lips nearly brushed mine. "You're making this one hell of a way to break my dry spell."

The words sent a thrill through me, then he pressed his mouth against mine and any sense I had went up in flames.

"Well, I'm flattered," I said breathlessly when he let me up for air. "It's been a while for me too, so I guess we're both due."

Shut up!

Something flickered behind the desire burning in his eyes. Surprise or disgust?

"Really?" he asked, his voice a little rougher than before.

I bit back a dejected sigh and decided that I might as well face it head on now. In for a penny and all that.

I nodded, my cheeks heating. "Yeah. Work's been crazy, and... I guess I haven't found the right person to take my mind off things."

He smiled, looking genuinely pleased. Just like that the tension upped and left me.

"I'm glad I could be that person for you."

We lapsed into a comfortable silence for a moment, just drinking each other in. Charlie was incredibly handsome, his chiselled features and rugged good looks making my body ache in all the best places.

With a sudden, determined movement, he tore the condom wrapper open with his teeth.

"As much as I want to ease you in," he said as he rolled the condom onto his thick cock. "I really need to be inside you. Right. Now."

My answering nod was just as frantic as his deep voice. He shifted over me, forcing my legs open and tugging me further down the bed. Then he leaned over me, that teasing but devilish smile curling his lips as he lifted one of my legs onto his shoulder.

He notched himself at my entrance but paused.

"Ready?" he asked, his voice hoarse.

"More than."

"Good."

He tilted my hips up and thrust into me with a slow deliberate pump of his hips that made me cross-eyed.

"Fuck," he muttered, his eyes closing for a moment as he pressed himself fully inside me.

Fuck was right. I knew I'd be tight, but this? Jesus. I could feel every inch of him. It bordered on overwhelming.

He began to move with a gentleness that took me by surprise. His thrusts were slow and deep, each one sending waves of pleasure coursing through my body. My climax started to build almost instantly.

"You feel so good, Emma," he groaned, his movements growing more urgent as he fucked me relentlessly.

My legs began to shake, my fingers digging into the sheets as the pleasure built and built.

Then he paused, his hazel eyes locking onto mine. I gritted my teeth against a crazed demand for him to keep going.

"You okay?" he asked softly.

I nodded, unable to form words.

A smug, satisfied smile tugged at his lips. "That good, huh?"

I laughed, but he still wasn't moving so it didn't last long. "Charlie!"

Smirking, he picked up the pace. Digging my one ankle into the mattress, I met him thrust for thrust, chasing the high that had escaped me before. The room filled with the sounds of our mingled breaths and low moans. It didn't take much to make me soar with how expertly he ground his pelvis against my clit and how his talented cock stroked the perfect spot inside of me.

How did I get so lucky?

The man was a beast in bed, gentle when it counted but gruff and commanding when the situation called for it. The exact sort of person I needed to break my dry spell.

If only he didn't live on the other side of the country...

I pulled him down for a searing kiss. "Charlie," I gasped against his lips. "I'm—"

"I know, love," he murmured. "Let go. I've got you."

And with those words, I did. Wave after wave of pleasure crashed over me, and I cried out, clinging to him.

Rather than stop, his thrusts grew even harder and more insistent as he pounded into me, chasing his own climax. The veins in his neck bulged as he held on for dear life.

Finally, with a low, guttural moan, he buried himself deep inside me, his body trembling as he came.

For a few moments, we just lay there, panting and sweating, our bodies still connected. Then, with a sated smile, Charlie withdrew and lay down beside me, pulling me close so that I was draped across his chest. He pressed a kiss to the top of my head, his fingers tracing lazy patterns on my back.

"That was..." I trailed off, unable to find the right words.

"Yeah," he agreed, and I could hear the smile in his voice. "It really was."

CHAPTER FOUR

EMMA

I smoothed down my dress for the millionth time, plastering on my best 'everything's under control' smile. Three months had flown by since Abi and Finn's wedding, and I'd thrown myself into work like it was going out of style. Anything to keep my mind off a certain charming Hollywood agent with a smile that could melt glaciers.

Considering how far I'd fallen from cloud nine ever since, it shouldn't have been hard to put the man behind me. Perpetual exhaustion followed me. If not for the vats of coffee I consumed daily, I'm not sure I would have been able to claw my way out of bed.

Even worse, I appeared to have picked up a stomach bug at some point and it refused to clear. I could rarely keep food down, my body ached like crazy, and I vomited at the absolute worst times.

And I meant the *worst* times.

Two weeks ago, I'd lost the battle with nausea and thrown up on a bride's dress. That bride had understandably been furious. Unfortunately, she also turned out to be well connected. Business was down. Like approaching the red down. Weddings were dropping off my calendar and I couldn't do anything about it. Between that and the exhaustion, every day had become an absolute struggle.

What should you do when you're sick and getting sicker? Take a break, right? A sick day at least. But what if you ran the business, and it couldn't function without you? Work through was my answer three weeks ago. At this stage, I was petrified that I'd be forced to take a break.

The Perier wedding was in full swing, the dance floor packed tighter than a subway car at rush hour. Despite the exhaustion, I'd outdone myself this time — if fairy lights and flowers could talk, they'd be singing my praises. Picture perfect, just like the bride wanted.

So why did I feel like I was one wobbly table away from disaster?

I shook my head, trying to clear the fog that had been creeping in all evening. Maybe this bug was getting worse? Or maybe it was karma catching up with me for surviving on coffee and granola bars for the past month.

Not that you had much success keeping those granola bars down.

I bit back a grimace at that reminder. Just the thought of food could set me off some days. It was so bad I'd started to lose weight. Something I would usually celebrate, but I just couldn't shake the suspicion that something was deeply wrong.

I made my way across the room, clutching my clipboard like it was my lifeline. One second I was 'fine.' Yes, my head felt a little fuzzy, but I could walk in a straight line. The next the music got louder, the lights intensified, my vision streaked, and my stomach did a somersault that would've made an Olympic gymnast proud.

"Emma!" The bride's voice cut through the noise. "There you are! I wanted to thank you again for everything. After all the chatter, I'll admit I was worried, but it's like you took a peek inside my brain and waved a wand. The day has been incredibly well organised. I had nothing to worry about."

I turned, mustering up a smile. "I'm so glad you're happy with everything. It's been my pleasure to——"

The room chose that moment to do its best impression of a tilt-a-whirl, and I stumbled, my trusty clipboard clattering to the floor. The bride's face swam in front of me, morphing from joy to concern faster than you could say cold feet.

Why is she falling?

"Emma? Are you okay?"

I opened my mouth to reassure her, but my body had other plans. I hit the floor and the world went black, sending me into an unscheduled nap on the ballroom floor.

*B*eep. Beep. Beep.

My eyes opened and I immediately regretted it. Harsh fluorescent lights assaulted my retinas. Great. A hospital room. Because nothing says successful wedding planner like fainting at your own gig.

Panic surged through me. The wedding. I needed to get back. Who was handling the cake cutting? The first dance? A million details raced through my mind, each more urgent than the last.

"Ah, Ms Sullivan. You're awake." A man in a white coat stepped into the room, looking far too chipper for someone working in a place that smelled like disinfectant and despair. "I'm Dr Stevens. How are you feeling?"

"Like I just went ten rounds with a bottle of tequila, minus the fun part," I croaked. "What happened?"

I glanced at the clock, mentally calculating how quickly I could get back to the venue.

Dr Stevens flipped through the chart in his hands, his expression turning serious. "You fainted at an event, Ms Sullivan. You were brought in with severe dehydration. Your electrolyte levels were dangerously low when you arrived."

I'd been pushing myself too hard, surviving on coffee and sheer willpower. Dehydration made sense. Nothing a quick IV drip couldn't fix, right? The doctor smiled sympathetically. "Yes, that's consistent with what we're seeing. It appears you're suffering from a condition called *hyperemesis gravidarum*, which is—"

His voice faded into background noise as I mentally drafted apology emails to the bride and groom. Maybe I could offer them a discount on their anniversary package to make up for this disaster. I'd have to work double-time to repair my reputation after this fiasco.

"—approximately ten weeks along."

I blinked, scrambling to catch up. What the hell did that mean? "I'm sorry, what was that?"

The doctor paused, studying my confused face. "You're pregnant. About ten weeks, based on our tests."

The word 'pregnant' sliced through my mental fog like a knife, snapping me back to the present with dizzying force.

Pregnant? How could I be pregnant?

Surely I'd heard that wrong. Maybe I had a concussion?

"I'm sorry, did you say pregnant? As in, there's a tiny human setting up shop in my uterus?"

His brow creased. "Yes—"

"You have to be wrong."

I couldn't be pregnant. I was always careful. Always used condoms. Refused to sleep with anyone who so much as grimaced at the thought of using them.

"I'm afraid you are definitely pregnant."

I winced as he uttered that word again. "How? I mean, I know how, but..." I covered my face as the enormity of it settled in. "Oh my god."

Charlie.

Memories of our night together hit me like a freight train

— his warm hands, the way he'd made me feel like the lead in my own rom-com. But we'd been careful. I mean, I wasn't exactly new to the birds and the bees and we'd used *a lot* of condoms that night.

"You're wrong. You have to be." My voice rose and I didn't even try to bite back the panic. "We used condoms. I can't be pregnant. Are you sure you didn't mix up my chart with someone else's? Maybe there's another Emma Sullivan who actually wants to be pregnant?"

Dr Stevens's expression softened, probably practised from years of delivering bombshells to unsuspecting patients. "I understand this must be a shock, but I can assure you, the tests are conclusive. You are indeed pregnant. While condoms are generally very effective, they're not 100% foolproof. There's always a small chance of failure."

I stared at him, scrambling for something, anything to disprove him. I couldn't afford to be pregnant right now. Not with the state of my business. I counted back the weeks, pinpointing my last period.

No matter how I twisted the maths, the facts didn't change.

The room shrank around me, until it was just me losing my mind and the patient but professionally caring doctor.

Pregnant.

With Charlie's baby.

A man I'd spent one night with, then mutually parted ways with the next day. A man who lived thousands of miles away from New York and would never cross my social pathways on a normal day.

Dr Stevens cleared his throat, drawing my attention back to him. "Ms Sullivan, I know this is a lot to process, but I do have some questions. Let's take things one step at a time, okay?"

I nodded numbly, unable to form words.

"First, we'll need to run some standard tests to ensure everything is progressing normally. I'd like to get an ultrasound to confirm the date of conception, and check for any potential complications."

"Complications?" My voice cracked on the word.

"It's just a precaution. Standard procedure for all pregnancies. We'll also check for a fatal heartbeat and rule out multiple fetuses."

"Now, while we wait for the nurse, I'd like to ask you a few questions about your family medical history. Do you know if there were any complications during your mother's pregnancy with you?"

I frowned, caught off guard by the question. "I... I don't know. My parents died when I was young. I never really asked about... that kind of thing."

He nodded. "I see. And your extended family? Any history of pregnancy-related issues?"

I shook my head, a lump forming in my throat. "I don't know much about my family's medical history at all. Is that... is that bad?"

Would Aunt Ginny even know?

"Not at all. We'll just need to monitor you a bit more closely, that's all." Dr Stevens made a note on his chart. "Now, let's discuss your current condition. The *hyperemesis gravidarum* you're experiencing is quite serious. We've given you a good dose of electrolytes, vitamins, and medication to help with the nausea."

All I could do was stare at him. Words came out of his mouth, but none of them made sense to me. My hand drifted to my stomach, still flatter than any attempt at humour I could make right now. There was a life growing inside me. A tiny being, half me and half Charlie. Half organised perfectionist, half clumsy charmer. God help us all.

Just the idea of it was insane. There was another human being *inside* of me. Could it hear everything I said? Feel what I did? Did it care what I ate, and that's why I hadn't been able to keep most foods down for weeks?

"We'll need to manage it carefully to ensure the health of both you and the baby."

I nodded, still struggling to wrap my head around the word 'baby'. "What exactly does that mean?"

"We need to address your dehydration and malnutrition before it develops further. The first step was getting some IV fluids and anti-nausea medication into you, but I'll prescribe you additional medication to take home." He checked his watch. "We've also run some additional tests, including checking your cortisol levels."

Why did that word sound familiar and why did I think it was possibly the worst word that could have fallen from his lips?

"It's a stress hormone," he explained. "Your levels are significantly elevated, which can exacerbate your condition. Have you been under a lot of stress lately?"

I laughed humourlessly. "You could say that. I run my own business, and things have been... challenging."

He nodded, his jaw tense. "I understand, but your cortisol levels, combined with the *hyperemesis gravidarum*, put you at high risk for complications. You'll need to make some lifestyle changes until it clears."

A knot formed in my stomach. "What kind of changes?"

"I'm recommending rest. At least for the next few weeks, possibly longer depending on how your condition progresses."

The words hit me like a physical blow. "Bed rest? But... I can't. I have a business to run. I can't plan weddings from bed!"

"I understand this is difficult, but your health and, if you want to carry to term, the health of your baby must come first. The elevated stress levels and severe morning sickness are putting both of you at risk."

I shook my head, panic rising in my chest. "How long? A few days? A week?"

"At minimum, several weeks," Dr Stevens said gently. "Possibly longer, depending on how you respond to treatment. In some cases, it clears up quickly but in others it can last throughout the pregnancy."

"But my clients, my business…"

"I know this is a lot to process, but I cannot stress enough how crucial it is that you follow these recommendations. Your condition is serious. Without proper rest and care, you risk severe complications, including preterm labour or worse." He stared at me, his gaze serious and unwavering. "There is another option, of course."

He didn't need to elaborate.

I always thought it would be black and white clear for me. If the timing or situation were wrong, I would have an abortion without a second thought.

I couldn't imagine a worse situation than this.

Yet, I hesitated.

Pragmatically, I knew it would make my life easier. Still just the thought of it stabbed me in the chest and an irrational voice whispered in the back of my mind, urging me to protect this tiny being at all costs.

What on earth was I going to do?

"I'm not sure if I want to…" I chewed my lip while contradictory feelings overwhelmed me. "You know? I'm still shocked and I think I need to process everything."

"That's perfectly fine," the doctor said. "You have a couple of weeks to make a decision."

The gravity of his words sank in, and tears pricked at my eyes. "I understand," I whispered. Maybe if I said it quietly enough, the universe would realise its mistake and hit the reset button on this whole mess.

But did I really understand? Nothing made sense.

How had I gotten pregnant if we used condoms? If I decided to keep it, how would I run a business while being unable to physically do my job? How could I get my reputation out of the toilet if I couldn't do the weddings I had left?

"It's hard to take in, I know." A sympathetic smile played at the corners of his mouth. "If you decide to keep the baby, I do recommend reducing your stress levels. Maybe try not working for a bit and we can reassess your condition in a couple of weeks. You could get lucky and be perfectly fine for most of your pregnancy."

"How long will I be here? Can I call my friend to pick me up?"

"We've run most of our tests. I just need an ultrasound and you're good to go." Dr Stevens handed me my phone from the bedside table. "The nurse will be in shortly to go over your care plan and schedule some follow-up appointments."

As he left the room, I fumbled with my phone, my fingers shaking. I pulled up Lila's number, praying she'd pick up and tell me this was all some elaborate prank. While I waited for her to answer, I sank back against the pillows and focused on my breathing. Anything to beat back the wave of panic trying to choke me.

"Hey!" Lila said, her voice as cheerful as ever. "How's the wedding going? Knock their socks off as usual?"

The sound of her, so normal and comforting, broke something inside me. A sob escaped my lips before I could stop it. So much for my usual iron control.

"Emma?" Her tone immediately shifted to concern. "What's wrong? Are you okay? Did the groom make a run for it? Because I swear, if I have to chase down another runaway groom—"

My eyes locked onto a framed print on the wall — a generic watercolour of a lighthouse against a stormy sea. I focused on the brushstrokes, willing the image to ground me as my world tilted on its axis.

I took a shuddering breath. "I'm... I'm at the hospital."

"What?!" Her voice rose. "Oh my god, what happened? Are you hurt? Do I need to come beat someone up? Because you know I will. I may be small, but I'm scrappy."

Despite everything, a tiny smile tugged at my lips. Leave it to Lila to offer violence as a solution. I traced the outline of the lighthouse with my gaze, clinging to its solidity as I formed the words.

"I fainted at the wedding." The words tumbled out as I filled her in, explaining how I'd been feeling weird for weeks. My focus darted between the painting's crashing waves and serene sky, mirroring the chaos in my mind. "But that's not... I'm pregnant."

There was a beat of silence on the other end of the line. I could practically hear the gears turning in Lila's head.

"Holy shit," she finally breathed. "Are you sure? I mean, not that I'm doubting you, but... holy shit."

I laughed, the sound edged with more hysteria than I'd like to admit. "Can you come get me?"

"Absolutely." I could practically see her running her hand through her hair, a nervous habit she'd had since college. "Which hospital are you at? Do you need me to bring anything? Chocolate? A time machine? A large bottle of wine that you probably can't drink?"

As I gave her the details, a wave of relief washed over me. Lila would know what to do. She always did. It was like her superpower, along with finding sample sales and always knowing which wine pairs best with a crisis.

"I'll be there in twenty minutes," she said. "Just hang tight, okay? And try not to panic. Maybe this is a blessing?"

I snorted, the sound wrong, hollow. *A blessing that might destroy the business I'd worked myself into the ground for years to establish.*

That wasn't quite right.

I mean it was the truth. Had I not been pregnant these last few weeks, I wouldn't have thrown up at the wrong moment and I wouldn't have struggled to stay awake on the job. My reputation wouldn't be in the toilet right now and my business in the red.

But the longer I sat with the news, the less it mattered.

Which in itself freaked me out even more.

That wasn't like me at all. All I cared about was my career. It's all I'd ever had.

But now, a tiny voice in my head whispered thoughts about soft baby skin and first smiles. I shook my head, trying to clear these unfamiliar, sentimental thoughts. This was ridiculous.

Yet... the image of holding a tiny hand, of teaching a little one how to tie shoelaces or ride a bike, kept creeping into my mind.

I ended the call and let my head fall back against the pillow, staring up at the stark white ceiling. The steady beep of the heart monitor filled the silence, a constant reminder of the new life growing inside me.

A life that was about to turn my carefully planned world upside down.

How had everything changed so quickly? Just this morning, my biggest concern had been making sure the wedding cake arrived on time.

It terrified me how quickly my priorities were shifting. The business I'd poured my heart and soul into for years suddenly felt... less important. Not unimportant, but no longer the centre of my universe. That centre was rapidly becoming occupied by the tiny life growing inside me.

I placed a hand on my stomach, a gesture that felt foreign yet oddly right. "Hey there, little one," I whispered, feeling slightly foolish but unable to stop myself. "You're certainly shaking things up, aren't you?"

Charlie's face flashed through my mind — his warm hazel eyes, the way his whole face lit up when he smiled. Would our baby have his eyes? His smile? His ability to charm the pants off anyone within a five-mile radius?

A jolt of panic rushed through me. How was I going to tell him? *Should* I tell him? Would he even want to know?

We'd both agreed it was just a one-night stand, and we'd

stuck to that. No phone numbers were exchanged. I hadn't looked him up on social media. The thought might have crossed my mind once or twice to ask Eva about him, since Abi had worked for him temporarily, but I'd held back, respecting our rules.

He probably wouldn't want anything to do with this mess. He'd run for the hills faster than I could break the news.

But a small, traitorous part of me whispered that maybe, just maybe, he'd be happy about it. The way he'd looked at me that night, like I was the only person in the world...

I shook my head, banishing the thought.

It was ridiculous to even consider. Charlie lived in a completely different world — one of red carpets and celebrity clients. He wouldn't want to be saddled with a baby and a wedding planner from New York.

This wasn't a Hallmark movie, after all.

The door opened and a nurse bustled in, breaking me out of my spiralling thoughts. She set up the device and pulled back the blanket covering me. All I could do was stare at the old machine. As much as I had accepted the doctor at his word, that thing was about to blow up every denial I could hold on to.

"This might be a bit cold," the nurse said as she squirted gel on my stomach. I flinched at the cool sensation, then held my breath as she pressed the wand against my skin.

For a moment, there was nothing but static on the screen. Then a grainy image appeared.

"There we are. See that little blob there? That's your baby."

I squinted at the screen, trying to make sense of the fuzzy shapes. "That's... that's my baby?" My voice came out as a whisper.

"Indeed it is. Let's see..." She moved the wand slightly. "Looks like you're right on track for ten weeks. Good size, developing nicely." She pointed out various features on the screen. "There's the head, and those little nubs will become arms and legs."

I stared at the screen, mesmerised. That tiny blob was my child.

"Now, let's check for the heartbeat," she said, flicking a switch on the machine.

The room filled with a rapid, rhythmic whooshing sound. My breath caught in my throat.

"Is that...?"

"That's your baby's heartbeat. Strong and steady, just as we like to see."

The sound washed over me, drowning out everything else. In that moment, all my doubts, all my fears about my career and the future, they all melted away. Nothing else mattered but that tiny heartbeat.

Tears welled up in my eyes. "Oh," I breathed, unable to form any other words.

"It's something else, isn't it?" She threw me a warm smile. "Now, let's just double-check...parenting came from my aunt. yes, I'm only seeing one baby here. Sometimes twins can hide, but it looks like you've just got one little one in there."

I nodded, still too overwhelmed to speak. One baby. My baby.

As the nurse finished up the ultrasound, wiping the gel off my stomach, a sense of calm settled over me. It all became crystal clear.

I was keeping this baby.

I didn't know how I was going to manage my business, or what I'd tell Charlie, or how I'd handle being a single mom. But I knew, with absolute certainty, that I wanted this child.

CHAPTER FIVE

EMMA

The taxi ride back to my apartment passed in a blur. Lila kept up a steady stream of chatter, filling the silence with updates on mutual friends and funny stories from her latest event. I was grateful for the distraction, even if I couldn't focus on her words. My mind was too busy playing a greatest hits compilation of 'Ways Emma's Life Is About to Implode.'

As soon as we stepped into my apartment, the dam broke. I collapsed onto the couch, burying my face in my hands as sobs wracked my body.

"Oh, honey." Lila wrapped her arms around me. "It's going to be okay. We'll figure this out. And if we can't figure it out, we'll fake it till we make it. That's gotten us this far, right?"

That only made me cry harder. Sure, that philosophy had worked with our businesses, but with a baby?

The optimistic euphoria I'd felt at the hospital after hearing the baby's heartbeat had worn off on the way home. Now I was left with exhaustion and my strategic mind, trying to poke and prod my life into some semblance of normal.

It refused to acknowledge that it would never be normal again. All it cared about was my promise to myself, if I was keeping the baby, it needed to make sense of how it fit into my world, but there was a roadblock to that.

I couldn't stop my business unravelling, put more money in my account or change the fact that I was about to be a single mother and raise a baby with a support network of one. Lila would help in any way she could. I knew that with certainty, but I also wasn't the type of person who liked to complicate other people's lives. My aunt would be no help and considering I barely remembered my parents, part of me feared that all I knew about parenting came from my aunt.

Yet another reason I'd always sworn I wouldn't have kids alone.

I'd had this totally unrealistic plan to find a man who had the perfect normal, stereotypical upbringing. The happy childhood, with two parents who loved each other and them and would move heaven and earth for their child.

I understood my thinking — find a man who would know how to be the parental figure and then learn from them — but none of that had ever happened.

And now I was alone. All of the responsibility of raising a normal, fully functional human on my own. What if I couldn't pull it off?

I cried until I had no tears left, clinging to Lila. When I finally lifted my head, her shirt was damp with tears.

"I'm sorry," I sniffled, gesturing at the wet patch. Usually, I had my emotions locked down. "Must be the hormones. Or the crushing realisation that my life is spiralling out of control."

She waved off my apology. "Please. What are best friends for if not to be human tissues?"

That startled a watery laugh out of me.

Lila patted my hand. "Now, why don't you go splash some

water on your face, and I'll make us some tea? Then we can talk about... everything. And by everything, I mean how we're going to turn this unexpected plot twist into the best damn story ever."

I nodded gratefully, hauling myself off the couch and shuffling to the bathroom. The face that stared back at me in the mirror was pale and drawn, eyes red-rimmed from crying. I splashed cold water on my cheeks, trying to pull myself together.

When I emerged, Lila stood in the kitchen with the kettle whistling on the stove. I joined her and happily sank into the familiar routine of making tea — picking out mugs, choosing our favourite blends. It helped ground me a bit. It was nice to know that even when your world is turning upside down, some things stay the same.

I reached for my usual mug, then hesitated. "Wait, can I even have tea? Is caffeine bad for the baby?"

Lila's eyes widened. "I don't know. I'll Google it." She whipped out her phone, fingers flying over the screen.

My stomach churned, and not from morning sickness this time. How many cups of coffee had I downed in the past ten weeks? I'd practically mainlined the stuff, especially on those long nights prepping for weddings. And the espressos... oh god, the espressos.

"Okay, so it looks like caffeine isn't great during pregnancy," Lila said, still scrolling. "They recommend limiting intake."

The mug slipped from my numb fingers, clattering on the counter. "Limiting? I've been guzzling the stuff like it's going out of style!" My voice rose, panic creeping in. "I had three shots of espresso today to get through the Perier wedding. And don't even get me started on how much coffee I've been drinking to fight off the exhaustion."

I sank into a kitchen chair, my head in my hands. "I'm already failing at this mother thing, and I haven't even given birth yet. What if I've hurt the baby? What if—"

"Em, breathe." Lila cut me off, her voice firm but gentle. "You didn't know. And one day of too much caffeine isn't going to hurt the baby."

"But it wasn't just one day," I whispered, the guilt washing over me. "It's been weeks. I've been so focused on work, on keeping everything together, that I didn't even notice…"

"Hey! Look at me." She crouched in front of me. Her dark curls framed her face, her blue eyes filled with concern and determination. The freckles across her nose, usually hidden under makeup, stood out in the harsh kitchen light. "You're going to be an amazing mother. You know how I know? Because you're already worried about doing the right thing. That's what good parents do."

I met her eyes, wanting desperately to believe her. "But what if—"

"No what-ifs," she said firmly. "From now on, we'll make sure you're doing everything by the book. I'll even drink decaf with you in solidarity. Deal?"

Despite everything, I felt a small smile tugging at my lips. "Deal."

As Lila bustled around, brewing a caffeine-free herbal blend, I took a deep breath. This was just the first of many changes, I knew. But maybe it could be okay. With friends like Lila, maybe I could handle it.

A few minutes later, we settled back on the couch, steaming mugs in hand. She fixed me with a gentle but determined look.

"Alright. Spill it all."

I took a deep breath, wrapping my hands around the warmth of the mug. "I'm about ten weeks along. I have this condition that causes extreme morning sickness." I pulled a face. I still didn't fully understand what that meant. Hopefully, the pamphlets would clear it up. "They want me on bed rest and I have to reduce my stress levels. Because apparently, the universe decided that running a business wasn't challenging enough. I needed to do it while confined to my bed like some Victorian heroine with consumption."

"What about the father? Please tell me it's not that guy from the speed dating event. The one who thought 'entrepreneur' meant he sold homemade slime on Etsy."

I winced, knowing this question was coming. "It's Charlie."

Her eyebrows shot up. "Charlie? As in, the hot Hollywood agent you had wild monkey sex with at that celeb wedding? That Charlie?"

"The one and only," I said, unable to keep the bitterness from my voice. "It was just supposed to be a one-night stand. We were careful, I swear. I don't know how this happened. Maybe it's karma for all those times I rolled my eyes at brides-maids complaining about their dresses."

"Well shit." She blew out a breath.

"My thoughts exactly."

"What are you going to do?" Lila set her mug down, turning to face me fully.

The million-dollar question. I'd been avoiding thinking about it since the doctor dropped the pregnancy bomb.

"And before you say 'curl up in a ball and pretend this isn't happening,' remember that I know where you hide your spare key."

Amusement tugged at my lips but quickly snuffed out as the sheer terror of my situation settled anew. What was I going to do?

"I don't know," I said, my voice small. "I always thought I'd want kids someday, but not like this. Not when I'm finally getting my business off the ground, not with a man I don't know who lives on the other side of the country. I mean, what am I supposed to do? Call him up and say, 'Hey, remember me? Surprise! I'm pregnant, and it's yours. I know we said it was one night but want to play house and raise a baby?'"

Lila winced. "Yeah, I can't see that going over well." She chewed her lip, studying me with a concerned expression. My stomach twisted, dreading her next words. "Have you thought about... other options?"

"I'm keeping it." I shook my head. "I know abortion is the right choice for some people, but... I don't think it's the one for me right now. Plus, knowing my luck, the kid would have grown up to cure cancer or something, and I'd spend the rest of my life feeling guilty."

"Okay," Lila said, no judgement in her voice. "Then we'll figure out how to make this work. First things first — your clients. We need to come up with a plan for them. Because let's face it, fainting at a wedding isn't exactly great for business."

I groaned. "I can't believe it happened before the first dance. Talk about unprofessional. I might as well have shown up in sweatpants and flip-flops."

"Don't worry about that." She waved my mortification away. "I called your bride while you were getting discharged. She was worried sick about you, by the way. I told her you had a bad case of food poisoning, but the rest of the night went off without a hitch. The hotel staff handled it. As far as she knows, you're a hero who tried to work through illness."

Relief hit me hard and I slouched lower on the sofa. "You're a lifesaver."

"I know." She grinned, but it was short lived. "Now, let's tackle your upcoming events. How many do you have booked? And please don't say a hundred, because even I have my limits."

I mentally ran through my calendar, wincing as I remembered the recent cancellations. "I have three weddings in the next month. After that..." I trailed off, my voice catching. "Well, let's just say my calendar isn't as full as it used to be."

Lila's brow furrowed. "What do you mean?"

I sighed, running a hand through my hair. "Remember that bride I threw up on? Word got around, and I've had four cancellations in the past week alone. If things keep going this way, I might not have any weddings left to plan by the time the baby arrives."

"Oh, Em." Lila's face fell. "I'm so sorry. But hey, it'll blow over, right? You're amazing at what you do. Once people remember that, they'll be lining up to book you again."

I appreciated her optimism, but I could see the doubt in her eyes. She knew as well as I did how quickly reputations could crumble in this business.

"Maybe," I said, not believing it for a second. "Anyway, I can handle the consultations for the one upcoming wedding from home. As for the rest... well, there might not be much left to handle."

Lila squeezed my hand. "Don't worry. We'll figure this out. I can take point on the upcoming weddings, and if any more come in, we'll tackle them together. Your business isn't going down without a fight, got it?"

I nodded, grateful for her support even as dread settled in my stomach. Between the pregnancy and my tanking business, I was running out of options fast.

"Okay." She blew out a breath. "So maybe five weddings. I can handle that. I'll deal with the ones next month, and we can reach out to some of the other planners we know to help with the later ones if more come in. You can still consult from home, right? Unless the doctor prescribed a strict regimen of daytime TV."

I nodded, hope unfurling inside of me. "Yeah, I think so. As long as I'm not on my feet all day, it should be fine. Though I might need you to be my stand-in for venue visits. Think you can handle pretending to be me?"

"Please, I've been practising your 'everything is under control' face for years. I've got this."

For the first time since my life started to crumble around me, I laughed. Real, genuine laughter.

"Perfect. We'll set you up with a killer home office — video calls, mood boards, the works. Your clients won't even know the difference."

As Lila continued laying out her plan, detailing how we'd divide up the work and rope in reinforcements, some of the tension left my body. This was what she did best — take a seemingly impossible situation and break it down into manageable pieces. If planning a wedding was like putting together a puzzle, she was the person who always found the corner pieces first.

But as she talked about coordinating with vendors and rearranging schedules, a cold realisation washed over me.

"I can't afford this."

She stopped mid-sentence, frowning. "What do you mean?"

I gestured around my small but stylish apartment. "This. All of it. My rent, my business expenses... I've been barely breaking even as it is, pouring everything back into growing the company. If I can't work full-time, if I have to pay other planners to take over my events..."

The reality of my situation hit me like a ton of bricks. I'd worked so hard to build my business from the ground up, scraping together every penny to make my dream a reality. And now, just when things were starting to take off...

"I'm going to lose everything," I whispered, tears welling up in my eyes again. "All those late nights, all those sacrifices... all for nothing."

Lila was quiet for a long moment, her brows drew together in thought. "What about moving in with me? My place is tiny, but we could make it work. It'll be just like college, but with more pregnancy hormones and less tequila."

The offer warmed my heart, but I knew it wasn't a real solution. "I love you, but your apartment is barely big enough for one person, let alone two and a baby. Plus, you work crazy hours at the gallery on top of wedding planning. It wouldn't be fair to saddle you with a pregnant roommate and then an infant. You'd end up hating me."

"Yeah, you're right." She sighed, her shoulders dropping. "But there has to be something we can do."

We sat in silence for a moment, the weight of my situation hanging heavy in the air. Then, almost in unison, we both turned to look at my phone, sitting innocently on the coffee table.

"You know," she said slowly, "there is one part of this equation we haven't discussed."

"No." I shook my head while my stomach did somersaults that had nothing to do with morning sickness. "Absolutely not."

"You have to tell him, Em." She threw me a sardonic look. "And not on the phone. No one drops the baby bomb over the phone. You'd have to go to Los Angeles."

I stared at her, my mouth hanging open. "Go to LA? Are you crazy? I can't just hop on a plane and show up at his office!"

But even as I said it, a tiny voice in the back of my head whispered, *Can't you?*

It takes two to tango. Why should my life be the only one turned upside down?

Lila shrugged. "Why not? You're pregnant with his kid. That gives you some rights, doesn't it? And he could help. Take the worry of medical bills out of the equation at least."

I groaned, burying my face in my hands. "This isn't how it was supposed to go. I had a life plan. And nowhere in that plan did it say get knocked up by a Hollywood agent and burn my business to the ground."

"Plans change," she said softly. "Sometimes for the better."

I stared at her, tears stinging my eyes. "How is this for the better? I'm about to lose everything I've worked for."

She scooted closer, wrapping an arm around my shoulders. "Not everything. You've still got me. And now you've got this little one." She poked my stomach gently. "And maybe, you'll have Charlie too."

I snorted. "Right. Because he's just going to welcome me with open arms when I show up on his doorstep, pregnant and broke."

"You don't know that he won't. From what you've told me, he seemed like a decent guy. And let's face it, Em — you don't have a lot of options right now. And just to be clear, I'm not suggesting you move in with him and play happy families. I just think your situation is half his fault so he should pay for at least half of it."

I hated to admit it, but she was right. I groaned, trying to imagine dropping the bombshell on Charlie. "I can't believe I'm even considering this."

I had to tell him.

"What if he doesn't want anything to do with us?" I whispered, voicing one of my deepest fears. "I don't want to force him into this. My aunt made it clear every day how much she resented being stuck with me. I can't do that to Charlie or our baby."

Lila's eyes softened. "Then we figure something else out. But you have to give him a chance, Em. You have to give yourself a chance."

"Okay, I'll go to LA."

CHAPTER SIX

CHARLIE

I leaned back in my chair, rubbing my temples as I stared at the mess of papers scattered across my desk.

A knock on my office door jolted me from my thoughts. "Mr Delacroix?" My assistant's voice filtered through. "There's someone here to see you. She doesn't have an appointment, but she's quite persistent."

I sighed, glancing at my watch. I had a conference call in twenty minutes and a stack of contracts to review. "Tell them to make an appointment like everyone else, Tammy. I'm swamped today."

"Her name is Emma Sullivan. She says you'll want to see her."

The name hit me like a punch to the gut, sending my heart into overdrive. Images of dark hair, gorgeous brown eyes, and a smile that could light up all of Hollywood flashed through my mind.

Emma.

Here.

In my office.

"Send her in," I said, my voice strangled with excitement.

I stood up, straightening my tie. I ran a hand through my hair while I waited, somehow resisting the urge to pace my office. Why was I so nervous?

It had been months since Finn and Abi's wedding, since that night we'd spent together. I'd tried to push her out of my mind, to focus on work and the endless parade of beautiful people that was my life in LA. Of course, it hadn't worked all that well.

The door opened and she slipped past my assistant with a small smile, looking even more beautiful than I remembered. Her hair was pulled back in a simple ponytail, and she wore a loose-fitting blouse and jeans instead of the knockout dress from the wedding.

But her eyes... those eyes still had the power to make my knees weak.

"What a surprise." A smile spread across my face and her steps faltered. "What brings you to my neck of the woods?"

I crossed the room, leaning in to kiss her cheek, enjoying the way she leaned into me. The scent of her perfume — light and floral, just like I remembered — washed over me, and for a moment, I was back on that dance floor, holding her close.

"Hi. I hope I'm not interrupting anything important," Emma said, her voice soft and a little shaky.

"For you? Never." I tried to keep my tone light despite the butterflies in my stomach, but failed. "Can I get you something to drink? Water? Coffee? Something stronger? It must be, what, noon in New York right now?" I was babbling, and I knew it. But I couldn't seem to stop myself. "Not that I'm encouraging day drinking, mind you."

Her lips quirked up in a small smile, but it didn't reach her eyes. "Water would be great, thanks."

I nodded, moving to the small bar in the corner of my

office. As I poured her water, my thoughts worked overtime. Why was she here? Had she thought about me as much as I'd thought about her?

"To what do I owe the surprise?" I handed her the glass. "Business or pleasure? Or maybe a bit of both?" I winked, trying to recapture some of that easy banter we'd shared at the wedding.

"I uh…" Emma glanced away, taking a deep breath. "I needed to talk to you about something important."

Her serious tone gave me pause. "Of course." I gestured to the sleek leather sofa against the wall. "Why don't we sit down?"

We sat and still she said nothing. I studied her, happy to just be in her presence for now. She was breathtaking, even with the worry etched across her face. I wanted to reach out and smooth away the lines on her forehead, to free her lip from the torture and tell her that whatever was wrong, I'd fix it.

"You're starting to worry me here."

She took another deep breath, her gaze meeting mine. "I'm pregnant."

The world seemed to tilt on its axis. I blinked, certain I must have misheard.

"You're... what?"

"Pregnant." She tilted her head, studying me with narrowed eyes. "And before you ask, yes it's yours. I know we used protection, but all I can assume is that the condoms were expired. I mean, they were yours, so…"

She continued talking, but her words faded into background noise as my mind raced. Pregnant. Emma was pregnant. With my child. A mix of emotions swirled through me — shock, fear, and underneath it all, an unexpected thrill of excitement. An absurd sense of pride swelled in my chest. I knew it was ridiculous to feel smug about being her only partner in years, but I couldn't quite squash the caveman-like satisfaction.

Focus, Delacroix. This is not the time for your ego.

"...and I haven't been with anyone else in years, so—"

"I wasn't going to ask."

But would I have if she hadn't beat me to it? I'd like to think not, but it hardly mattered now. God knows my law degree scoffed at me for not even asking for paternity.

I trusted her.

But what if I'm not cut out for this? What if I turn out to be just like my old man?

Emma stared at me, stunned. "You... weren't?"

"No, I wasn't." I shook my head, meeting her gaze steadily. "I trust you. If you say it's mine, then it's mine."

"Oh." Her eyes widened, a mix of surprise and something that looked almost like relief flashing across her face. "I... thank you."

I offered her a small smile. "You don't need to thank me for basic decency. So, what can I do?"

She blinked at me for a couple of seconds, seemingly thrown by my easy acceptance. "I have something called *hyperemesis gravidarum*. From what I understood, it's morning sickness on steroids. I can't work. My business is collapsing and I can't afford my apartment in New York. I'll have to move in with my best friend..."

She filled me in on everything that had happened in the last few days, the words falling from her lips at speed. The vulnerability in her voice snapped me out of my shock. Without thinking, I reached out and took her hand.

"Hey, it's okay. Whatever you need, it's yours."

Relief washed across her face. "Thank you. I was so scared you'd..."

"What? Run for the hills?" I smiled, my thumb tracing circles on the back of her hand. "No, I'm not going anywhere."

I hope I'm not.

A baby. My baby. Our baby. It was terrifying and exhilarating all at once.

"If you could just help with some of the costs, I might be able to keep myself afloat with my savings."

"But doesn't bed rest mean you won't be able to work?"

She nodded and her brown eyes shimmered with unshed tears.

"What if you moved in with me?" The wheels began to turn in my head. "I've got plenty of room at my place. We can set you up in the guest room, make sure you've got everything you need until the baby comes."

Her eyes widened, but I interrupted before she could refuse.

"I'm not taking no for an answer. It makes the most sense." I squeezed her hand, keeping my voice gentle but firm. "I've got the space, and this way I can make sure you're taking care of yourself. And the baby." The word felt foreign on my tongue, but not unpleasant.

"Are you sure?" She bit her lip, looking uncertain. "I don't want to impose. This is all so sudden, and I know it's a lot to take in. If you just want to support me with the medical bills, that would be enough."

"You're not imposing. I'm offering. Insisting really." I squeezed her hand. My smile faltered as a thought struck me. "If you hadn't needed help, would you have ever told me about the baby?"

She looked away, guilt flashing across her face. "No, probably not."

An awkward silence fell between us. Emma started to apologise, but I cut her off.

"It's okay. I understand. But I'm glad you did tell me. I want to support you both."

Her shoulders sagged and tears shimmered in her eyes again. "I would find a good guy to drag into this mess, huh? I'm sorry."

"You're not dragging me in. I want to help. But let's focus on you." I flashed her a smile, hoping it would calm her down. "Tell me more about your condition. What do we need to do to keep you both healthy?"

As she explained the details of her condition, I hung on her every word. The way her hands moved as she talked, the little furrow between her brows, it was all so achingly familiar and yet new at the same time.

"... and the doctor says I'll need to be careful about reducing my stress levels, staying hydrated and keeping food down," she was saying. "It's all a bit overwhelming, to be honest."

"We'll handle it." A list had already begun to form in my mind. "I'll make sure you have everything you need. We can set up a home office for you in the guest room, so you can still work on your wedding planning stuff. And I'll be there to help with anything else you need."

She blinked back tears again. "Charlie, I…" She swallowed. "Thank you. You have no idea how much this means to me. I was so scared to come here, to tell you all this."

I reached out, gently wiping a tear from her cheek. "Hey, no more tears, okay?"

She nodded, still looking slightly unsure. Her face paled and she clapped a hand over her mouth, looking panicked.

"What's wrong?"

Alarm shot through me. Was she having some kind of complication? Oh god, what if something was wrong with the baby?

She shook her head, eyes wide. "I think I'm going to be sick."

For a split second, I froze, my mind racing. Sick? Was this normal? Should I call a doctor?

Right. She literally just told me her morning sickness was worse than normal.

I sprang into action, grabbing the wastepaper basket from

beside my desk and thrusting it into her hands just in time. As she retched, I gathered her hair back with one hand, rubbing circles on her back with the other.

"It's okay," I murmured. "I've got you. Just let it out."

When the wave of nausea passed, Emma sat back, looking embarrassed. "I'm so sorry. This is mortifying."

I shook my head, reaching for a box of tissues on my desk. "Hey, none of that. It's not your fault you're dealing with morning sickness." I glanced at the clock. "Although I guess it's more like all-day sickness."

She laughed weakly, accepting the tissues. "Yeah, whoever came up with the term 'morning sickness' clearly never experienced it themselves."

She dabbed at her mouth, her cheeks flushed with embarrassment. The need to not let her down burned inside of me with a fierce and terrifying desperation.

"I know this isn't how either of us planned things." I hesitated, then gently tucked a stray strand of hair behind her ear. "But I want you to know that I'm here for you. For both of you. It might take some time to adjust, but whatever you need, I'm in."

She met my gaze, her eyes filled with a mix of gratitude and something else I couldn't quite place. "Thank you. I don't know what I would have done if you hadn't come around."

I grinned, trying to lighten the mood. "What, you mean if I'd fainted dramatically or tried to escape out the window? Not my style, darling. Though I can't promise I won't freak out again a little later when it all sinks in."

She laughed, the sound warming me from the inside out. "Fair enough. I'm still freaking out myself, to be honest."

"Well, we can freak out together then."

Emma smiled, and for a moment, it was like no time had passed at all. We were back at that wedding, sharing jokes and stolen glances across a crowded room.

Just this morning, my biggest concern had been negotiating

a new contract for one of my A-list clients. Now, I was preparing to become a father and let an almost-stranger I couldn't stop thinking about move in with me.

It was surreal, and I'd need days, maybe weeks, to get used to it.

But what if we didn't work out? What if I screwed it up?

And what if, after the baby was born and the hormones settled, she didn't want me? I'd be devastated. I'd lose them both.

I was grasping at straws, trying to protect myself from... what? Responsibility? Commitment? Or maybe from the terrifying possibility that I might actually want this?

Maybe it was better this way. Keep her at arm's length. Don't get too attached. It's safer that way, right? For both of us. But why did the thought of her walking out that door limit the air in my lungs?

"I don't want you to feel pressured into anything, especially with everything else you're dealing with. Maybe we should keep things platonic, at least for now."

For a second, she stiffened and something flickered across her face, but then I blinked and it was gone. She smiled at me. Had I imagined it?

"Right, platonic. Of course. I understand."

*O*nce she'd left, I collapsed back onto the sofa with my head in my hands. I'd screwed up already. But what else could I have done?

She was vulnerable, pregnant with my child. The last thing I wanted was for her to think I was trying to take advantage of the situation.

The memory of our night together came rushing back too easily. I could shut my eyes and be there again effortlessly. Remembering the way she'd felt in my arms as we danced, the spark in her eyes when she laughed at my terrible pick up lines.

Platonic. Right. Because that was totally going to work when I was already halfway in love with her.

One step at a time.

First, get her settled.

Then figure out how to co-parent.

And maybe, just maybe, I'd figure out how to navigate these feelings without screwing everything up.

CHAPTER SEVEN

EMMA

The cab ride back to my hotel took longer than I'd expected. I was used to New York traffic, but it had nothing on Los Angeles.

My thoughts consumed me as I replayed every minute detail from seeing Charlie again.

It had not gone to plan.

The door clicked shut on my hotel room and I almost sagged against it in relief. The room screamed 'generic hotel chic' — all sleek lines and muted colours, about as personal as the ER room they'd put me in in New York. Nothing like the organised chaos of my New York apartment, with its over-flowing bookshelves and the ever-present scent of fresh flowers. I missed my space. I could have really done with my safe haven right then.

I tossed my purse onto the bed, watching it bounce slightly on the too-firm mattress before I collapsed onto the edge of it. My hand unconsciously drifted to my stomach, a habit I'd developed scarily fast.

Was it aware of anything yet? Could it sense my stress? Did it know how close it came to not having a father? If I were aware of something like that before I'd even experienced the world, I'd have been upset.

"I know things are a bit crazy right now," I whispered, feeling slightly foolish but pushing through. "But I'm going to figure this out, okay?" Maybe this talking thing wasn't so bad after all. "It'll all work out for the best in the end."

In the meantime, I needed to do something with my racing thoughts.

How did everything spiral so quickly? A week ago, I was just an insanely overworked wedding planner. Now? Now I was… what exactly? Soon-to-be roommate of a Hollywood agent who probably thought I was trying to pull a fast one on him but was too nice to say anything?

The shrill ring of my phone cut through my pity party, making me jump. I contemplated rejecting it, desperately needing a minute to breathe without honking cars surrounding me. Then I read the caller ID and decided that being alone with my overactive imagination was the last thing I needed.

"Hey," I answered, aiming for nonchalant and landing somewhere between mildly hysterical and one step away from a full-blown meltdown.

"Emma! Finally! I've been on pins and needles here. How did it go? What happened? Did you tell him? What did he say? Are you okay? Do I need to hop on a plane and come kick his ass?"

Lila's rapid-fire questions hit me like a welcome tidal wave, washing away some of the loneliness that had been creeping in. Her familiar voice engulfed me, grounding me.

"Whoa, slow down, Speedy Gonzales." A shaky laugh escaped me, but I shot to my feet, unable to stay still and talk about the mess my life had become in less than a week. "One question at a time. My brain can only just keep up with my own thoughts right now, let alone your interrogation."

"Sorry, sorry." She didn't sound sorry at all. "I'm just worried about you, Em. You've been radio silent since you left, and I've been imagining all sorts of scenarios. Most of them end with me having to dispose of a body, by the way." She cleared her throat and lowered her voice. "I've got a guy. If you need one, that is."

I snorted. "As much as I appreciate your willingness to commit murder on my behalf, I don't think that'll be necessary. At least... not yet."

"Ooh, ominous. What happened?"

I took a deep breath, trying to figure out where to even begin. How do you sum up a day that felt like it lasted a lifetime? "Well, I told him. About the baby, I mean."

"And? How did he take it? On a scale of 'fainting Victorian lady' to 'cool as a cucumber', where did he land?"

"Somewhere between 'deer in headlights' and 'man who just realised he left the stove on'," I said, the look on Charlie's face when I'd dropped the bombshell fresh in my mind. "For a minute there, I thought he might actually faint. Or throw up. Or both."

"Men," Lila scoffed, her eye roll practically audible through the phone. "Always so dramatic. You'd think we were telling them we're growing a second head, not a baby."

"Says the woman who threatened bodily harm not two minutes ago."

"Hey, that's different. I'm being protective, not dramatic. There's a very important distinction."

I laughed, some of the tension in my shoulders easing.

"So, what happened after the initial shock wore off?" Her tone shifted from playful to serious. "Did he step up? Please tell me he stepped up. Because if he didn't, I wasn't kidding about that disposal guy."

"He did." I sank into the armchair by the window, my legs too weak to hold me up. "Though I'm still shocked he didn't ask for a paternity test. For all he knows, I could be anyone, pretending to be something I'm not."

"Oh, honey." Lila sighed, her tone softening. "Is that what you're worried about? That he thinks you're trying to trap him?"

I swallowed hard, fighting back the tears that threatened to spill over.

"Maybe? I don't know."

"Men are idiots sometimes. Especially when they're caught off guard."

"Maybe." I couldn't keep the doubt out of my tone. I squeezed the throw cushion.

"Emma Jane Sullivan," she said, her tone stern and reminiscent of my third-grade teacher when she caught me doodling wedding dresses instead of paying attention to maths. "I've known you for years, and I can say with absolute certainty that you are the least opportunistic person I know. You're practically a saint."

"You would say that." I rolled my eyes. "You wouldn't be my best friend if I were a snake."

"You're right. I have good taste in people, and you're good people."

I grunted at her confidence.

"My point is anyone who spends more than five minutes with you knows you're not capable of that kind of deception. You can barely lie about liking someone's ugly bridesmaid dresses without breaking out in hives. If Charlie can't see that, then he's an idiot who doesn't deserve you or this baby. Hell, he doesn't even deserve to breathe the same air as you."

Her words wrapped around me like a warm blanket. But the nagging voice in the back of my mind refused to be silenced completely. "But what if—"

"Enough with the what-ifs."

My mouth snapped shut at a tone I'd only ever heard her use with service providers who dragged their feet.

"Now, tell me what really happened. Is he going to help, or do I need to book a flight and bring my baseball bat?"

I stared up at the unfamiliar ceiling and sighed. The popcorn texture mocked me, each little bump a reminder of how far I was from home.

"He is. He also insisted I move in with him."

"Good. Maybe he's a decent guy after all. Colour me surprised. I was all ready to hate this guy, and now he's being all responsible and shit. I don't know what to do with my murder energy now."

It took me a second to realise she'd pulled a one-eighty on me.

Then I laughed. It didn't last long, I had too many fears crowding in and shouting for attention.

"I barely know him. What if we end up hating each other? What if he resents me for turning his life upside down? What if he snores, or leaves the toilet seat up, or has a secret collection of creepy clown dolls? How am I meant to raise a baby with a total stranger?"

"Hey, hey. One step at a time, okay?" She spoke slowly, almost like you would when trying not to spook a wild animal that could easily rip out your throat. "Right now, you need a place to stay that isn't going to bankrupt you, and he's offering. Take the win, Em. We can worry about the creepy clown dolls later."

I shuddered, even knowing she was joking. Nobody liked clowns.

"I've got your back."

"How are they doing?" I asked, guilt eating at me for not checking in sooner. Some perfectionist I was, letting the pregnancy brain make me forget about my clients. "The brides, I mean. Are they okay with the changes? Has anyone threatened to leave scathing Yelp reviews?"

"They're fine." Her voice crackled through the phone, warm with amusement. "Everyone bought the story about you having to go to Florida to look after your sick aunt. They were all very understanding and so far, no one's talking about replacing you."

"My aunt?" I raised an eyebrow, even though she couldn't see me.

I almost laughed. The last thing Aunt Ginny would want was me putting a kink in her routine.

"I'm sure she'd love to know she's being used as a cover story."

"Anyway, everything is on track and you don't need to worry about anything."

"Thanks, Lila." My body sagged into the mattress, the tension seeping from me for the first time since I woke up to the news a week ago. "Words can't express how grateful I am for your help."

"Anytime, babe. That's what I'm here for — bad jokes and unwavering support."

We fell into a comfortable silence for a moment, and I found myself wishing she had come with me. I could have used one of her bone-crushing hugs right about now.

"So," Lila said after a beat, her tone turning serious again. "Back to Charlie. What's the plan? When are you moving in? And more importantly, how fancy is his place? I need details, woman. Paint me a picture of this Hollywood hotshot's bachelor pad."

"Tomorrow, I guess." I sighed, the reality of my situation crashing back down on me. "He said he'd have the guest room ready for me. As for how fancy it is, I have no idea. Knowing my luck, it'll be some ultra-modern monstrosity with more glass than walls and furniture that looks pretty but is impossible to actually sit on."

Now that I'd uttered the words, I regretted it. A place like that would be a nightmare to child-proof and I'd just jinxed myself with the universe. Shit.

"Wow, he's not wasting any time, is he?" A hint of approval

crept into her voice. "That's a good sign. It means he's taking this seriously. He's not just all talk."

"Yeah, I guess, but what if he's only doing this out of obligation? What if he doesn't really want this baby, or me, in his life?"

"Is that what you're really worried about? That you're forcing yourself into his life?"

I nodded, forgetting for a moment that she couldn't see me. "It's just... he suggested we keep things platonic."

"Maybe he's trying to be respectful? I mean, think about it. You show up out of the blue, tell him you're pregnant, and that you need help. Maybe he's trying to show you that he's not expecting anything in return for his help. That he's not some creep who's going to take advantage of the situation."

I blinked, considering this possibility.

"Or maybe," she continued, her words coming in a rush as she warmed to the idea, "he's as scared as you are. Maybe he's worried about screwing things up, moving too fast. I mean, you guys are kind of doing this whole relationship thing backwards, aren't you? Baby first, then living together, then... who knows?"

Lila had a point.

"But what if—"

"No more what-ifs," Lila cut me off. "You're driving yourself crazy with all these hypotheticals, Em. The only way you're going to know for sure what Charlie's thinking is to talk to him. Use your words, like we taught the flower girls at the Patterson wedding."

I groaned, throwing an arm over my eyes. "I know, I know. You're right. It's just... I'm terrified. Like really terrified. What if I'm making a huge mistake? What if this all blows up in my face?"

"Stop. I can play this game too. What if you're not? What if this is the start of something amazing? What if Charlie turns out to be the best thing that ever happened to you? What if this baby is the beginning of your own fairytale?" She took a deep breath and her silence spoke volumes, screaming at me to calm my jets. "You'll never know if you don't give it a chance."

I sighed, knowing she was right.

"I'll try."

The conviction in my voice was a lie. My mind was still racing with all the possibilities, all the things that could go wrong. What if Charlie's house was a bachelor pad nightmare? What if he expected me to be some 1950s housewife? What if—

"Good, but I'm not buying it. You're still spiralling." She chuckled, the sound frustrated but in a loving way. "You're going to be fine. It's all going to work out, and if it doesn't, you have a best friend with connections who will make sure it's all fine."

"I know. Thank you, Lila. Really."

"Anytime, babe. Now go get some sleep. And call me tomorrow after you've moved in, okay? I want all the details about Charlie's place. I bet it's disgustingly luxurious. Like, 'gold-plated toilet paper holder' levels of extra."

I hoped not. Imagine raising a baby in that.

"I will. I'll give you the full MTV Cribs tour rundown."

"You better. Night, Em. Love you, you neurotic mess."

"Love you too, you bossy weirdo."

I dropped the phone on the bed and hauled myself back to my feet. I wandered to the window, looking out at the unfamiliar Los Angeles street. The city sprawled out before me, so different from the New York cityscape I was used to. It was beautiful, in its own way. Different, but not necessarily bad.

Like my life.

Maybe different didn't have to mean disaster. Maybe it could mean opportunity.

CHAPTER EIGHT

EMMA

The next morning, I stood on Charlie's doorstep, my oversized suitcase at my feet, feeling like I'd stepped into an alternate reality. How had my life taken such a sharp turn? One minute, I was planning other people's happily-ever-afters, and the next, I was pregnant and about to move in with a virtual stranger.

My finger hovered over the doorbell. I could still turn back, hop in a cab, and catch the next flight back to New York. But then what? Go back to my tiny apartment, with no job and a baby on the way?

"You've faced down bridezillas with spray tans gone wrong," I muttered to myself. "You can handle this."

Before I could think it through, I pressed the bell. The chime echoed through the house, my heart pounding in sync with it. Footsteps approached, and then the door swung open, revealing Charlie in all his casual, California glory.

Did the man ever have a bad hair day? As if his perpetually perfect locks weren't enough, he'd grown a beard since New

York. The neatly trimmed facial hair accentuated his strong jawline, making him look somehow more rugged and refined at the same time. My fingers twitched and I fought the urge to reach out and run them through it.

Like it wasn't too much to ask that he got knocked down a couple of steps on the handsome ladder, right? Instead, he'd gone and climbed a few rungs higher. The beard was just unfair — a devastating addition to his already unfairly attractive appearance.

"Emma!" His face lit up with a smile that made my insides do a little flip. "Come in, come in."

He reached for my suitcase, but I held onto it. "I've got it, thanks."

His eyes widened as he took in my single piece of luggage. Who cared about the luggage, right? I didn't. Yet I fought him on it.

"Come on." With a gentle but firm movement, he took my suitcase despite my protests. "Let's get you settled in."

I followed him up a sweeping staircase, trying not to gawk at the opulent surroundings. The house wasn't over the top or gaudy, but it was a far cry from my cosy New York apartment, all sleek lines and modern art. It was beautiful, but it didn't feel like a home. At least, not yet.

A knot formed in my stomach. How could I ever fit into this world? Charlie led me to a door at the end of the hallway.

"This will be your room," he said, pushing it open.

I stepped inside and my jaw dropped.

"Is this good enough?" he asked, his tone almost uncertain.

"You can't be serious." I turned to him, incredulous. "It's bigger than my whole apartment in New York. Are you sure this isn't *your* room?"

He shrugged, a sheepish smile playing on his lips. "Well, it was. But I figured you'd be more comfortable here. It has its own en-suite and everything."

"I can't take your room."

"Of course you can."

I glanced around, taking in the dark, masculine colour palette. "I appreciate it, but—"

The reality of the situation hit me anew, leaving me momentarily breathless.

"Emma? You okay?"

I nodded, blinking back the tears that burned the back of my eyes. "I'm fine. It's just... a lot to take in, you know?"

"I know. But it'll all be okay. I'll make sure of it."

I managed a smile, touched by his reassurance. "Okay."

As the day wore on, I unpacked my meagre belongings and tried to settle into my new surroundings. The house was quiet, almost too quiet compared to the constant bustle of New York. As ridiculous as it sounded, I missed the honking horns and distant sirens that had been the soundtrack to my life for so long.

Despite the drastic change in scenery, some things remained frustratingly constant. Like clockwork, the now-familiar wave of nausea hit me, sending me scrambling for the en-suite bathroom.

As I knelt over the pristine toilet, retching, I couldn't help but feel out of place. The marble floors and gleaming fixtures seemed too perfect.

Wiping my mouth, I eyed the plush towels hanging nearby.

What if I ruin it?

The irrational worry nagged at me as I rinsed my mouth. It was just a towel, but in this house, everything felt valuable, breakable. I settled for patting my face dry with some tissue, vowing to ask Charlie about designated throwing up towels later. By evening, hunger finally drove me from the sanctuary of my new room. I padded downstairs, following my nose to the kitchen. To my surprise, I found Charlie bent over the stove, a look of intense concentration on his face.

The nausea hit me almost instantly. The smell of cooking chicken, usually appetising, now turned my stomach. I swallowed hard.

He looked up, a grin spreading across his face. "Perfect timing. Dinner's almost ready."

I forced a smile, silently praying I could keep it together. The baby, it seemed, had other ideas.

I tried to focus on my surroundings and ignore the bubbling in my stomach. Charlie Delacroix was cooking me dinner. And not just heating up a frozen pizza, but actually cooking what appeared to be a proper meal. I almost rubbed my eyes, the sight before me was so strange.

"You cook?"

He chuckled. "Don't sound so shocked. I'm a man of many talents."

The aroma wafting from the pans made my stomach growl audibly. His grin widened.

"Hungry?"

I nodded, a bit embarrassed. "Starving, actually. What are you making?" The words left my mouth automatically, even as my stomach churned.

I eyed the chicken warily, knowing I'd struggle to eat it. The baby's needs came first, but how could I explain this without hurting Charlie's feelings?

"Grilled chicken with quinoa and steamed non-starchy vegetables." Something started smoking and he hastily removed the pot from the burner before turning the whole thing off. "All approved by the dietitian."

I froze. "The what now?"

He'd started pulling pans from the oven, but stopped long enough to throw me a sheepish look over his shoulder. "Oh, uh, I hired a dietitian. To help with meal planning, you know? For the pregnancy."

I stared at him, speechless. He'd hired a dietitian. For me. The thoughtfulness of the gesture overwhelmed me, and tears pricked my eyes.

When had he even had the time?

"Emma?" Charlie's voice was soft, concerned. "Are you okay?"

I nodded, furiously blinking back tears. "It's really sweet of you to put in so much effort. You didn't have to."

"I just want to make sure you and the baby are taken care of." He shrugged, his back turned as he plated up the food. "It's no big deal."

But it was a big deal.

"Thank you," I said softly, meaning it with every fibre of my being.

He turned and our gazes clashed again. This time the air between us crackled with an unnamed energy. Then he smiled, breaking the spell.

"You're welcome. Now, how about you set the table while I finish up here?"

Grateful for something to do, I busied myself with plates and cutlery, trying to ignore the warmth blooming in my chest. I couldn't let myself get carried away by a few kind gestures.

But I couldn't help but wonder if maybe, just maybe, this could work out after all.

The next morning, I woke disoriented, the unfamiliar surroundings and the strength of sunlight streaming through the windows throwing me off. Then it all came rushing back — the pregnancy, the move, Charlie.

I stretched, relishing the feel of the luxurious sheets against my skin. Despite my initial reservations, I had to admit the bed was incredibly comfortable. Maybe too comfortable. A glance at the clock told me it was nearly ten — I'd slept far later than usual.

So much for being a responsible adult.

My stomach growled, reminding me that I'd missed my usual breakfast time, something the pile of pamphlets had agreed was a bad idea. I climbed out of bed, my legs a little shaky. I ran a hand through my tangled hair and took a deep breath while I adjusted to the feeling of my blood sugar being low. At some point, I'd probably take this new hyperawareness of my body for granted, but for now, it was a weird sensation.

I opened the door, conceding that I probably looked a mess and stepped into the hallway.

Surely Charlie's seen worse.

I promptly collided with a wall of warm, damp skin.

"Whoa!" Hands shot out, steadying me before I could stumble. "Good morning, sleepyhead."

I glanced up, ready to apologise, but the words died in my throat.

Wow, that's a lot of skin.

Charlie stood before me, wearing nothing more than a towel slung low on his hips. Water droplets clung to his chest, tracing tantalising paths down his abs. His hair was damp and tousled, giving him a boyish charm that contrasted sharply with his very adult body.

Holy mother of...

A familiar pull of attraction tugged at me, quickly followed by a wave of panic.

"Emma?" His voice broke through my hormone-induced haze. Amusement creased his brow. "You have got to stop doing this to me, darling. I'll go grey before the baby even kicks."

I blinked and tore my gaze away from the expanse of bare skin.

"Fine!" My voice came out as a squeak and heat rushed to my cheeks as I took a hasty step back. I cleared my throat, willing my sex-starved hormones to chill the fuck out. "I'm fine. Just, uh, still waking up."

He grinned, seemingly oblivious to my discomfort. Or the fact that he was practically naked. "No worries. I was just about to start breakfast. Pancakes and fruit sound good?"

I nodded, not trusting my voice. My eyes betrayed me, drifting down to where the towel sat precariously on his hips.

"Great!" he said, running a hand through his damp brown hair. The movement caused his muscles to ripple in a way that made my mouth go dry. "I'll meet you downstairs in a few."

"Sure," I managed to croak out. "I'll just... go... down…"

I turned and fled down the stairs, my heart pounding. What was wrong with me? I was acting like a teenager with a crush, not a grown woman about to have a baby.

In the kitchen, I splashed cold water on my face, trying to regain my composure. This was ridiculous. So what if Charlie was attractive? Lots of people were attractive. It didn't mean anything.

Yeah, keep telling yourself that.

CHAPTER NINE

EMMA

Fifteen minutes later, I was sitting at the breakfast bar with a cup of ginger tea and a notepad full of scribbles. Turns out being left alone with my thoughts resulted in lists. Long lists. I'd compiled at least three pages of questions I needed to ask him.

He'd mercifully — or unfortunately — covered up. I couldn't decide if I was relieved or disappointed.

You're here to co-parent, not drool over his abs.

Only, the t-shirt he wore didn't do all that good a job at hiding the sculpted chest beneath. It was practically skin tight, making my mouth water and my core ache.

I forced my eyes away from his muscular arms as he reached for a mixing bowl.

Focus, Emma. You're here to ask questions, not ogle the father of your child.

His eyes instantly zeroed in on the notepad. "What's all this?"

I took a deep breath, bracing myself for his reaction. "We

barely know each other, and that's weird for two people having a baby. I figured we should just rip the Band-Aid off, rapid-fire style, and get it out of the way."

His brows shot up, but he nodded. "Makes sense. Alright, hit me with your best shot while I whip up those pancakes."

As he moved around the kitchen, gathering ingredients, I launched into my interrogation. "Are you religious? Should we get the baby christened? Does your family do the godparents thing? I don't, but if you really insist on it, Lila will throw herself in as a sacrifice, happily, I imagine."

"Whoa, slow down!" Charlie laughed, cracking eggs into a bowl. "One at a time, please. I'm not particularly religious, but I'm open to discussing it if you are. As for christening and godparents, that's something we'd need to decide together if you're religious?"

"I'm not." I crossed those questions off the lists, happy I didn't need to worry about the embarrassment of a christening when my side of the church would literally feature one person — two, if my aunt bothered to check her messages and then get on a plane.

Charlie nodded, pouring batter onto the pan. "Alright, next question?"

I watched his forearms flex as he tilted the bowl, the muscles rippling under his skin. *Jeez, this man is distracting.* I shook my head, trying to clear it.

Bracing myself, I waited for the familiar wave of nausea to hit as the smell of cooking pancakes filled the air.

My stomach clenched in anticipation, but to my surprise, the scent was almost... appetising?

Don't get your hopes up.

"Okay, here's a big one. How are we going to co-parent without being a couple?" I asked, my pen poised over the notepad. "We're not together, and we don't need to pretend so we can be good parents. But we do need a plan."

Charlie flipped a pancake, his brows knit together in

thought. "That's a good point. I suppose we'll need to communicate a lot, make decisions together about the big things. Maybe set up regular 'parent meetings' to discuss any issues?"

I stared at him for a second, my eyes narrowing as I tried to work out if he was saying all the right things to please me or if he meant it. A man who would willingly commit to open communication and proper discussions? Where had he been hiding all my life?

LA, of course.

His sincerity seemed genuine, but I couldn't help but wonder if this was just another performance from the charming Hollywood agent.

Stop it. He's trying. Give him a chance.

I scribbled his response down. "And what about when I don't need constant monitoring anymore? Where will I live then? How will we share custody if I go back to New York?"

He paused, spatula mid-air. "I... hadn't thought that far ahead yet. I guess we'd need to figure out a custody arrangement. Maybe alternating weeks or months?"

"We'd need to consider the baby's routine, schooling…" I muttered, adding more notes. "In the first few years, yeah alternating every few weeks could be possible. Expensive though," I grimaced. "But when she or he starts school, I wouldn't really want to pull them out of their routine."

"You could stay in LA." He side-eyed me as he flipped another pancake. He sounded nonchalant, but there was an edge to his voice that made my attention sharpen. "Do you have any reason to go back to New York? Do you have family there?"

He must have already known that answer. I wouldn't be here if I had family in the city.

I shook my head, pushing away the twinge of loneliness that threatened to surface. "No, I don't have family there. Just Lila and my business."

Not that my business would survive the next six months.

Charlie nodded, sliding a plate of steaming pancakes in front of me. "Well, let's table that discussion for now. We've got time to figure it out. What's next on your list?"

"I think we should probably set some ground rules for living together."

He raised an eyebrow, intrigued. "What kind of ground rules?"

"Like me contributing to bills." I straightened in my seat, trying to look more confident than I felt. "I know you said not to worry about it, but I need to feel like I'm pulling my weight." Charlie opened his mouth to protest, but I held up a hand. "Please, it's important to me."

"Alright." He nodded reluctantly. "We can work something out. Anything else?"

I bit my lip, hesitating before plunging ahead. "No... um, no bringing dates home. I think that would be awkward."

A flash of something — annoyance? — crossed Charlie's face before he nodded. "Agreed. This should be a comfortable space for both of us."

"We should probably discuss chores too. I don't want to feel like a guest in your home, so I'd like to help out where I can."

He waved his hand, brushing it away. "I have a cleaner. She comes in twice a week. No chores necessary."

"Oh."

I still didn't know how much money he made. The question was in my notebook, but I'd never utter it. He'd assured me hospital bills wouldn't be a problem. In fact, he refused to let me even see the invoices. Beyond curiosity, I didn't need nor want to know how much money he made.

His gaze dropped to my notepad. "What else do you have in there?"

"Enough to keep us talking for weeks," I muttered, glancing down at my notes, scanning for the next important question. "Okay, here's a big one. What kind of parent do you want to be? How do you feel about discipline?"

He leaned against the counter, his brow furrowed in thought. "I want to be involved, supportive. As for discipline, I believe in setting clear boundaries and consequences, but not in physical punishment. What about you?"

Something about the tense set of his jaw gave me pause. "Same here. No spanking or anything like that. Time-outs and talking things through seem more effective."

"Agreed," he said, pouring himself a cup of coffee. I missed coffee. It hadn't even been a week, and I craved it.

Charlie took another sip, and I found myself staring at his lips.

"What else?"

"Education." I forced my attention back to my notepad and tapped my pen against it. "State or private school? How do you feel about extracurricular activities?"

Charlie took a sip of his coffee before answering. "Private. With my job…." He grimaced. "I'm not saying something would happen, but I do have a number of high-profile clients. I don't think public school would be in ours or our kid's best interest. As for extracurriculars—"

"Hold up." I held up a hand, something like fear arrowing through me. "Not in their best interests, how?"

Oh my god, did I let a man who could have a hit out on him get me pregnant? Panic surged through me.

"Nothing like that." His eyes widened as he realised how his words had come across. "I just meant that being in the public eye can be tough on kids. Paparazzi can be relentless, and some of my clients have had issues with their children being harassed or photographed at school. Private schools tend to have better security and privacy measures in place."

I took a deep breath, letting the relief sink in.

"I'm sorry, I should have explained that better. I didn't mean to scare you." He ran a hand through his hair, looking sheepish. "There's no danger, just potential annoyances that I'd rather our child not have to deal with."

"Okay, that makes sense. But we should probably discuss security measures at some point, just to be safe."

Charlie nodded. "Absolutely. We can go over all that when the time comes. But as I was saying, I think we should leave the extracurriculars discussion until they're born and see what they take a liking to."

He continued explaining his thoughts on after-school activities, but I was only half-listening. Some stranger sticking a camera in my child's face had not been on my list of worries. Paparazzi, public scrutiny… it was a lot to take in.

I absently placed a hand on my stomach. This wasn't just about me and Charlie anymore. We were responsible for a whole other person. The weight of it was both terrifying and exhilarating.

"If it's a boy," Charlie said, something about the excitement in his voice catching my attention. "And he wants to skate, I'll teach him."

"You skate?" I smiled at the thought of Charlie teaching our child to skate. It was such a normal, domestic image — one I hadn't allowed myself to imagine until now.

"I'm Canadian, darling." He chuckled, a hint of pride in his voice. "I played hockey growing up. Made it to the junior leagues before I decided to pursue a career in entertainment instead."

"Wow." I jotted that tidbit down. "So you're telling me our kid might end up being a hockey prodigy?"

"Could be." He grinned. "But let's not get ahead of ourselves. Eat at least a bite before they go cold."

He nudged the plate towards me and I obliged, picking up the fork and cutting off a piece from the stack. I tentatively popped it in my mouth and chewed. Every muscle in my body tensed while I waited for my stomach to flip the switch.

It didn't happen, and I sagged in my seat with relief.

"What's next on that list of yours?" Charlie asked, a note of satisfaction in his voice.

I glanced down at my notepad, scanning for another important question. "Alright, how about this: what's your relationship with your parents like? And do you have any siblings?"

"I have a younger sister in Toronto." His expression softened as he flipped another pancake. "She's a lawyer. I don't see her much, but we get along. So well, she sends me care packages from home."

I laughed. "Why would you need a care package from Canada?"

"You'd be surprised." He grinned, a nostalgic glint in his eye. "There are some things you just can't get here. Ketchup chips, Coffee Crisp, proper maple syrup…"

"Proper maple syrup?" I raised a brow. "Are you saying the syrup here isn't up to your Canadian standards?"

"Not even close." He winced, shaking his head. "But your chocolate is far worse."

I gasped. "What's wrong with our chocolate?"

"Nothing. Unless you like some actual cocoa with your high fructose corn syrup."

I laughed at Charlie's disdain for American chocolate. "I'll have you know our chocolate is perfectly fine. But I'll humour you and try some of this supposedly superior Canadian chocolate sometime."

"Deal." He slid another pancake onto my plate.

I took a bite to appease him. "What about you parents?"

He sighed. "My relationship with my parents is… complicated. I don't talk to my dad anymore, but I have an okay relationship with my mom. I go home for Christmas every year to see her and my sister."

A twinge of envy slithered through me. "What about your extended family? Any aunts, uncles, cousins we should know about?"

Charlie shook his head. "Not really. My mom's an only child, and my dad's side… well, we don't really keep in touch."

"Okay." I nodded. "Now, what about—"

"Whoa, slow down there, detective." Charlie pushed the plate closer to me again. "You need to eat. We've got months to learn everything about each other."

I glanced at the stack of pancakes, my stomach growling in response. "Right, sorry. I guess I got carried away."

And I really should take advantage of this surprise reprieve from morning sickness. Who knew when it would hit again.

As I took a bite, Charlie leaned against the counter with a satisfied glint in his hazel eyes. "My turn for a question. What about your family? Any traditions or holidays you want to incorporate?"

I swallowed hard, both from the pancake and the question. "Not really. It's just me and my aunt, and we're not close. No real traditions to speak of."

"I'm sorry to hear that." His tone softened. "Well, maybe we can start some new traditions with our little one."

Those words falling from his lips did funny things to my insides. It was a dangerous path to let my mind wander down, but I couldn't help it.

"I'd like that," I said softly, taking another bite of pancake.

Charlie smiled, his eyes crinkling at the corners. "So, what else is on that mega list of yours?"

I glanced down at my notepad, but he shook his head.

"Actually, hold that thought. Eat a few more bites first. You need your strength."

I rolled my eyes but complied, savouring the fluffy pancakes while I could. As I ate, Charlie puttered around the kitchen, keeping a close eye on me. The man seemed to be at total ease in the kitchen.

After a few moments of comfortable silence, Charlie spoke again.

"Tell me about your childhood. Where did you grow up?"

I swallowed my bite, surprised by his interest. "New York, mostly. I was born in England, but my aunt moved me to the States after my parents died."

"I'm sorry to hear that. How old were you?"

"Nine."

"What about your favourite subject in school?"

I couldn't help but smile. "Art, believe it or not. I loved drawing wedding dresses even back then."

"Really?" His eyes lit up. "So you were always destined for the wedding business, eh?"

"I guess so." I laughed. "What about you? What were you like in high school?"

Charlie grinned. "Hockey obsessed, of course. But I was also in the drama club. Bit of a theatre nerd, if I'm honest."

"I can't picture that at all."

We continued exchanging questions and answers and I found myself relaxing more and more. His easy manner and genuine interest in my responses made me feel... seen. "Earth to Emma," Charlie's voice broke through my reverie. "You still with me?"

I blinked. He stared at me, his brow creased with concern. I'd been staring. Oops.

"Sorry. Just got lost in thought for a moment."

He smiled, a softness in his eyes that made my heart skip. "No worries. I was just asking if you had any allergies."

"Oh, um, no." I shook my head. "You?"

"Nope," he said, popping the p. "Lucky us, eh?"

I nodded, trying to regain my focus. "So, um, what's your favourite season?"

As Charlie launched into an enthusiastic defence of winter — "The best season for hot chocolate and hockey, obviously" — a smile tugged at my lips. I placed a hand on my stomach, excitement and fear rushing through me. This man, with his easy charm and kind eyes, was going to be the father of my child, and the more I learned, the more I wondered if I could have made a better mistake.

CHAPTER TEN

CHARLIE

"So, what do you think?"

Emma bit her lip, her gaze darting around the buzzing arena. "It's… loud."

I laughed. "Just wait until someone scores. Then you'll see loud."

I might have quit playing hockey before college, but I'd never stopped living and breathing the game. The chill in the air, the roar of the crowd, the scrape of skates on ice, it all felt like coming home.

When one of my clients had let slip that he had season tickets and he'd be in Romania all summer, I'd snapped them up. I'd have gone anyway, but Emma hadn't really left my house since she'd arrived. I wanted her to experience some of the great things about this city. I'd left Canada for Los Angeles, and I loved it, flaws and all. This game was the first of many. Hopefully, it would get her mind off her business.

She raised a brow. "I'm not sure my ears can handle that."

"Trust me, you'll love it." I leaned in closer, pointing to the ice. "See that guy there? Number 87? Keep an eye on him. He's a magician with the puck."

Emma squinted, trying to follow my finger. "They're moving so fast. How can you even tell who's who?"

"Years of practice. And an unhealthy obsession with the sport."

As the first period got underway, I found myself splitting my attention between the game and her reactions. Her brow furrowed in concentration as she tried to follow the action.

"Okay, so explain this to me again," she said during a lull in play. "Why did they just stop?"

I suppressed a chuckle. "Offside. See that blue line? If an attacking player crosses it before the puck does, play stops."

"And that's… bad?"

"Very bad. Kills the momentum of the attack."

She nodded slowly. "Right. Got it. I think."

I launched into a more detailed explanation of the rules, gesturing animatedly as I spoke. Emma listened intently, her eyes flicking between me and the ice.

"You really love this, don't you?" she asked, a small smile playing on her lips.

"Yeah, I do. It's been a part of my life for as long as I can remember."

"Tell me about that," Emma said, turning to face me fully. "What was little Charlie like, discovering hockey for the first time?"

I leaned back in my seat, shuffling through my memories, trying to pinpoint the exact moment. I couldn't find it. "Honestly? I can't remember a time when hockey wasn't a part of my life. My dad had me on skates before I could walk."

Her eyes widened. "Isn't that dangerous?"

I chuckled, shaking my head. "Nah, not really. It's common for hockey families. He had me bundled up like a little marshmallow. I couldn't have hurt myself if I tried."

Emma frowned. "I guess. But still, a baby on ice skates…"

"Trust me, it's fine. I turned out okay, didn't I?" I winked, trying to lighten the mood.

She rolled her eyes, but I caught the hint of a smile. "Jury's still out on that one."

I laughed, then turned my attention back to the ice as the Toronto Timberwolves scored. The crowd around us erupted, and I joined in, whooping and clapping.

Emma winced at the noise. "Okay, you weren't kidding about it getting loud."

"You'll get used to it. Maybe." I leaned in closer, speaking directly into her ear to be heard over the din. "Want some earplugs? I always bring a pair."

She shook her head. "No, I'll tough it out. When in Rome, right?"

"That's the spirit!" I clapped her on the shoulder, then quickly pulled my hand back. Touching her, no matter how innocently, always sent a jolt of electricity through me. "Just wait until you hear the goal horn. It'll blow your mind."

Emma raised an eyebrow. "Is that a good thing or a bad thing?"

I laughed. "Depends on which team scores."

On the ice, a Timberwolves player deked past two Stingers defenders, faking left before cutting right. With lightning speed, he fired a shot that sailed over the goalie's glove and into the top corner of the net.

The crowd around us erupted.

"Damn it!" I groaned, running a hand through my hair. "Come on, Stingers! Get it together!"

Emma watched me with amusement. "I take it that wasn't good for our team?"

"Definitely not," I grumbled. "We're down by one. They need to step up their game."

"But the Canadian team scored."

"Ah, well…" I rubbed the back of my neck sheepishly. "It's

a bit complicated. My dad played for the Toronto Timber-wolves back in the day."

Emma's eyebrows rose. "So shouldn't you be cheering for them?"

"Not a chance. After he left us, I made a point of cheering for any team playing against the Wolves. Petty, I know, but..."

"But it feels good." Emma finished for me, her voice soft with understanding.

I nodded. "Yeah. It's like my own little act of rebellion, I guess. Every time they lose, it feels like a tiny victory against him."

Emma reached out and squeezed my hand, her touch unexpectedly comforting. "That's not petty, Charlie. It's human."

"Now, let's hope the Canadians don't score again." I grinned. "Or I might have to disown my entire country."

As the players reset for the face-off, Emma pulled a small stack of notecards from her purse.

"What's that?"

She looked slightly embarrassed. "Oh, um... just some of the questions we haven't gotten to yet."

"You brought study cards to a hockey game?"

"I did." She stared at me, a determined glint in her gorgeous eyes.

It was stupid to love a stubborn streak in a woman, right? It probably spelled trouble for me down the line, but I couldn't make myself care when she looked at me like that.

"Alright, hit me with your best shot. But fair warning, I might get distracted if something exciting happens on the ice."

She nodded, shuffling through her cards. "Okay, here's an easy one to start. Did you have any hobbies growing up besides hockey?"

I side-eyed her. "Who says hockey was a hobby? It was more like a religion."

She laughed, but I really wasn't joking. In my house growing up, hockey had been all we worshipped.

"Alright, alright. Well, my sister and I used to spend hours exploring the woods near our house. We'd build forts, pretend we were on grand adventures, that sort of thing."

"That sounds nice," Emma said, an odd catch in her voice. "How old is she?"

"V is three years younger than me."

Her brow creased. "V?"

"Veronica."

She studied me with a critical eye. "And how old are you?"

I snorted. "Maybe you should have asked me that before you jumped into bed with me."

Emma shook her head, chuckling. "I just had the exact same thought."

"I'm thirty-two. You?"

"Twenty-eight."

"A year younger than V." I nodded.

Is it weird that I knocked up a woman my sister's age?

I really didn't want to know the answer, so I brushed it away and focused on what we'd originally been talking about. "Anyway, V might have been younger but she always kept up. Our mom never worried about us when we were kids, you know? We'd disappear into those woods for hours, and she'd just assume we'd come back when we got hungry."

"Was that a generational thing or what? My aunt never knew where I was. I'm not sure she actually cared."

I shrugged. "Different times, I guess. It's funny though, as soon as we hit our teens and started getting into typical Canadian teenage stuff — parties, drinking in fields, that kind of thing — suddenly Mom got all protective. It was bizarre."

"Maybe she just started feeling more responsible," Emma said. "Where was your dad then?"

"Fucked off with some z-list actor when I was twelve." A familiar tightness formed in my chest and I rubbed at it. "I think after that, Mom felt like she had to be both parents, you know? But by then, we were used to our freedom. Made for some interesting arguments."

Emma was quiet for a moment, then said, "I'm sorry about your dad."

I waved it off. "Don't be. He was an ass. We were better off without him."

She looked like she wanted to say more, but the crowd erupted. I turned my attention back to the game, grateful for the distraction.

"Oh, come on! That was clearly interference!" I shouted, jumping to my feet along with half the arena.

Emma tugged on my sleeve. "What happened?"

I sat back down, still fuming. "The ref missed a call. Our guy got checked illegally, but they're letting it slide."

She nodded, but that adorable furrow between her brows told me she didn't have a clue what any of that meant. "And that's... bad?"

I couldn't help but laugh at her earnest attempt to engage. "Yeah, it's bad. But it's part of the game. Sometimes calls go your way, sometimes they don't."

As play resumed, Emma shuffled through her cards again. "Okay, here's another one. What's your favourite childhood memory?"

I thought for a moment, a smile spreading across my face. "Oh man, that's a tough one. But I'd have to say... probably the time V and I built this massive snow fort in our backyard. We spent days on it, and it was like our own little ice castle. We even slept out there one night, bundled up in sleeping bags and drinking hot chocolate."

Emma's eyes softened. "That sounds wonderful. I wish I had memories like that."

Her wistful tone made me curious. "You don't?"

"A lot of my early memories are kind of fuzzy."

"But there must be something."

She hesitated, her brow knitting slightly. "My parents took me to the beach once. I must have been about five or six. We built sandcastles and flew a kite. It's not much, but it always makes me smile when I think about it."

There was something in her voice, a hint of uncertainty that made me wonder if the memory was entirely real or if it was something she'd constructed over time. But the way her face lit up as she described it, I didn't have the heart to question it.

"That sounds great to me," I said softly.

Our moment was interrupted by another roar from the crowd. I turned just in time to see a Stingers player score, tying up the game.

"Yes!" I shouted, jumping to my feet and pumping my fist in the air. "That's what I'm talking about!"

Emma laughed, clearly amused by my enthusiasm. "I take it that was good?"

"It was freaking awesome!" I grinned, caught up in the excitement. Without thinking, I grabbed her hand and squeezed it. "We're back in this!"

As soon as I realised what I'd done, I let go, feeling a mix of embarrassment and something else I couldn't quite name. "Sorry," I muttered. "Got carried away."

Emma's cheeks were slightly flushed, but she smiled. "It's fine. I'm glad you're enjoying yourself."

"So," I said, clearing my throat. "Any more questions on those cards of yours?"

She shuffled through them, her brows drawing together. "How about... did you have any pets growing up?"

I chuckled. "Not unless you count the raccoon family that lived in our garage for a while. Mom was too soft to call animal control, so we just kind of... coexisted with them for a summer."

Emma's eyes widened. "Are you serious? Weren't you worried about rabies or something?"

"Nah, they mostly kept to themselves." I shrugged. "V named them all, of course. The mom was Bandit, and the babies were Rascal and Trouble."

Emma laughed, shaking her head. "That's insane."

"What about you?" I asked. "Any pets in your past?"

She shook her head. "No, my aunt was allergic to pretty much everything with fur. I always wanted a dog, though."

"Maybe someday." It sounded too much like a promise, like we were planning a future together beyond our current arrangement. A future I wouldn't mind bringing to life.

As the second period came to an end, the arena buzzed with excitement. The score was tied, and the tension was palpable.

"So, what happens now?" Emma asked as people started getting up from their seats.

"Intermission. Time for a bathroom break, grab some snacks, that kind of thing. Want anything?"

"I'm good, thanks." She shook her head. "But I might take you up on those earplugs now."

I laughed, reaching into my pocket and pulling out a small case. "Here you go. Just don't put them in too tight, or you'll miss all the fun."

I watched her as she adjusted the earplugs, unable to stop myself from enjoying the sight of an adorable line of concentration forming between her brows, the slight pout of her lips as she tried to get comfortable. Was there anything this woman could do that I wouldn't find endearing?

The crowd around us started to get rowdy as the Kiss Cam made its rounds on the jumbotron. Couples were being highlighted, some eagerly locking lips while others shyly pecked each other's cheeks.

"What's going on?" Emma asked, her voice a bit louder than necessary due to the earplugs.

I chuckled. "It's the Kiss Cam. They put random couples on the big screen and—"

My explanation was cut short as our faces appeared on the enormous screen above the ice. The crowd around us erupted in cheers and whistles.

Her eyes widened in panic. "What do we do?" she half-shouted.

My heart raced, caught between the desire to kiss her and the knowledge that we'd agreed to keep things platonic. "We don't have to do anything," I said, leaning close to her ear so she could hear me. "They'll just boo and move on."

She hesitated for a moment, then asked, "And if we do?"

I shrugged, trying to appear nonchalant even as my pulse quickened. "Then we give them a show and go back to watching the game."

Emma bit her lip, glancing between me and the screen. The crowd's chanting grew louder, urging us on.

"Oh, what the hell," she muttered, and before I could react, she grabbed the front of my jersey and pulled me in.

What started as a gentle, soft brush of her lips, transitioned to a full on inferno. An explosion of sensation, a burst of pent-up desire that had been simmering between us for a week.

I tilted my head, taking complete control and deepening the kiss as one hand cupped her cheek while the other wrapped around the nape of her neck. The taste of strawberry invaded my mouth, her lip balm.

Emma responded with a passion that matched my own, her fingers twisting in my jersey as her tongue duelled with mine. The world around us faded into oblivion, replaced by the sound of our breaths mingling and the cheers of the crowd that felt like they were a million miles away.

One touch, and I forgot everything, including why this was a terrible idea.

CHAPTER ELEVEN

EMMA

How could something as simple as a kiss shake me to the core?

Charlie's lips moved against mine with a passion I hadn't expected, igniting a fire that spread through my entire body. I clung to him, desperately trying to anchor myself as our tongues danced. I forgot about the crowded arena, the game, everything except the man in front of me.

But it didn't last.

A deafening roar jolted me back to reality. The crowd. The Kiss Cam. Oh god.

I pulled away, breathless and dizzy. He stared into my eyes, his gaze dark and intense, before he glanced up at the jumbotron. Our faces filled the enormous screen, both of us looking flushed and slightly dazed.

Heat crept up my neck and into my cheeks as I became acutely aware of the thousands of eyes on us. People clapped and whistled, grinning in our direction. I wanted to sink into my seat and disappear.

"How... how many people saw that?" I whispered.

Charlie chuckled, running a hand through his hair. "You probably don't want to know."

"What do you mean?"

He hesitated for a moment before answering. "Well, these games are televised, so..."

My eyes widened in horror. "Oh no. No, no, no." I buried my face in my hands, mortification washing over me in waves. "You mean to tell me that kiss might have been broadcast to... what? Millions of people?"

"Hey, it's okay." He placed a hand on my shoulder, trying to be comforting. All it did was remind my body that I'd been seconds away from crawling into his lap. "Nobody's going to remember it by tomorrow. These things happen all the time at games."

I peeked through my fingers at him. "Really?"

He nodded, directing a reassuring smile at me. "Promise. It'll be old news before the final buzzer."

I took a deep breath, trying to calm my racing heart. As the game resumed and the crowd's attention shifted back to the ice, I found myself replaying the kiss in my mind almost obsessively.

I snuck a glance at Charlie, who'd become engrossed in the game once more. His brow creased in concentration as he watched the players zip across the ice. Confident that he was fully focused on the game, I openly admired his profile, the strong line of his jaw, the intensity in his eyes.

Stop it.

I tried. Oh, how I tried, but my mind kept wandering. I shuffled through all the things I'd learned about Charlie tonight — and yes, the kiss featured, again and again. Those dangerous what-ifs coming out to play again.

What if he had lived in New York when we met? What if, after that night at the wedding, we'd dated? Three months of getting to know each other, of falling in love slowly instead of being thrown into this whirlwind of unexpected parenthood.

Would we be a real couple now? Committed to raising our baby together, not out of obligation, but out of love?

A pang of sadness hit me in the chest. Because as much as I tried to deny it, I wanted that. I wanted the fairytale, the happily ever after. I wanted Charlie to look at me the way he looked at the ice — with passion, excitement, and unwavering focus.

Charlie leapt to his feet, pumping his fist in the air as the Stingers scored another goal. "Did you see that?" he shouted over the roar of the crowd, his eyes alight with joy. "What a beautiful shot!"

I nodded, forcing a smile. "Pretty impressive."

He laughed, dropping back into his seat. "Pretty impressive? That's like calling the Sistine Chapel a nice finger painting."

"Well, excuse me for not being fluent in hockey-speak," I teased, nudging him with my elbow.

Charlie's smile softened. "Sorry, I get a little carried away sometimes. It's hard not to when you love something this much, you know?"

My chest ached and those pesky what-ifs tried to rear their heads again. I squashed them, focusing only on his face. Not on how handsome he was, or how much I wanted to feel the brush of that beard between my legs.

I studied him for a moment, curiosity getting the better of me. "Can I ask you something?"

"Shoot."

"Why did you quit?" At his confused look, I elaborated. "Hockey, I mean. You said you played as a kid, but now you're an agent. What happened?"

Charlie's expression clouded over, and for a moment, I regretted asking. But then he sighed, running a hand through his hair.

"It's... complicated." His gaze fixed on the ice while he rubbed his thumb across his lips. "I loved the game. Still do, obviously. But I got tired of everyone sucking up to me because of my dad."

"Why were they sucking up?"

"He's in the Hockey Hall of Fame. Big deal in Canada. Everyone wanted to be my friend, but it wasn't really about me. I was just a means of getting to my dad."

My heart ached for him. "That must have been hard."

"It sucked. So I quit. Bonus points for making my old man angry, which I loved at the time."

"Do you ever miss it? Playing, I mean."

He shrugged. "Sometimes. But I'm happy being a fan now."

His attention shifted back to the ice.

CHAPTER TWELVE

CHARLIE

"There's your baby," the doctor said, her tone warm as she pressed the wand against Emma's exposed belly.

I'd been expecting graining black and white images. Instead, the picture was surprisingly clear. I leaned forward, my breath catching as I made out the distinct shape of a tiny human.

"That's really our baby?" I asked, my voice thick with emotion.

The doctor smiled knowingly. "Yes, it is. Let me point out some details for you."

As her finger moved across the screen, outlining the head, the tiny arms and legs, tears welled in my eyes. Holy shit. That was our baby. Our actual, real-life, growing-inside-Emma baby.

"Look at those little fingers," I whispered, a ridiculous smile spreading across my face. I turned to Emma, overwhelmed with emotion. "Can you believe it?"

Her eyes were wide, filled with a mix of wonder and shock.

Before I could think better of it, I leaned over and kissed her full on the lips.

It was brief, just a peck really, but it felt like touching a live wire. Her breath caught, her body tensing for a split second before she relaxed into me. For that brief moment, everything else faded away.

We were back in New York, the night stretched out before us, seemingly endless. No complications. No strings. No future.

Except you wanted the future.

Yeah, part of me had, but what would we have done? Dated long distance, rarely seen each other because we were both workaholics? It would have never worked.

But now, I wished I'd leapt and taken the chance that it would have.

I pulled back and reality crashed over me. What was I doing? We'd agreed to keep things platonic, to focus on co-parenting. She couldn't leave me if we didn't have a romantic relationship for me to fuck up.

She stared at me, her mouth slightly open in surprise, her cheeks flushed a deep pink. Her fingers touched her lips, as if trying to hold onto the sensation.

"I'm sorry. I got carried away and…"

Smooth move. Real fucking smooth.

She blinked, dazed. Her mouth opened as if to say something, but no words came out. The air between us crackled with unspoken tension.

"Would you like to hear the heartbeat?" the doctor asked, saving me from my own awkwardness.

I nodded eagerly, aware that Emma was watching me with a knowing smile. Had she heard it before?

Of course she had. They would have checked everything out in New York. The realisation that she'd experienced this without me, that she'd had to find out alone, pierced me with a sharp stab of regret. I shoved it aside.

I was here now, and that's what mattered.

The second she'd left my office, I'd had my assistant chasing down every possible connection we could use to our advantage. The dietitian was the first call, then this doctor's office.

Some men had a little black book filled with fuck buddies. I now had one filled with paediatricians, gynaecologists, family therapists, play centres, elementary schools and more. Before I got home, I'd already booked us spots on a parenting course I knew Shaun and Mona Martin were using and submitted our interest for the best nursery and elementary school in LA. If my assistant was to be believed, it was never too early to start booking things.

Maybe I was losing my mind, but nothing could go wrong. I wouldn't allow it.

I held my breath as the doctor flipped a switch, and the room filled with a rapid, whooshing sound.

Thump-thump-thump-thump.

My eyes widened, and a lump formed in my throat. "Is that...?"

"That's your baby's heartbeat." The doctor smiled.

Joy surged through me, quickly followed by a wave of emotion so strong it nearly knocked me off my feet. Tears spilled down my cheeks, and I didn't even try to hide them.

I was going to be a father.

Then fear sunk its claws into me. What if I screwed this up and she left me? Emma would never forgive me. I would never forgive myself.

I glanced at her, unable to keep my eyes off her. She blinked rapidly, fighting back tears. Apparently I'd learned nothing today because without thinking, I reached out and took her hand, giving it a gentle squeeze. To my relief, she squeezed back.

Having her move in had been... an adjustment, to say the least. I'd gotten used to the freedom of coming and going as I pleased. But now there was Emma, with her meticulous organisation and her habit of humming while she worked.

I'd tried to be a good host, to make her feel welcome. I'd cut back on my work hours, determined not to be the absentee father my own dad had been. I'd learned to cook her favourite meals, surprising even myself with my new repertoire of dishes. I'd stocked the cupboards with all her most loved things, including an almost endless array of decaffeinated teas.

But the last week had also been an exercise in restraint.

She was a constant temptation, even in the most innocent moments. From the way she padded around the kitchen in the morning, hair mussed from sleep wearing nothing but tiny shorts and a strap top, to the sound of her laughter echoing through the house when she was on the phone with Lila. Everything about her drew me in. I found myself looking for excuses to be near her, to make her smile, to hear her voice.

It was torture of the sweetest kind.

And sometimes not so sweet...

Take the morning she'd caught me coming out of the bathroom, wearing nothing but a towel. The look in her eyes had been... intense. Hungry, even. It had taken every ounce of willpower I possessed not to drop that towel right then and there.

But I had to be strong. My stupidity with the condoms had already changed her life.

Emma's grip on my hand tightened and fresh tears spilled from her eyes. Without hesitation, I sat on the edge of the exam table, tucking her into my side, wrapping my arm around her shoulders. She cuddled into me, burying her face in my shirt as she sobbed.

"These are happy tears, right?" I asked, my tone hesitant.

"Yes." She chuckled, the sound choked with emotion. She eased back, sniffling as she brushed her fingertips across her damp cheeks. "It's incredible."

She stared at the screen again, a hazy look entering her

glistening eyes. My chest ached and I couldn't even begin to explain why.

As we listened to the steady rhythm of our baby's heartbeat, a wave of emotion crashed over me. Love, fierce and protective, surged through my veins. This tiny life, no bigger than a peanut, was ours. The enormity of it all hit me like a freight train.

I might not have planned any of this, but I'd be damned if I failed.

"The baby's heart looks perfect," the doctor said. "Everything is developing beautifully."

"Really?" I asked, my voice cracking. "Everything's okay?"

She nodded reassuringly. "Absolutely. Your baby is healthy and growing exactly as it should be."

"That's great news." My shoulders sagged with relief. "See? Our little peanut is a fighter, just like its mom."

Emma rolled her eyes, but a smile played at her lips. "Peanut? Really?"

I shrugged, grinning. "Well, it does look like a peanut right now. But don't worry, we'll come up with a better nickname once it starts looking more human and less legume-like."

"You're ridiculous." She laughed, the sound warming me from the inside out.

"Only for you." I winked at her, falling easily into our usual banter. It felt good, normal, even as everything around us was changing.

The doctor glanced between us. "Would you like to know the sex of the baby?"

"You can tell already?" Emma asked, tinged with surprise.

She nodded. "We can make an educated guess, though it's not 100% certain."

I turned to Emma, struggling to find the right words. "Do you... I mean, do we want to know? I realise we haven't discussed this."

Emma bit her lip, looking hesitant. "Actually, if it's okay with you, I'd rather wait. Make it a surprise?"

Relief flooded through me. "Yeah, that sounds perfect. Let's wait."

"That's fine." The doctor smiled, but her expression quickly turned serious. "Now, Emma, how has your *hyperemesis gravidarum* been? Any improvement?"

Emma sighed. "It's not much better, but I'm managing to keep more water down at least."

"That's good to hear," the doctor said. "We'll continue to monitor it closely and do some more tests before you leave today to check your hydration and nutrition."

While the doctor talked to Emma about her condition, my mind was still reeling. There was so much we needed to figure out — our living situation, our relationship (or lack thereof), how we were going to balance our careers with parenthood. But in that moment, looking at our baby on the screen, none of that seemed to matter.

I couldn't tear my eyes away from the image of our child. Those tiny hands, the curve of the spine, the rounded head — it was all so perfect, so miraculous. I found myself imagining holding this little person, teaching them to walk, to talk, to laugh, to skate. The future stretched out before me, filled with possibilities I'd never dared to dream of before.

"Here you go." The doctor held out a small envelope to me. "Your baby's first photos."

I took it with trembling hands. Carefully, I pulled out the black and white ultrasound pictures. They were clear and detailed, showing our baby from different angles. To me, they were the most beautiful thing I'd ever seen.

I stared at the images, tracing the outline of our little one with my finger. "I can't believe we made this," I murmured, the words escaping me on a shaky breath. "Our perfect little... peanut."

She laughed again, the sound music to my ears. "You're really sticking with peanut, huh?"

I grinned at her, feeling lighter than I had in weeks. "For now. We can workshop it, come up with something better. How about 'the reason mommy can't keep down her breakfast'?"

"Charming," Emma deadpanned, but amusement danced in her eyes.

CHAPTER THIRTEEN

CHARLIE

"Any update on that preschool application, Tammy?" I shouted, my voice carrying through the open office door.

I'd spent what felt like hours shuffling through an endless pile of paperwork, my mind a million miles away from contracts and deal memos.

It had been nearly two weeks since Emma dropped the baby bomb on me, and I still felt like I was walking through a dream. The ultrasound appointment yesterday had only intensified that feeling. I couldn't stop staring at the picture of our little peanut, marvelling at the tiny hands and feet.

A snort of laughter sounded outside the door before my assistant appeared, her brow arched in amusement. "I'm sorry, did you just ask about a preschool application? Who are you, and what have you done with my boss?"

"What? Can't a guy show some interest in early childhood education?"

"Not when it's you." Tammy crossed her arms and leaned

against the doorframe. "You're giving me whiplash. Last week, you were shouting for contracts and directors. This week, you're panicking over preschool positions? What alien abducted you, and when can I get the real Charlie back?"

"Trust me, I'm asking myself the same question." Even as the words fell from my lips, I reached for the ultrasound picture in my pocket. The reality of impending fatherhood was both exhilarating and daunting.

Her eyes narrowed and I could see the questions brewing behind her eyes. Thankfully, my phone rang before she could get any of them out. Jesse's name flashed on the screen, relief and dread battled for dominance in my chest. He never called me out of the blue.

"I've got to take this." I reached for the phone, throwing Tammy a grin. "Don't forget to check in on the application."

She rolled her eyes good-naturedly as she left, closing the door behind her. I took a deep breath and answered the call.

"Hey, Jess. What's up?"

"Oh, not much," he said, his voice light, but failing to conceal the undercurrent of excitement. "Just calling to see if the rumours are true. Is Charlie 'I'll-never-have-kids' Delacroix really going to be a dad?"

I groaned, sinking lower in my chair. The leather creaked in protest, matching my internal grumbling. "How did you find out?"

"A friend of mine vets the applications for Celestial Heights Preschool."

Shit. I'd been so focused on trying to get all the pieces in place I hadn't stopped to wonder if any of Tammy's contacts could be trusted.

"When he called me, I said he must have the wrong guy. The Charlie I knew swore he'd never have kids." He chuckled, utterly delighted with my life's unexpected turn. "Imagine my surprise when he starts reciting your phone number. So now, I'm confused. When did you fall so hard for a woman that she could convince you to have a kid, and why the fuck haven't you introduced her to your friends?"

I sighed, running a hand through my hair. Leave it to Jesse to cut straight to the chase. "It's complicated, Jess. I didn't exactly plan this."

"Oh, this I've got to hear." Pure amusement dripped from his voice. "How did you end up knee-deep in diapers and baby bottles?"

"Remember Finn McCarthy's wedding?"

"The one where you swore you'd behave yourself? Yeah, I remember. Don't tell me you knocked up a bridesmaid."

My face burned. "It was the wedding planner."

There was a moment of silence, then Jesse burst out laughing. "The wedding planner? Oh man, that's rich. You're telling me you went to a wedding and came back with a baby on the way? That's some next-level irony right there."

"Yeah, yeah, laugh it up," I grumbled, but a small smile tugged at my lips. When he put it like that, it did sound ridiculous.

"So what happened? Did she slip and fall on your dick?"

I rolled my eyes. "Very funny. No, we just... connected. It was supposed to be a one-night thing, but..."

"But now you're picking out onesies and researching the best brand of organic baby food?"

"Something like that." I pinched the bridge of my nose, wishing I wasn't having this conversation. "I know it's crazy. I'm still trying to wrap my head around it."

"I get that, but how far have you gotten in that wrapping?" he asked, his tone softening.

I leaned back in my chair, staring at the ceiling as I tried to sort through the jumble of emotions in my chest. "Honestly? I'm terrified. But also... excited? I mean, I look at Emma, and it's like... shit, Jess, I'd do anything for her. For her and the baby."

"Well, well, sounds like someone's found their one. Never thought I'd see the day."

"Yeah, maybe." Warmth spread through my chest at the thought. "I'm such an idiot."

"What did you do?" Jesse asked, his tone a mix of amusement and concern. "Please tell me you didn't try to negotiate a contract for shared custody or something equally Charlie-like."

"Worse." I cringed at my own stupidity. "I told her we should keep things platonic."

A bark of laughter escaped Jesse. I held the phone away from my ear and waited for him to get it out of his system.

"You're a fucking idiot."

"I thought it would be easier, you know? Less complicated."

Less room for her to change her mind after the baby came and blame all of her feelings for me on pregnancy hormones.

"But now..."

"Now you're realising that ship has sailed."

"Yeah." I sighed. "We started talking about what happens after the baby comes and she mentioned going back to New York." My heart rate picked up just thinking about it. "How I kept a straight face I don't know, but I don't know if I could ever let them go."

"Charlie, my friend, you're in deep."

"Tell me about it," I muttered. "I keep thinking about ways to show her how I feel without pressuring her. But what if it's just the pregnancy hormones making her receptive? I don't want her to wake up one day and feel like I took advantage of her vulnerable state."

"Have you considered, I don't know, talking to her about it?" Jesse's voice dripped with sarcasm. "Novel concept, I know. But I hear it works wonders in personal relationships. Not that you'd know much about those, Mr I-don't-do-feelings, I-do-deals."

"Very funny," I grumbled. "But seriously, what should I do?"

"Be honest with her," Jesse said. "Tell her how you feel. Let her make her own decisions."

I snorted. "Yeah, because that always works out so well in my line of work."

"This isn't work. It's your life and your family. Sometimes honesty is the best policy."

Family. The word sent a jolt through me. A family with Emma. The thought was terrifying and exhilarating all at once. I wanted it with a ferocity that unnerved me.

"I'll think about it," I said finally.

"You do that," Jesse said. "In the meantime, when do we get to meet this miracle woman who's managed to domesticate you? Lukas is also pissed at you for not sharing the news, by the way."

"Why the fuck did you tell Lukas?" I scrubbed a hand across my face, cursing the fact my friends had turned into gossips as soon as they met their other halves.

"Someone had to confirm I wasn't hearing things." Amusement shook the words. More like he couldn't keep it to himself. "So when do we get to meet her? Zoey is busting my balls for dinner and then a girls night once she susses her out. I don't know how much longer I can hold her off."

I hesitated as a protective urge hit me. "I don't know. It's all still new and..."

"And what? You're afraid we'll scare her off with stories of your misspent youth?"

I laughed, but it sounded hollow even to my own ears. "No, it's not that. It's just..."

Why *was* I so reluctant to introduce Emma to my friends?

"Just give us some time to figure things out, okay?" I said finally. "This whole situation is... delicate."

"Alright, alright. I'll hold off the hounds for now. But you have to answer something truthfully for me."

My eyes narrowed. "What?"

"How are you really feeling about all of this?" His tone

shifted from teasing to something more serious. "And don't give me that PR-approved bullshit. I want the real deal."

I leaned back in my chair, closing my eyes as I tried to sort through the tornado of emotions swirling inside me. The image of our peanut on the ultrasound screen flashed in my mind and my chest ached. But right on its heels came the familiar spectre of doubt.

"What about the last answer was PR-approved bullshit?"

He snorted. "The part where you avoided any mention of your old man."

I winced. "Low blow, man."

"Someone's gotta keep you honest," he said, his words careful and measured. "And because it's my job as your best friend to keep your head out of the sand, try again and don't gloss over it like you're facing a horde of reporters."

I sighed, rubbing my temples. "I'm... overwhelmed. Hearing that tiny heartbeat, those little fingers... it's like nothing I've ever experienced. But at the same time, I can't shake this fear that I'll mess it all up."

Jesse's voice softened. "You're not your dad, Charlie. The fact that you're even worried about this proves that."

"Logically, I know that, but I'm still terrified."

"And that's okay. Being a parent is the most terrifying, amazing thing you'll ever do. Trust me, I know."

Jesse and Zoey had triplets, now three years old and absolute terrors if the stories were to be believed.

"How do you do it? How do you not mess it up?"

"I'm just there. Always," Jesse said simply. "You love them, you try your best, and you hope it's enough. And most of the time, it is."

I let his words sink in, feeling a strange mix of fear and hope. "I never thought I'd be in this position, you know? I mean, Emma and I barely know each other."

"I can promise you that's going to change real fast."

Was I fretting for nothing? I already knew Emma better

than my dad had known my mom before he put a ring on her finger. The great Jason Delacroix, hockey legend turned deadbeat dad, had swept my mother off her feet with his fame and charm.

He'd married her faster than he could score a hat trick, only to betray her and then abandon us all when I was twelve.

"Every time I think about holding this baby, about being responsible for another human life, I feel like I can't breathe."

"Welcome to fatherhood, my friend," Jesse said, his voice warm with amusement and understanding. "That feeling? It doesn't go away. But it does get easier. And you learn to breathe through it."

I took a deep breath, trying to imagine it. Me, a father, changing diapers and singing lullabies. It was terrifying and exhilarating all at once.

"I hope so," I whispered.

"We're all just making it up as we go along. But you've got something your dad could never appreciate."

Common decency?

"Your girl."

I smiled, Emma's beautiful face filling my mind. As much as I loved my mother and how hard she'd tried, mothering didn't come naturally for her.

"Speaking of parenting," Jesse's voice broke through my reverie, "Remember how terrified you were to hold the triplets when they were born? I thought you were going to pass out."

"Don't remind me." I groaned at the memory. "I was convinced I was going to drop them. Or break them. Or both. They were so tiny."

"And now look at you. Applying for preschools before the kid's even born. You're going to be a great dad, Charlie. A neurotic, overprotective, probably slightly insane dad, but a great one nonetheless."

His words sent a rush of warmth through me, along with a fresh wave of terror. "You really think so?" Even though half of my genetic makeup came from one of the biggest assholes in the hockey hall of fame? "Because right now, I feel like I'm one panic attack away from buying a lifetime supply of bubble wrap and child-proofing the entire city of Los Angeles."

"I know so," Jesse said confidently. "And hey, if you want some practice, Zoey and I would be happy to let you and Emma babysit the triplets for a night. You know, to help you prepare. Think of it as a trial run for parenthood, only with the option to give the kids back at the end of the night."

I laughed. "You just want a night off from your little hellions. What's the matter, the terrible twos extending into the terrifying threes?"

"Can you blame me?" Jesse chuckled. "Seriously though, the offer stands. It might be good for you and Emma to get some hands-on experience. Plus, it'll give you a chance to see each other in parent mode. Nothing sexier than a man who can handle a diaper blowout with grace and minimal gagging."

"I'll think about it," I said, making a mental note to discuss it with Emma later. "Thanks, Jess. For everything."

"Anytime, man. Just promise me if you're going to name a kid after someone, you pick me and not Lukas." He sniggered. "I need something new to wind him up."

I laughed, feeling lighter than I had in days. Maybe Jesse was right. Maybe I wouldn't fuck it up. And maybe, just maybe, we could be more than just co-parents.

With a renewed sense of purpose, I turned back to my paperwork. But this time, instead of contracts and deal memos, I found myself sketching out nursery designs in the margins, each one more and more outlandish. Maybe I could hire a muralist to make the design better and paint whichever Emma loved most.

With a sigh, I pushed the paperwork aside and pulled out my phone. Maybe it was time to have an honest conversation with Emma.

Before I could overthink it, I sent her a text.

CHARLIE

How are you feeling? Everything okay at home?

EMMA

I'm fine, just craving the weirdest food.

CHARLIE

How long have you been having these cravings?

EMMA

Honestly? Since before I even knew I was pregnant. Started with an obsession for pineapple on everything. Even pizza. Probably should have figured it out then.

CHARLIE

Pineapple on pizza? Please tell me that's just a pregnancy thing and not a regular occurrence.

EMMA

What if I said it was a lifelong love?

CHARLIE

Then I'd have to seriously reconsider this co-parenting arrangement. There are some things I just can't overlook.

EMMA

Hey, don't judge until you've tried it with anchovies and jalapeños.

Absolutely not. But if she needed solidarity, I'd force myself to eat it.

CHARLIE

You're killing me, Sullivan. Next thing you'll tell me you put ketchup on steak.

EMMA

Now that's just blasphemy.

CHARLIE

Good to know you have some culinary standards. Though I'm still side-eyeing that pineapple pizza situation.

EMMA

Keep it up, and I'll make you try it.

CHARLIE

What are you craving today?

EMMA

Green mangoes with spicy peanut sauce. And pickles on the side.

CHARLIE

Your wish is my command. Be home soon.

I shut my laptop lid, grinning like an utter fool.

CHAPTER FOURTEEN

EMMA

"Listen here, little peanut." I tossed the sad excuse for a snack aside and flopped back on the couch, one hand resting on my slightly swollen stomach. "You need to cool it with these cravings, okay? "

The sound of a key in the lock made me sit up straight.

No. He didn't actually...

"Special delivery!" he called out as he stepped through the door with grocery bags in hand, looking for all the world like he'd just won the lottery. "One order of green mangoes and spicy peanut sauce, coming right up!"

He made his way to the kitchen.

I followed him, torn between gratitude and mortification. "You didn't have to do this. It's the middle of the day, don't you have work?"

He shrugged, already pulling out a cutting board. "Work can wait. This is way more important."

I watched, dumbfounded, as he expertly sliced the mangoes and whipped up a quick peanut sauce. I should have stopped him, but I couldn't stop watching. And those pesky cravings sat up and took notice at the first sniff of tart, slightly acidic fruit.

"Is this okay for the baby?" I eyed the spicy sauce.

Charlie paused, knife hovering over a mango. "I think so. The books said most cravings are fine unless it's, you know, coal or something non-edible."

I laughed, patting my belly. "Hear that, little one? Daddy's been doing his homework."

"Of course." He shook his head. "I am not being caught unawares, thank you very much."

He went back to prepping the mangoes, but I couldn't stop staring at him. Never in my wildest dreams did I think he'd come around this well.

"I can't believe you actually left work for this," I said, my voice thick with emotion. "You shouldn't have to cater to my crazy cravings."

"Hey, it's okay." He turned to me, his expression softer than I'd ever seen it. "My assistant already thinks I'm losing my mind, so we might as well go crazy together, right?"

A laugh bubbled up, surprising me with its intensity. "Your poor assistant. She's probably wondering what drug brainwashed you and turned you into my domestic god."

"God, huh?" Charlie wiggled his brows. "I like the sound of that."

I shook my head, amused despite myself. "Well don't let it go to your head."

He chuckled. "Too late."

He plated the chopped mango and drizzled sauce over it. I stared at him, overwhelmed but frozen to the spot. Then he pulled out a jar of pickles and a wave of emotion hit me. What had I done to deserve any of this? "You know, the only person who's ever gone out of their way for me like this is Lila."

His hands stilled, and he turned to face me, his features serious. "What do you mean?"

I shrugged, trying to play it off as nothing while my heart

worked on twisting itself into a knot in my chest. "Growing up, I didn't have many people in my corner. My aunt, she wasn't..." I trailed off, memories flooding back.

"Your aunt wasn't what?"

I took a deep breath. "She raised me after my parents died. But she wasn't exactly... maternal." I bit my lip and willed the burn in my eyes to take a hike.

No one had cared about that though. All the British social services saw was a nine-year-old with no family in the country and two passports. They'd contacted my aunt within a day of my parents passing. She'd jumped on a red-eye, freed me from temporary foster care, taken care of my parents' funeral and then flown us back to the US hours after the last piece of dirt covered their casket.

"Once in high school, I got really sick. Had to spend the whole day in the nurse's office because she had taken off on some last-minute road trip and wasn't answering the school's calls. Didn't even tell me she was leaving."

His eyes widened. "Jesus, that's awful. I'm so sorry."

"It's fine. Ancient history, right?" I shook my head, forcing a smile. "I just... I guess what I'm trying to say is, thank you. For the mangoes, for everything. It means more than you know."

"You don't have to thank me, Em." Charlie stepped closer, his hands capturing mine and squeezing. "This is what partners do, right? We take care of each other."

Partners.

One word should not be able to turn me inside out. The joy that rushed through me should have terrified me. Instead, I embraced it, basked in the warmth of it. I know I'd barrelled in with this unfounded hope that he'd help me, but the last few weeks had defied my expectations. Maybe everything would work out.

"I guess so. I'm just not used to it, you know? Having someone to lean on."

"Well, get used to it," he muttered. "Because I'm not going anywhere."

Our gazes locked and the world faded away while I got lost in Charlie's hazel eyes. Something about him pulled me in, made me feel safe.

The urge to close the distance, to taste his lips again, screamed through every fibre of my being.

Charlie cleared his throat and took a step back. "So, uh, want to eat these mangoes before they turn brown?"

He picked up the plate, while I laughed, grateful for the break in tension.

"God, yes. I've been dreaming about them all day."

He placed them on the breakfast bar and pulled out a stool for me. I took a seat, happily settling in to devour the fruit. We chatted, that sense of comfort I hadn't experienced in years continuing to consume me. It was nice, this little bubble of domesticity we'd created.

As I savoured a particularly juicy piece of mango, I felt a flutter in my stomach. "I think the baby approves," I said with a grin.

His eyes lit up. "Really? Can you feel it moving already?"

I shook my head. "Not exactly. It's more like... a flutter. Like butterflies."

His face transformed, a mix of awe and excitement washing over his features. His eyes widened, and he leaned forward, as if he could somehow see or hear the flutter himself.

"That's... wow," he breathed, his voice filled with wonder.

"Can I ask you something?" I said, licking peanut sauce off my fingers in a way that was decidedly unladylike.

Charlie nodded, his gaze fixed to my lips. "Shoot."

"Are you scared? About... all of this?" I gestured vaguely at my stomach. "Being a parent, I mean."

Silence reigned, and I worried I'd overstepped.

He released a shuddering breath and smiled. "More terrified than words can convey, actually."

"Really? You seem so put together about all this. Like you've got it all figured out."

He let out a soft, self-deprecating laugh. "Trust me, half the time I'm convinced I'm going to royally screw this up."

His honesty caught me off guard. It was both comforting and unsettling.

"But you've been amazing." I gestured to the plate of mangoes. "You're already doing all these thoughtful things. I mean, who leaves work in the middle of the day to cater to pregnancy cravings?"

"A guy who's trying really hard not to mess up the most important thing that's ever happened to him."

My heart did a little flip. He meant the baby, not me. "You won't mess up." Hell, he was practically perfect. "I've seen how dedicated you are. You're going to be a great dad."

Charlie threw me a smile that didn't quite reach his eyes. "I appreciate your faith in me. I just hope I can live up to it."

I wanted to reassure him further, to wipe away the doubt clouding his eyes, but before I could form the words, a wave of nausea struck me out of nowhere. The mangoes, which had tasted like heaven moments ago, now churned in my stomach.

"Oh god," I groaned, clapping a hand over my mouth.

Charlie's eyes widened in alarm as I pushed the stool back. He tried to reach for me but I shook my head, unable to speak as I bolted from the kitchen. I barely made it to the bathroom before emptying the contents of my stomach into the toilet. "Em?" His soft voice filtered through the door, filled with concern. "Can I get you anything?"

I wanted to tell him to go away, to leave me to my misery, but another wave of nausea hit, and all I could do was groan. The door opened and I waved a hand blindly, trying to silently tell him I was fine. Of course, it would have helped sell the image if I wasn't hugging the toilet and heaving.

His hand landed on my back and he crouched down beside me, rubbing gentle circles as I continued to retch. When I finally finished, he handed me a damp washcloth without a word.

"Thanks," I mumbled, wiping my face. "Sorry you had to see that."

"Hey, no apologies needed." Charlie shook his head, his expression a mix of concern and... was that amusement? "I signed up for this, remember? Morning sickness and all."

"Come on, let's get you to the sofa. I'll grab you some water and crackers."

Charlie settled me on the couch and wrapped a soft throw blanket around my shoulders. Then he disappeared into the kitchen, leaving me to sink into the plush cushions and shut my eyes. I tried to will the lingering nausea away. It would clear eventually, but I hated these moments of uncertainty, waiting for it to overpower me and catch me unawares.

"Here you go." He placed a plate of plain crackers on the coffee table and took a seat next to me, his thigh brushing against mine.

The casual contact sent a jolt through me. He pressed a glass of water against my lips. "Small sips, okay?"

"Thanks," I said when I'd emptied half the glass. "You didn't have to do all this."

"You've got to stop thanking me for basic human decency."

"I'm just not used to this. Having someone around when things get messy. Literally and figuratively."

"Well, get used to it. Because I'm not going anywhere."

"What's your favourite food?"

He laughed. "I was wondering if you'd forgotten." He shook his head, but chewed his lip, giving it serious thought. "I'd have to say my mom's poutine. It's this Canadian dish with fries, gravy, and cheese curds. Sounds weird, but it's amazing."

I wrinkled my nose as my stomach rumbled. "That does sound weird. But oddly appealing right now."

"Pregnancy cravings strike again?"

"Maybe. I don't know, but something tells me you'd be insulted if the baby hated your favourite dish."

"Nah, I'd just start converting them to Canadian food after birth." He grinned. "What about you?"

"Probably a really good New York style pizza. Thin crust, lots of cheese, and yes, sometimes with pineapple."

He groaned dramatically. "I can't believe I'm having a baby with a pineapple-on-pizza person. What have I gotten myself into?"

I swatted his arm playfully. "Hey, don't knock it till you've tried it. Maybe the baby will inherit my superior pizza tastes."

"God help us if that happens."

CHAPTER FIFTEEN

EMMA

I wiped the condensation from the bathroom mirror, grateful the vanity wasn't any deeper. A couple more weeks and I wouldn't have a hope in hell of leaning over it.

Dropping the towel, I stepped back and took it all in.

My hair hung in messy waves around my face, still damp from the shower. Dark circles shadowed my eyes, a testament to the restless nights I'd been having.

My hands traced the more than noticeable curve of my stomach. The bump had well and truly popped. I stared at my reflection, the sight both foreign and familiar all at once. A mix of wonder and anxiety swirled in my chest. Just fifteen weeks pregnant and I could hardly recognise myself.

My eyes drifted lower, catching sight of the faint silvery lines stretching across my hips. Stretch marks. I'd known they were coming, but seeing them made my throat tighten.

I reached for my robe, wrapping it tightly around myself. As I cinched the belt, my hand lingered on my stomach. A flutter of movement, so slight I might have imagined it, brought a small smile to my lips.

"Hey there, little one," I whispered, the words barely audible over the hum of the bathroom fan. "You're certainly making your presence known, aren't you?"

The smile faded as quickly as it had come, replaced by a familiar ache of longing. I wished I could share this moment with someone. With Charlie. But he'd been so careful lately, maintaining a respectful distance. I wasn't sure he'd want to feel her move.

At some point in the last three weeks, I'd convinced myself that it was a girl. I had zero logical explanation. It was just a feeling. One that I happily indulged when I lay alone at night, dreaming of our future.

A lump formed in my throat as I stared at my reflection. Who was this woman looking back at me? She bore a resemblance to me, but there was something different in her eyes. A vulnerability, a fear I wasn't used to seeing.

I closed my eyes, taking a deep breath. This was temporary. My body was doing something amazing, creating a whole new person. I needed to embrace it, not fight against it.

Opening my eyes, I forced a smile at my reflection. "You're growing a human," I said, trying to inject some confidence into my voice. "That's pretty badass."

The words rang hollow in the quiet room. I sighed, turning away from the mirror and I exited the bathroom, the cooler air of the bedroom raising goosebumps on my skin. My clothes lay neatly folded on the bed, a silent reminder of another challenge. Getting dressed had become an exercise in patience and creativity.

I eyed the pile warily for a couple of seconds, psyching myself up.

I gritted my teeth and got it done, working extra hard to ignore how the elastic of my underwear dug into my skin, leaving angry red marks and the once comfortable bra now felt constricting. I tugged at it, trying to find a position that didn't make me want to rip it off.

My jeans posed the biggest challenge. I skipped them, opting for yoga leggings and a loose fitting top instead.

I ran a hand over my swollen belly and forced myself to focus beyond the issues, to search for the positive. Despite the discomfort, the mood swings, and the constant worry, a wave of love washed over me. This little one, still barely more than a flutter beneath my palm, had already changed my life in ways I never imagined.

"You're worth it all, peanut," I whispered, a small smile tugging at my lips. "Every stretch mark, every sleepless night, every moment of doubt. You're the best thing I've ever done."

The realisation hit me then — no matter what happened with Charlie, no matter how my body changed or how difficult things got, I had this incredible little person to look forward to. My baby. Our baby. And that love, pure and unconditional, would be enough to get me through anything.

A knock at the door startled me. "Yeah?"

"You okay in there?" Charlie called through the door. "I've got everything set up for the movie."

"Yeah, I'll be right out."

"Hey," he said, his eyes crinkling at the corners as he smiled. "I was starting to think you'd fallen asleep in there."

I forced a laugh, hoping it sounded more natural than it felt. "No, just... having a bit of a wardrobe crisis. Nothing fits right anymore."

His concern flickered in his eyes. "We can go shopping this weekend if you want. Get you some more comfortable clothes."

The offer, so casually made, sent a warmth spreading through my chest. This was the Charlie I'd come to know over the past few weeks — thoughtful, caring, always ready to help. That didn't mean I would rush to agree. Something told me he'd try to pay for everything and then I'd feel even more reliant on him. And for what? Clothes that wouldn't fit me in two weeks or a month? No. I'd wait until not even my leggings could contain me and then I'd deal with my wardrobe.

"I'm okay for now. Thanks."

*C*harlie had set up the couch with an assortment of pillows and blankets, creating a cosy nest that looked incredibly inviting.

"So, what are we watching?" I asked, settling into my usual spot on the couch.

"I thought we'd go classic tonight." Charlie grinned, flicking through the options on screen until he came to a familiar title: *When Harry Met Sally*. "I remember you mentioning it was one of your favourites."

He'd remembered that?

"It is," I said, unable to keep the surprise out of my voice. "But I didn't think it'd be your kind of movie."

"I'm broadening my horizons." He shrugged, popping the disc into the player. "Plus, I figure I should probably watch more rom-coms if I'm living with a wedding planner, right?"

I laughed, the sound coming easier this time. "Fair point. Though I hope you don't think real life weddings end with dramatic New Year's Eve confessions of love."

"You mean they don't?" Charlie gasped in mock horror, settling onto the couch beside me. "My whole worldview is shattered."

As the movie started, I found myself relaxing into the familiar banter. About halfway through, a particularly romantic scene came on. Harry and Sally, dancing close at a New Year's Eve party, their faces inches apart. The sexual tension between them was palpable, even through the screen.

I shifted in my seat, my body thrumming with a familiar ache, desire pooling low in my belly.

Before I could talk myself out of it, I turned towards him. The soft glow of the TV illuminated him, his eyes fixed on the screen. This close, it was hard not to appreciate how handsome he was.

Just do it.

I took a deep breath, my heart pounding.

All I had to do was lean in...

But as I moved, Charlie sat forward, and my lips met empty air. I jerked back, mortification washing over me in a hot wave. He grabbed the remote and settled back into his seat, increasing the volume.

Had he seen what I was about to do? Had he deliberately moved to avoid me?

He glanced at me, a small smile playing on his lips. "You okay? You look a bit flushed."

I nodded, not trusting my voice. My cheeks burned with embarrassment, and I wished the couch would open up and swallow me whole.

The movie continued, but I registered none of it. My mind raced, replaying the moment over and over. The more I thought about it, the more I was convinced he'd caught me moving from the corner of his eye and dodged me.

Maybe he was just being respectful, sticking to our agreement to keep things platonic. Maybe he hadn't even noticed what I was trying to do.

Or maybe... maybe he really didn't want me anymore.

The credits rolled, startling me out of my spiralling thoughts. Charlie stretched beside me, his shirt riding up to reveal a strip of tanned skin. I quickly averted my eyes, heat rising to my cheeks.

"That was good," he said, turning to me with a grin. "I can see why you like it so much."

I managed a weak smile. "Yeah, it's a classic for a reason."

His brow furrowed, concern evident in his eyes. "Are you sure you're okay? You've been quiet for a while."

"I'm fine," I lied, forcing more enthusiasm into my voice. "Just tired, I guess."

"Of course. You should get some rest. We can do this again another night if you want."

"Goodnight," I said, pausing at the doorway. "Thanks for the movie night."

He smiled, warm and genuine. "Anytime, love. Sleep well."

CHAPTER SIXTEEN

EMMA

"I've got a late meeting today," Charlie said, sliding a plate of dry toast in front of me. "Might not be home until after eight."

I nodded, my stomach churning at the smell of his pancakes. "No problem. I'll probably just catch up on some reading."

Three weeks had passed since our movie night and I hadn't tried to kiss him again. Charlie sat at the kitchen table across from me, sipping his coffee. Nothing seemed to have changed with him.

"Oh, there's a premiere next week for one of my clients. Want to come? It could be fun."

My hand froze halfway to my mouth, a piece of toast dangling in the air. A premiere? With my swollen ankles and ever-expanding waistline? I pictured myself waddling down the red carpet, feeling like a beached whale next to the stick-thin starlets.

"Thanks, but I'll pass." I forced a smile. "I've got a video call with a client that night."

It was a lie, but Charlie didn't need to know that. I wanted the man to be attracted to me — pointing out my flaws would be the absolute worst thing to do.

He nodded. "For the next one then. Feels like there's one nearly every week through the summer."

"Do you have to go to them all?"

"Fuck no. I'd never get anything done. My calendar already scares me." He grimaced, shaking his head. "I have to attend my clients' premieres, but the rest are a choice. Sometimes I go to others if I'm interested in the project or I need to make a connection."

The thought of him at those events with beautiful starlets made my stomach twist uncomfortably. I ignored it. Or tried to.

"How is the business going?" he asked, his brow creasing with concern. "Any luck getting those clients back?"

I sighed, setting down my toast. "Not great. Two more weddings dropped this week. At this rate, I'll be out of business before the baby arrives."

Charlie's face fell. "I'm sorry, Em. Is there anything I can do to help?"

I shook my head, fighting back tears. Damn hormones. "Unless you can magically make me not pregnant and fix my reputation, I don't think so."

I clamped my mouth shut, horrified at my own words. I didn't mean that. Not really. My hand instinctively moved to my belly, a silent apology to my little peanut.

I want you, I promise. I just... wish you were here already.

The thought of holding my baby, of finally being free from the constant nausea, the swollen ankles, the backaches — how could I be so selfish?

"Maybe you could set up business here after the baby comes?"

I forced a smile, trying to mask the turmoil of emotions churning inside me. "Maybe. I don't know if LA is ready for my brand of New York wedding magic."

Twenty-three weeks. That's how long I had left of this pregnancy. Twenty-three weeks of feeling more and more like a stranger in my own skin. The image of a leggy blonde draped over his arm at a premiere flashed through my mind. She'd be wearing something slinky and sophisticated, not struggling to fit into stretchy leggings. She wouldn't have to worry about morning sickness or heartburn or any of the million other indignities of pregnancy.

Stop it. You're being ridiculous.

But was I? He was handsome, successful, kind. What was stopping him from finding someone who didn't come with all this baggage?

"You okay? You zoned out there for a second."

I blinked, tearing my gaze away from the plate I'd been staring at for who knew how long. I glanced up to find Charlie watching me with a concerned line between his brows. The urge to reach over and smooth it away made my fingers twitch.

"Yeah, sorry. Just thinking about... the baby."

It wasn't entirely a lie.

"I was just saying that with your talent, I'm sure you could corner the market on celebrity weddings out here."

That ugly twisting feeling hit my stomach again.

"Right, because every starlet dreams of having her wedding planned by a washed-up New Yorker with a baby on her hip."

Charlie's brow furrowed. "Hey, don't talk about yourself like that. You're incredibly talented, Em. Any bride would be lucky to have you plan their wedding."

"Thanks," I murmured, dropping my gaze to my plate. "I appreciate the vote of confidence."

"It's more than that, love." He smiled at me. "I'd be happy to hook you up with some of my contacts. I'm sure between me and my assistant we could have you back up and running in no time."

Why would I stay in LA once the baby came?

"I ordered you something." He grinned, that excitement lighting up his face again. "A pregnancy pillow. Read they help with getting comfortable in bed."

"Thanks," I murmured, forcing a smile. "That's really sweet of you."

As Charlie rambled on about the pillow's benefits, a spark of determination ignited within me. No way in hell was I going to let some Hollywood starlet or leggy model swoop in and steal him. Time to pull out the big guns. If subtlety wasn't working, maybe it was time to go nuclear. I'd make him see me as more than just his pregnant roommate, even if it killed me.

CHAPTER SEVENTEEN

CHARLIE

"Damn it, Tammy, I don't care if he's the next big thing. We're not taking on any more clients right now," I grumbled at my tablet, scrolling through the endless stream of emails.

"Morning," Emma said, her sleep-filled voice dragging me out of my email-induced trance.

I glanced up from my tablet, my usual greeting dying on my lips as I took in the sight before me. Emma stood in the doorway, clad only in a thin silk robe that clung to her curves, accentuating her growing belly.

"Morning," I managed, my mouth dry. "Everything okay? You're not usually up this late."

"Oh, I'm fine." She padded across the tile floor, bare feet silent against the cool surface.

I couldn't tear my eyes away from her. My cock began to stir, a slow, steady ache that grew with each step she took.

As she slid into the chair opposite me, the robe gaped slightly at her chest. Her hard nipples were easy to spot through the thin fabric. For a second, all I could think about was sucking them into my mouth and listening to her beg for more.

I averted my eyes, guilt gnawing at me for even looking. But the image was seared into my brain, fuelling the fire consuming me.

"Slept through my alarm, I guess. Figured I'd eat before showering."

"Are you sure?" I frowned at her, concern overriding my inappropriate thoughts. "The morning sickness isn't acting up again, is it? We could call the doctor if—"

Emma laughed, the sound light and carefree. "Relax, Charlie. I promise I'm fine. A girl can't sleep in once in a while?"

She reached for the plate of plain toast I'd laid out for her. The movement caused her robe to slip open further, revealing a tantalising glimpse of skin, and I choked on my coffee, my mind instantly filled with images of laying her out on the table and enjoying a very different kind of breakfast.

"Charlie? Are you okay?"

I coughed, trying to regain my composure. "Fine," I wheezed. "Coffee went down the wrong way."

She eyed me sceptically but didn't press the issue. Instead, she launched into a discussion about her plans for the day, seemingly oblivious to the effect she had on me.

I tried to focus on our conversation, I really did. But my traitorous eyes kept drifting to the V of her robe, to the soft curve of her neck, to the swell of her stomach where our child grew.

My fists clenched beneath the table as my cock hardened painfully, straining against the confines of my pants. It had been months since I'd fucked a woman and there was only so much my fist could satisfy me. I wanted nothing more than to push her down on the table, tear away that damn robe, and bury myself inside her.

But guilt was a bitter pill, one I choked on with each filthy thought. I shouldn't be thinking about her like this. We'd agreed to keep things platonic, to focus on co-parenting. But with every passing day, it became harder to remember why I'd suggested that in the first place.

"Anyone in there?" Emma waved her hand in front of my face, snapping me back to reality.

"Sorry," I mumbled, heat creeping up my neck. "What did you say?"

She smirked, amusement dancing in her eyes. "I asked if you had any big plans for the day. But you seemed lost in thought there. Care to share with the class?"

I scrambled for an excuse, anything to explain away my distraction. "Oh, uh, work stuff. You know how it is."

Something flickered across her face, an emotion I struggled to place. Sadness? Disappointment? It was there and gone before I could pin it down, her smile firmly back in place as she nodded sympathetically.

"Must be intense if it's got you this preoccupied. Anything I can help with?"

The offer, so innocently made, sent my mind spiralling in directions it definitely shouldn't go. I stood abruptly, needing to put some distance between us before I did something stupid.

"Thanks, but I've got it handled," I said, perhaps a bit too quickly. "I should probably get going. Traffic is always a nightmare."

I dumped the remains of my coffee in the sink, placed the cup in the dishwasher, and grabbed my keys. All of it on autopilot. My mind was fixed on that damn robe. The curve of her breast, the softness of her skin, the way the silk hugged her growing belly.

✳

"So, if we replace this glass with a solid wood bannister, it'll be much safer when the baby starts crawling."

The contractor nodded, scribbling notes in his little notebook. "Shouldn't be a problem. We can match the wood to your existing trim for a seamless look."

A floorboard creaked, and Emma appeared at the top of the stairs, wearing yoga leggings and a loose top, her dark hair tousled from sleep. She rubbed at her eyes, a sleepy smile curling her lips.

"Charlie?" she asked, surprise colouring her voice. "I didn't expect you home for lunch."

I smiled, an ache forming in my chest at the sight of her. "Trying to cut down on office hours before the baby comes. How's the nap?"

"Exactly what I needed," she replied, descending the stairs. "Oh! Since you're here, I wanted to run something by you."

I raised an eyebrow, curious. "Sure, what's up?"

Emma beamed, practically vibrating with excitement. "I've been thinking about doing a nude maternity photoshoot. You know, to celebrate my changing body and this amazing journey we're on."

My brain short-circuited. "A... nude... what?"

"A photoshoot," she repeated, oblivious to my shock. "And the photographer would see you naked?" The words tumbled out before I could stop them, my voice strangled.

The contractor chuckled beside me, and I remembered we weren't alone. Heat crept up my neck as I struggled to control the instant 'no' desperately trying to escape.

Emma's smile faltered, and her face paled. "Well, yeah. That's kind of the point, Charlie."

The contractor cleared his throat, amusement clear in his voice. "I think I've got everything I need here. I'll order the supplies and we can get started next week." He clapped me on the shoulder. "Good luck with that, mate."

I barely registered his departure, my mind too busy conjuring images of Emma posing naked, her belly round and full, skin glowing in soft lighting. The idea of another person — even a professional — seeing her like that sent a surge of jealousy through me.

"It's not as scandalous as you're making it out to be," Emma continued, her voice lacking its earlier conviction. "Lots of women do these shoots. It's empowering, you know? A celebration of what our bodies can do."

I nodded mechanically, trying to keep my expression neutral as my imagination ran wild. Emma, draped in sheer fabric. Emma, cradling her belly, a serene smile on her face. Emma, completely bare, vulnerable and beautiful.

"I get that," I managed, my voice hoarse. "But have you really thought this through? Once those photos are out there, you can't take them back."

A faint line formed on Emma's forehead. "I'm not planning on plastering them all over billboards. They're for me. To remember this time."

Guilt twisted in my gut. Of course I wanted her to feel empowered and beautiful. But the idea of someone else capturing her in such an intimate moment... it made my blood boil.

"I'm not saying don't do it," I backpedalled, running a hand through my hair. "I want you to feel good about yourself and your body. I do. I guess I'm wondering if there might be other ways to celebrate that don't involve... you know..."

"Nudity?"

I nodded, desperately trying to find the right words. "I support you, one hundred percent. I only want to make sure you're comfortable with everything. Maybe we could look into some alternatives? Something a bit more... private?"

Emma studied me for a long moment, her face unreadable.

"I appreciate your concern. But this is something I really want to do. For me."

I swallowed hard, forcing a smile. "What if I took them?"

Emma's brows shot up and she grew paler. "You? As the photographer?"

I nodded, trying to look more confident than I felt. "Why not? I've got a decent camera."

She hesitated, biting her lip. "As sweet as that offer is, I want these photos to be... professional. Plus," she added, her attempt at a playful tone falling flat, "Thanks, but I'd rather keep you on diaper duty than camera duty. You'll have plenty of chances to take pictures once the baby's here."

"Fair point." I sighed. "Okay. I support you, no matter what."

As Emma headed back upstairs, I slumped against the wall, letting out a shaky breath. The image of her naked, posing for some stranger, refused to leave my mind. I'd have to find a way to deal with this growing attraction before I did something we'd both regret.

A few hours later, a soft knock on my office door interrupted my concentration. "Charlie? Can I get your help with something?" Emma called through the door.

"Sure." I pushed away from my desk, curious. I rushed across the room, happy that she'd come to me instead of hurting herself in the kitchen. "Sure, what's up?"

I opened the door to find Emma standing there, looking slightly embarrassed. She was topless but for a bra she held to her breasts. It was unhooked, the straps slipping down her arms.

My mouth went dry, then she spoke and it got so much worse.

"This is kind of awkward," she began, biting her lip. "But I can't seem to clasp my bra."

I hesitated, torn between the desire to help and the knowledge this could cross a line we'd carefully drawn.

"Oh," I managed, my voice sounding strangled even to my own ears. "Um, sure. I can... help with that."

Emma smiled gratefully, turning her back to me. "Thanks. I feel silly asking, but..."

"No, it's fine," I assured her, somehow forcing words past the lump in my throat. I stepped closer and the scent of her shampoo — something floral and light — enveloped me. My dick hardened and my mind took a trip back to New York and the way I'd buried my face in her hair after coming so hard I saw stars. "Happy to help."

I reached for the clasp, my fingers trembling slightly. The warmth of her skin radiated against me. I tried to focus on the task at hand, but the intimacy of the moment overwhelmed me. I missed the clasp a couple of times.

The irony wasn't lost on me.

I could take the thing off one-handed but putting them on took multiple tries.

Never mind the voice in the back of my mind begging me to just turn her around, throw the bra away and kiss her.

"There," I murmured, finally managing to fasten the clasp. My fingertips brushed against her spine as I pulled away, sending a shiver through me.

Emma turned, her cheeks flushed. "Thanks. You're a lifesaver."

I nodded, not trusting myself to speak. The urge to pull her close, to feel her body against mine, nearly overpowered me. I needed to get out of there before I did something stupid.

"Glad I could help," I managed, already backing towards the door. "I should get back to work. Let me know if you need anything else."

I retreated to my office, closing the door behind me and

leaning against it. My heart raced while I took several deep breaths, trying to calm myself and will my erection to go away.

Fuck. All I wanted to do was rip the door open and fuck her until she understood that she would only ever be mine. But I couldn't. I slumped into my chair, running a hand through my hair. How long could I keep this up? Pretending I didn't want more, pretending the sight of her didn't set my blood on fire.

a week passed with more of the same, every day it got harder and harder to resist her. I stopped working from home but for one day a week, hoping that would help me maintain my self-control.

At the breakfast table, I scrolled through my emails, absently munching on toast and sipping coffee. My regular morning routine.

I tried to enjoy the quiet kitchen filled with the aroma of fresh coffee and the gentle hum of the refrigerator. But movement in my peripheral vision caught my attention, and I tensed before glancing up.

My breath caught in my throat. Emma walked across the kitchen, wearing nothing but one of my dress shirts. The white fabric barely skimmed the tops of her thighs, leaving her long legs bare. The buttons strained across her growing belly, threatening to pop open at any moment.

My mind instantly filled with images I had no business conjuring. Unfortunately, neither my body nor my brain cared for my logic.

Instead it flooded me with visions of Emma, crawling out of my bed, hair mussed from sleep — or other activities. The shirt sliding off her shoulder as she reached for me, a mischievous glint in her eye. My hands, pushing the fabric aside to reveal more of her soft skin.

"Morning," Emma said, oblivious to my internal struggle.

I swallowed hard. "Morning."

Forcing my gaze back to my tablet, I took a sip of coffee, willing my body to behave.

She rose up on her tiptoes, reaching for a mug from one of the cupboards and my eyes betrayed me, following the curve of her legs. The hem of the shirt inched higher, revealing more tantalising skin. My fingers itched to trace the path my eyes travelled, to feel the softness of her thighs beneath my hands.

One wrong move and I'd see everything. Part of me — a part I tried desperately to ignore — hoped for exactly that.

"Whoa there." I pushed my chair back and rushed over to her. "Let me help you."

"I'm okay. I've got it."

I wrapped an arm around her waist to steady her while my other hand shot out, grabbing the mug she'd been reaching for. The warmth of her body against mine sent electricity coursing through my veins, but concern overrode any lingering desire. I set her back on her feet and handed her the mug, unable to keep the worry from my voice.

"You need to be more careful, Em. What if you'd fallen?"

Her eyes widened with surprise. "I... I didn't think—"

"No, you didn't," I cut her off, immediately regretting my harsh tone. I softened my voice, trying to mask the fear that still gripped me. "I'm sorry. You scared me. Please, promise me you'll be more careful? If you need something out of reach, ask me."

For the first time, I regretted my kitchen design. It had been built for my six-foot-four height.

She nodded, a strange expression crossing her face. "Okay. I will."

As Emma cradled the mug in her hands, staring up at me, I became acutely aware of how close we stood. The scent of her shampoo enveloped me, and the warmth of her skin radiated through the thin fabric of my shirt. The urge to pull her closer, to capture her lips with mine, nearly over-whelmed me.

Instead, I stepped back, putting some much-needed distance between us.

❄

The opening credits rolled across the TV screen as Emma and I settled into our usual spots on the couch for our weekly movie night. A bowl of popcorn sat between us, a physical barrier I both appreciated and resented. The past two weeks had tested my restraint to its limits. Every innocent touch, every shared laugh, every moment of domestic bliss pushed me closer to the edge of breaking my promise to wait until after the baby's birth.

I'd tried to ask Jesse for advice but he'd just laughed and called me an idiot and hung up on me. So I'd been left working overtime trying to avoid touching her and limit how much time we spent together. My reasoning being that if I only saw her at mealtimes, it should be easy to resist her. There was nothing sexy about food.

Unless you slathered it over her naked body and—

I stiffened and slammed the box shut on that thought. Nope. Not going there.

I glanced at Emma, her profile illuminated by the soft glow of the TV. She wore leggings and an oversized sweater, her hair piled messily on top of her head. Even like this — or perhaps especially like this — she took my breath away.

And that was allowed. As long as I didn't touch. Though some days I needed to literally recite the reasons why that was a bad idea to remind myself.

Her body and emotions surged with pregnancy hormones, leaving her vulnerable.

What if she decided later I'd taken advantage of her state?

Or worse, what if she realised after the baby came she

didn't want me at all? And then she'd leave and I wouldn't have the joy of seeing her sleepy expression every morning.

Or catastrophic: she moved back to New York.

The thought of that left me cold.

I forced my attention back to the movie, but movement beside me caught my eye. Emma's gaze had drifted to her phone, her thumb swiping in a familiar pattern. My stomach dropped as I recognised the telltale interface of a dating app.

Panic surged through me, constricting my chest.

When did she start scrolling the apps? Why was she scrolling the apps? Had she met someone?

The sight unlocked a new fear. That I'd lose her to someone else before our baby even arrived.

Who would she choose over me? What could they offer I couldn't? My mind raced with possibilities, each more devastating than the last.

Should I say something? Ask her about it? The words formed on my tongue, but I swallowed them back. What right did I have to question her dating life? We'd agreed to keep things platonic, after all. I had no claim on her beyond our child.

I tried to focus on the movie, but the images blurred before my eyes. All I could think about Emma finding someone else, building a life and a family excluding me. The thought tore at my heart, leaving me raw and aching.

I cursed my own shortsightedness. How had I not seen this coming?

CHAPTER EIGHTEEN

EMMA

I clutched my oversized tote bag to my chest as Charlie and I stepped into the birthing class. The room was filled with soft mats, plush pillows, and an array of strange-looking props that I couldn't begin to identify. The scent of lavender hung in the air, presumably to create a calm and inviting atmosphere.

It wasn't working.

Not on me, at least.

One foot in that room and panic like I'd never known infused me. Something about the concept of practising to have the baby made it all the more real.

Not to mention the stress of waiting for the test results to confirm the baby's health. The doctor had assured us that the tests were routine, but the anxiety gnawed at me constantly. I wanted to share my fears with Charlie, but he seemed so focused on being supportive, in the most clinical way possible, that I didn't know how to broach the subject.

"You okay?" Charlie asked. "You look a little pale."

His hand hovered near the small of my back. I could almost feel it. The ghost of his touch. But it rarely came these days.

When had his touch become so rare that even this near-contact sent a jolt through me? The warmth of his palm used to be a constant, reassuring presence. Now, it seemed he couldn't bring himself to bridge that final inch.

I forced a smile. "I'm fine. Just... processing."

In a few short months, I'd be responsible for a tiny human. Processing the reality that I was about to learn how to push said human out of my body. Processing the fact that ever since my baby bump had really popped, Charlie hadn't touched...

Like I was nothing but a duty and it was the baby he really wanted.

Of course, I'd understood all of that before now. I just thought I had a handle on it.

These days it was hard for me not to fixate on what went wrong. The kiss we shared at the hockey game six weeks ago had been off the charts, but ever since he'd put a distance between us. He treated me more like a roommate than... whatever we were supposed to be.

It had occurred to me more than once that I could be imagining the whole thing. That maybe nothing had actually changed and I was the one making too much out of a situation.

But then he'd started going out of his way to avoid squeezing past me in the kitchen or shifting his hands on the car door to stop our hands touching as I got in. There were too many little things not to make something of it.

"Charlie?"

I turned at the vaguely familiar voice, my eyes landing on a petite pink-haired woman waddling towards us, her belly prominently displayed in a form-fitting maternity top. I recognised her instantly. Mona Martin. From Abi's wedding. She hadn't looked ready to pop back then, but not much else had changed. Shaun followed close behind her, his grin widening as he glanced from Charlie to me.

"Oh my god, what are you doing here?"

"Mona! Shaun!" Charlie's hand dropped to his side. "What a surprise," he said, his voice an octave higher than usual.

I glanced at him, surprised at the panic that flickered across his features before he schooled them into a friendly smile. His eyes darted between them and me.

Mona's gaze shifted to me, her brow furrowing slightly. "And who's this?"

Charlie cleared his throat and finally placed his hands on me. Granted, it was just my shoulder, but that touch burned through my dress. My traitorous nerve endings lit up, while my mind rebelled against the false intimacy. I fought to keep my expression neutral, but my heart leapt at the touch, even though it felt like a performance for our audience.

"Mona, you remember Emma? She was the wedding planner for Abi and Finn's wedding."

Recognition dawned on her face, quickly followed by shock. "Of course! It's so good to see you again. What are you doing in LA?"

I opened my mouth to respond, but Charlie beat me to it. "Emma's staying with me for a while. We're, uh, expecting." He gestured vaguely towards my midsection.

"Oh." Mona's eyes widened, darting between Charlie and me. "Oh! Wow, that's... congratulations!"

Shaun's grin grew even wider. "No wonder you've been so scarce lately. You knocked up the wedding planner?" His shoulders shook. "Does Finn know?"

Charlie's hand tensed on my shoulder, and I could practically hear the gears in his head grinding to a halt. "Uh, not yet. We haven't really told anyone..."

I forced a smile, trying to diffuse the awkwardness. "It's all still new. We're just... figuring things out."

Figuring things out.

When would we move out of that phase? I'd grown tired of this limbo a while ago. Also how could this be new still? We'd been living together for weeks, sharing a home but not a life despite my subtle attempts to change that. I'd lost count of how many times he'd rejected or ignored my advances at this point. The distance between us seemed to grow with each passing day, as insurmountable as the swell of my belly.

Mona's eyes lit up, and she clasped her hands together. "Oh, this is so exciting! We can be pregnancy buddies!" She reached out and grabbed my hand, pulling me closer. "How far along are you? I'm six months, but I swear this little one's trying to make me look like I'm carrying twins."

"Twenty-two weeks."

"That's fantastic!" Her enthusiasm was overwhelming, especially given that we'd only met briefly at Abi's wedding. "Oh, we have to get together for lunch sometime. Or even better. I know all the best prenatal yoga spots in LA. We could take a class together."

Before I could respond, the instructor called for everyone's attention. "Alright, let's get started!"

Saved by the bell.

"Find a comfortable spot on the mats, and we'll begin with some breathing exercises."

Charlie's hand slid from my shoulder to the small of my back, guiding me towards an empty mat. The touch shocked me but simultaneously sent a shiver up my spine, and I tried to ignore the warmth that spread through me at his proximity.

It should have been comforting. Instead, it highlighted every moment he hadn't touched me in the past weeks. I settled onto a mat and tried my hardest to shake off the negative energy. I had to stop obsessing over his actions. We were having a baby, what did it matter if he didn't touch me, kiss me or really look at me anymore?

A tapping sensation started in my lower abdomen and I smiled, imagining little feet bouncing inside of me. The sensation, growing more pronounced with each passing week, never failed to amaze me.

"You okay?" Charlie whispered, his breath warm against my ear.

I nodded, not trusting my voice. He was so close, yet it felt like there was an ocean between us. How could I tell him that I wanted more than this platonic arrangement we'd agreed on? That every time he touched me, my skin caught fire with need?

I guessed the better question was: could I handle more rejection?

I'd never been the type to throw myself into romantic relationships without a thought. I'd grown up watching my aunt flit from one man to another, cycling through the highs of falling in love to the lows of heartbreak. Watching that, having her as a role model, I'd been extra careful vetting the men I dated. Didn't do casual. No one night stands.

Until Charlie.

Maybe I should try dating apps for real. "Dads, I want you to sit behind your partners, legs on either side to support them. This position will help you both feel connected and allow you to provide physical support during labour."

Shaun and the other expectant fathers in the room seamlessly moved into position, clearly having done this before. Charlie, however, hesitated.

"Uh, should I...?"

"I guess so."

Charlie shuffled behind me, his movements awkward and unsure. "Is this okay?" he asked, his hands hovering near my waist.

"It's fine," I said, trying to keep my voice steady. But my heart was racing. The stark contrast between Charlie's uncertainty and the other fathers' easy confidence stabbed at my insecurities. As he settled in behind me, his chest pressed against my back. It was torture being this close, knowing that for him, it was just part of the class.

The instructor began leading us through breathing exercises, but I couldn't focus. All I could think about was his proximity, the way his hands rested lightly on my hips, the rise and fall of his chest against my back. Every inch of contact tingled and made my frustrating hormones sit up and take notice.

"Remember, moms," the instructor said, "your partner is your rock during this process. Lean into them, both physically and emotionally."

I wanted to laugh at the irony. How could I lean on Charlie when I was terrified that one wrong move would shatter this fragile co-parenting arrangement we'd built?

As the class progressed, we moved through various positions and exercises. Charlie was attentive, following the instructor's directions to the letter. But there was a clinical precision to his touches. It was nothing like the loving caresses Shaun bestowed on Mona, or the tender looks the other couples shared.

Each carefully placed hand, each perfectly executed movement only served to remind me of what we lacked. Charlie's attentiveness felt more like a well-rehearsed performance than genuine care. During a break, Mona waddled over to us, Shaun in tow. "Isn't this class great? Shaun and I have been coming for weeks. It's really helped us feel prepared."

I nodded, forcing a smile. "It's... informative."

"Oh, you two are naturals," Mona said, beaming at Charlie and me. "You look so in sync already."

If only she knew. I glanced at Charlie, expecting to see discomfort or maybe amusement at Mona's assumption. Instead, he was grinning, looking every bit the proud father-to-be.

"Thanks," he said. "We're just taking it one day at a time."

As we moved into the next set of exercises, I couldn't shake that pesky thread of inadequacy that had woven into my thoughts. Loving couples surrounded me and I felt like a fraud, pretending to be one half of a partnership that didn't really exist.

As if the session couldn't get any more humiliating, the instructor demonstrated a massage technique for easing lower back pain during labour. Charlie's warm hands settled against my lower back and began to rub at a pretend ache.

I bit my cheek, holding back a groan of pleasure that would not be appropriate in a room full of strangers.

But my body's reaction couldn't overshadow the doubt — fear really — that we'd lost some sparkle in the last four weeks. Right around the time I started to really show. Only there had been something. A tension. A barely restrained need.

Now we were just… comfortable.

"Is the pressure okay?" Charlie asked, his fingers working out a knot in my muscles.

"It's fine," I said, hating how my voice caught.

Everything was fine. It had to be fine.

As the class wound down, the instructor had us practise different labour positions. In one, I was supposed to lean back against Charlie's chest, his arms supporting me.

"Relax into your partner," the instructor said. "Trust them to hold you up."

I tried. I really did.

"Emma, you need to relax," the instructor said gently, coming over to us. "Your body is rigid. Remember, your partner is here to support you."

I don't rely on other people. I'd always managed on my own, and this wouldn't be any different.

CHAPTER NINETEEN

CHARLIE

I sat at the kitchen table, laptop open, trying to focus on the latest contract negotiations for a new blockbuster trilogy. But I couldn't keep my eyes on the screen. Instead, they kept wandering to the woman currently rummaging through the fridge.

She'd been at it for at least five minutes, humming and mumbling to herself while jars clinked together. I bit my lip. Why did she need to reorganise the fridge again? Hadn't she got it right the first three times?

Ever since the birthing class, she'd become very particular. Despite arguing that she didn't need to buy things to decorate, she'd started filling my living room with bright, colourful pillows and throws. New mugs and dishware had appeared in the cupboards.

Another five minutes ticked by before she emerged with a jar of pickles in hand, and bumped the door shut with her hip. I couldn't help but stare.

She was... glowing. No other word for it. Her skin had a radiant quality, her eyes sparkled with life and her breasts…

I bit off a groan and tore my gaze away.

Pregnancy suited her, even if she hadn't realised it yet.

This week marked eleven weeks since she'd moved in with me. I thought we'd settled into our new life with relative ease. If I wasn't working, I was reading every pregnancy and parenting book I could get my hands on. Emma's body continued to change and I constantly found myself desperately grasping for self-control.

My resolve to keep things platonic was crumbling by the day. The promise I'd made to wait until after the baby was born felt increasingly impossible to keep. But I had to try, for Emma's sake and for our child's.

Something about being able to visibly see the effects of my baby growing inside of her did funny things to me. One look at her and I got hard. It made zero sense, but I couldn't act on it no matter how much I now regretted uttering those damn words.

She wanted this to be uncomplicated and I would do everything in my power to give her that until she delivered the baby. Then all bets were off.

Even if it gives me the worst case of blue balls in history.

It felt like I'd been walking on eggshells for a week since I caught her swiping on a dating app. She hadn't gone on any dates yet, but that didn't stop the dread growing inside of me, waiting for the day she'd come downstairs dressed up for one.

I studied her. Would I be able to tell if she had met someone? Her demeanour hadn't changed, though I had made it a point to stay away as much as possible in the last week.

The cravings had well and truly set in. She seemed to take it all in stride, including accepting that she'd developed a liking for pickles. There hadn't been any middle of the night snack runs like some of the films I'd watched had warned would come. But then I had taken extra care to stock the kitchen with every food I could imagine her wanting.

She hummed happily as she plucked one of the green wedges from the jar. One bite and she moaned. My cock instantly responded.

Friends. You're just friends.

I bit my cheek.

For the last few weeks, I'd gotten used to the sight of her biteable ass in yoga leggings. Today, she'd traded them in for jeans.

Maybe she's going out.

With a guy? My eyes narrowed while panic tried to close off my airways. Other than the jeans there were no other differences. Her brown hair hung in loose natural waves around her face like usual, no makeup covered her face and her purse still sat on the side table where she'd dropped it a few days ago.

If she were meeting a guy, wouldn't she do her hair and makeup?

"Are you going out?" I asked finally, somehow keeping my voice level.

She glanced at me, almost noticing me for the first time. Her brow wrinkled. "No, why would you think that?"

Relief slammed into me. I nodded to the jeans and her confusion cleared.

"Oh, I was just checking the fit." She shrugged. "I promised Mona I'd get coffee next week. Didn't think I should do that in yoga leggings."

My gaze dropped to her waist again. Her shirt had ridden up, revealing a sliver of skin. A fucking hair tie held her jeans closed.

Why hadn't she said anything? I could have taken her shopping days ago.

Then she reached for a glass on a high shelf.

"We've talked about this." I pushed my seat back and

rushed over to her. "Ask me for help when you can't reach something."

"I've got it." She turned slightly towards me, waving me off. "I'm fine."

"Maybe." I gently pushed her out of the way. "But I'd rather you not risk hurting yourself when I can help."

I plucked the glass off the shelf and handed it to her, my gaze never wavering from her amused but frustrated eyes.

We stood so close, her growing baby bump brushed against me. How had I not realised how much her body had changed already? She'd always been petite, but now there was a definite curve to her belly, a roundness that hadn't been there before last week.

I backed away, intending to return to my work, but I couldn't tear my eyes from her and that ridiculous hair tie, much less my mind.

"Get your things." I shut my laptop and snatched my keys off the table. "We're going shopping."

Emma turned, pickle halfway to her mouth, her brow scrunched with confusion. "What? Why?"

I gestured to her makeshift jeans fastener. "You need maternity clothes."

A blush crept up her cheeks, and she tugged her shirt down self-consciously. "Oh, that. It's fine, really. I don't need—"

"Yes, you do." I took the jar of pickles from her and set them on the counter. "I'm buying you a whole new wardrobe."

Her eyes widened. "Charlie, no." With a firm but gentle hold, I guided her out of the kitchen. "You don't have to do that. I'm only going to get bigger, so I might as well wait a little longer."

"Not taking no for an answer, Sullivan."

"Stop." She dug in her heels and I stopped, my brows raising. She glanced away, her expression sheepish. "I can't afford it. My savings will only cover so much and I need to be strategic if—"

"That's easily fixed. I'm paying."

She stared at me, her eyes rounding. "No. You can't."

"It's my fault your clothes don't fit. Buying you new ones is the least I can do."

She opened her mouth to protest again, but I was already ushering her towards the door.

"Come on, it'll be fun. Promise."

Thirty minutes later, we were standing outside a trendy maternity boutique that had come highly recommended. My clients and assistant found it hilarious that I'd gone from asking them for restaurant recommendations and hot tickets to requesting **OB-GYN** contacts and parenting tips. I, on the other hand, considered myself smart. Why struggle when we had a fount of knowledge within easy reach?

Emma's eyes widened as she took in the white and gold rimmed window display. "This place looks expensive. I really don't need—"

"Nope," I cut her off, guiding her towards the door with a hand on the small of her back. "No more protests. Your comfort is worth every penny to me." I opened the door and ushered her in. "Take your pick of the store, there's no limit."

She bit her lip, looking torn. "But they'll only fit for a couple of months, and then they'll just get thrown out. It's such a waste."

I turned her to face me with a hand on her shoulder. "You deserve the best, and that includes comfortable, stylish clothes. Please, let me do this for you."

"I don't know." She continued to chew her lip.

"I've got some work things coming up and it would be amazing to have a date for once."

It wasn't a lie. It felt like my clients had gotten together and agreed to release all of their projects in the same month. Add the charity events and dinner engagements to the mix and my summer was about to get very busy. It would be nice to not have to fend off some attention-seeking starlet masquerading as my date for the night.

When she didn't bite, I added: "And my friends want us to go on a double date." I winced the second the words fell from my lips. "Not that I — I didn't tell them that we were—"

She tilted her head, staring at me with utter confusion. Sighing, I gave up trying to explain myself and focused on the true purpose.

"Don't you want to feel comfortable when you meet them?"

Finally, she nodded. "Okay. But I'm putting everything but the essentials back once I try it on."

I grinned, knowing I'd won this round. "Whatever you say, darling."

The bell above the door jingled as we stepped into the boutique, a chic little place tucked between a juice bar and a yoga studio my assistant had recommended. The shop assistant, a blonde with a pixie cut and a bright smile, greeted us with clasped hands.

"Welcome! How can I help you today?"

I smiled. "We're looking for a whole new wardrobe for this gorgeous mama-to-be. She's just starting to show, and we want to make sure she has everything she needs to feel comfortable and beautiful."

Emma stiffened under my touch, and I mentally kicked myself.

Too much. Dial it back.

The shop assistant didn't seem to notice the tension, her smile only widened. "Congratulations. You make such a stunning couple."

"Oh, we're not..." Emma shook her head. "I mean, he's not my..."

"Thank you." My gaze trailed over the nearby racks,

avoiding Emma's at all costs. I didn't need to look to feel the daggers she directed at me. "We need a complete wardrobe overhaul, from basics to formal wear. Clothes that'll fit right now but also in a few months time."

"Understood."

"There's no limit." I fished my wallet out of my pocket and pulled out the black Amex I rarely used. The assistant's eyes widened a fraction. "Whatever Emma wants, it's hers."

"Yes, sir." The assistant grinned and took the card.

"Okay, stop." Emma turned on me, her eyes wide and frantic. "This isn't necessary. Seriously, Charlie. I'll get a couple of bits but we—"

"Need to present a unified front. What would my clients and friends think if they saw you spilling out of your clothes?" My brows rose as her eyes narrowed. I hated pulling the image card on her. To me, she looked gorgeous no matter what she wore, but I needed her to accept my offer. "We might not be in a relationship, Em, but you are carrying my baby and my clients do expect me to uphold a particular image."

For a moment, she just stared at me. Then she growled, "Fine," and stormed off between the racks of flowy dresses and stretchy leggings.

Relief briefly washed over me, though I knew that wouldn't be the end of it. The damn woman was too stubborn for her own good sometimes. No, I fully expected her to fulfil part of the order while watching every single penny.

For now, I trailed after them, content to let Emma take the lead. I watched as she ran her fingers over soft fabrics, her eyes lighting up at a particularly cute top or a cosy-looking pair of joggers. Every so often, she'd glance back at me, holding up an item with a questioning tilt of her head. I'd nod encouragingly, giving her a thumbs up or a wink.

But as the pile of clothes in her arms grew, I noticed an unsurprising pattern. She kept gravitating towards the sale racks, her brow puckering as she checked price tags and put items back with a sigh.

I caught the shop assistant's eye, motioning her over while Emma was distracted by a display of nursing bras.

"She's holding back." I glanced at Emma, making sure she was out of earshot. "Anything you see her put back, grab it and add it to a fitting room."

"Got it." She nodded, understanding dawning in her eyes. "Don't worry, I'll make sure she gets everything that makes her eyes light up."

I grinned, grateful for her perceptiveness. "You're a lifesaver."

She wandered back to Emma and I let my gaze wander the store, taking in the racks of colourful clothes and the soft, soothing background music. It was a world away from what I was used to, but there was something comforting about it.

My attention landed on a display in the corner, and my breath froze. Nestled between the racks of sensible nightgowns and stretchy yoga pants was a collection of maternity lingerie. Delicate lace and shimmery satin in soft, muted shades that made my mouth go dry.

Before I could stop myself, an image of Emma in one of those wispy little numbers filled my mind. The way the fabric would stretch over her new curves, the lace framing her collarbones and brushing against her thighs...

I hardened instantly. Heat rushed through me, desire and shame warring in my gut.

What the hell was I thinking? I'd agreed to keep our relationship strictly platonic. I couldn't have these thoughts. We hadn't even talked about the kiss in the doctor's office. I had no business picturing her like that, no matter how beautiful she was.

But god, she was beautiful. Even more so now, with the glow of pregnancy softening her features and rounding her hips. I'd always thought she was gorgeous, but something about seeing her body change, knowing it was because of our child growing inside her... it did things to me. Things I wasn't ready to examine too closely.

I swallowed hard, tearing my gaze away from the lingerie display. I needed to focus on being her friend, her support system. Not some creep who fantasised about her in skimpy underwear.

EMMA

as there nothing budget-friendly in this entire store? Nearly every item I pulled cost far too much money to waste on a piece of clothing that would only be good for a month, two at most.

But as much as I desperately wanted to leave and find the nearest Target, I knew Charlie wouldn't let me. A wishful part of me hoped that if I got enough to fill a bag, he'd be appeased and then I could sneak out to a more affordable store when he was at work.

That didn't mean I wasn't grateful. No, I appreciated everything he tried to do for me. This just wasn't necessary. Particularly when no amount of pretty clothing would change the fact my ankles were swollen and my dress size had exploded in less than a month. I'd read that some lucky women didn't show until the third trimester, but my frame showed every new development.

Every time I looked in a mirror, discomfort arrowed through me. My body felt foreign, like it belonged to someone else. I sifted through another rack of flowing tops, trying to ignore the price tags that made my eyes water. A soft, maroon blouse caught my eye, and I reluctantly added it to the pile in the assistant's arms. I'd need to sell a kidney to afford half of these clothes.

Charlie was chatting with the shop assistant, his expression relaxed and easy. Like he couldn't care less that the mother of his child was slowly morphing into a human incubator.

Stop it!

I handed the top to the assistant with a forced smile, reminding myself that Charlie was being supportive. It was a good thing.

But was it really?

The past few months had been a rollercoaster of emotions. Living with Charlie was both heaven and hell. He was attentive, always making sure I had everything I needed. But that was just it — he treated me like a task to be completed. But he always pulled back at the last second, leaving me feeling confused and frustrated. I'd pulled out all of the stops in the last two weeks, trying to get him to react, to really see *me*. All of it had failed.

"Find anything you like?" Charlie's voice startled me, and I nearly dropped the pair of stretchy jeans I was examining.

"Oh, um, yeah. Just a few things," I mumbled, avoiding his gaze. I couldn't bear to see the indifference in his eyes, the way he looked at me like I was just another responsibility to manage. I gestured to the pile of clothes the assistant was holding instead. "I should probably try these on."

"Great idea."

I nodded and made a beeline for the fitting room. Charlie followed and I stopped short.

"You don't have to come. I can manage."

He pouted, actually pouted, like a kid denied ice cream.

"But I want to see what you picked out. Come on, Em. Let me be involved in this."

I sighed, torn between wanting to maintain some privacy and not wanting to seem ungrateful. After all, he was paying for all of this.

"Fine," I conceded. "But no laughing if something looks ridiculous, okay?"

His face lit up with triumph. "I could never laugh at you."

I lifted a brow but chose not to comment. What good would it do?

Instead, I walked into the fitting room with anticipation and dread swirling in my gut. On one hand, I was excited to try on new clothes that might actually fit comfortably. On the other, I was terrified of seeing Charlie's reaction to my changing body.

But as I closed the fitting room door behind me, leaving him waiting outside, I took a deep breath. I could do this. I'd planned weddings in hurricanes and wrangled bridezillas on the verge of nuclear meltdowns. Trying on some maternity clothes in front of the father of my child? Piece of cake.

Right?

CHAPTER TWENTY-ONE

CHARLIE

*E*mma stepped out of the fitting room, wearing a simple black dress, the fabric stretchy and soft-looking as it hugged her curves. It skimmed over her belly, highlighting the gentle swell, and dipped low in the front to showcase her new cleavage. She looked stunning. Radiant.

"Well?" She did a little spin, the skirt flaring out around her legs. "What do you think? Too much for everyday?"

I shook my head, struggling to find my voice. "No. No, it's perfect. You look stunning."

She ducked her head, a blush staining her cheeks. "You're just saying that because you have to."

"Hey." I stepped closer, dipping my head to catch her eye. "I'm saying it because it's true. You're gorgeous, Emma. Pregnancy suits you."

She met my gaze, her eyes searching mine for any hint of insincerity. I held steady, willing her to see the truth in my words. The air between us crackled with tension. I couldn't stop myself leaning in, drawn to her like a magnet. Her breath hitched, her lips parting slightly.

Why is this a bad idea?

"I've got a few more items for you to try on," the shop assistant said, breaking the spell. She brushed past us and hung another load of clothes in the fitting room.

Emma blinked, stepping back. She noticed the items the assistant added and frowned. "I put all of this back."

"You didn't want to." The assistant shrugged, before directing a sly smile at me. "I'm just following orders."

"Charlie." Her eyes narrowed on me, her tone beseeching.

"I told you there was no limit." I pointed to the fitting room. "Go on. I can't wait to see what you really picked."

With a grumble and a look that said the conversation wasn't over, she disappeared back into the fitting room, I let out a shaky breath. I'd been seconds away from kissing her again. If the assistant hadn't interrupted, I would have.

The next hour passed in a blur of outfit changes and compliments. Emma tried on everything from casual leggings and tunics to elegant dresses that made my heart race. With each new outfit, I fell a little bit more for this incredible woman.

When total silence fell, I should have known trouble was coming.

The fitting room door burst open, and Emma stormed out, her face flushed and eyes blazing. She clutched a piece of midnight blue lace that made my heart stop. It was the lingerie I'd been eyeing earlier, the one I'd tried desperately to push from my mind.

"What the hell is this?" she asked, her voice dangerously low. "And why is it in my pile?"

I opened my mouth, but my brain short-circuited, caught between the image of Emma in that scrap of lace and the very real, very angry woman standing in front of me.

"I... uh..."

Her eyes narrowed. "Did you put this in there? Is this some kind of joke?"

"No!" I finally managed, holding up my hands in surrender. "I swear, I didn't—"

A soft chuckle interrupted my fumbling explanation. The shop assistant stepped forward, a sly smile playing on her lips. "Sorry, that was my doing. You said to add anything she looked at longingly, and well... you spent a good five minutes staring at that piece." She shrugged. "So I figured what applied for her should apply for you too."

If the floor could have opened up and swallowed me whole, I would have gladly let it. Emma's gaze swung back to me, a mix of confusion and something else I couldn't quite name in her eyes.

"You... looked at this? Longingly?" Her tone softened.

I ran a hand through my hair, searching for the right words. "It's a nice piece, that's all. I thought you might like it."

Emma's face fell, and she looked down at the lingerie in her hands. "Right. Well, I appreciate the thought, but there's no way I could pull this off. Especially not with my waistline the way it is now."

Something in me snapped. All the pent-up frustration, the desire I'd been trying to suppress, the overwhelming need to make her see how beautiful she was — it all came rushing to the surface.

"Stop," I growled, stepping closer to her. "Stop talking about yourself like that."

Her eyes widened, and she took a step back. But I followed, closing the distance between us until her back hit the mirrored wall of the fitting room.

"Charlie, what are you—"

"You want to know what I think about your body?" My voice was low, intense. "I think you're gorgeous. Every curve, every new inch — it's enough to drive a man crazy with want."

CHAPTER TWENTY-TWO

EMMA

"What are you talking about?"

I stared at Charlie, my back pressed against the cold mirror of the fitting room. His words echoed in my ears, impossible to process.

"You've barely touched me in weeks. Lately, it feels like you go out of your way not to look at me. How can you say I drive men crazy?"

"Are you kidding me?" His jaw clenched, a muscle ticking in his cheek. "You're glowing. Every day, you become more radiant. Men can't help but notice."

"No, that's... that's not true. You—"

"I've seen the way people look at you," he said, his voice low and intense. "At the grocery store, at the park. You might not notice it, but trust me, they do."

"I..." My voice faltered. What could I say? That I'd been too afraid to hope for any positive attention?

"I didn't think anyone would find me attractive like this."

Charlie's features softened, but the intensity in his eyes

remained. "Emma, pregnancy is beautiful. It's a miracle, and it shows in every inch of you."

He stroked my jaw, his touch almost reverent. "Your body is doing something incredible, creating life. How could that not be attractive?"

Heat flooded my cheeks, spreading down my neck and across my chest. His words ignited something deep within me, a spark of hope and desire I'd been trying to smother.

"You're just saying that," I whispered, but even to my own ears, it sounded weak, unconvincing.

Frustration flashed in his eyes. "Why would I lie about this?"

"To make me feel better?" I hated how small and insecure I sounded. "Because you feel guilty?"

His hands dropped from my face, and for a moment, I thought he was going to step away. Instead, he gripped my shoulders, gently but firmly turning me to face the mirror.

"Look," Charlie commanded, his voice soft but brooking no argument. "Really look at yourself and see what I see."

But I couldn't. All I could see were the changes that had been haunting me for weeks. The roundness of my belly, the fullness of my breasts, the slight puffiness in my face. I squeezed my eyes shut, unable to bear the sight. Not wanting to confront the changes in my body that had been causing me so much anxiety.

He sighed. "I think this might be the most painful part."

Confusion consumed me and my mouth opened, words forming but never escaping. What was painful? Looking at me? Hadn't I been trying to drive that point home for the last five minutes?

"I've spent weeks watching you stare into the mirror with disgust, and it kills me," he said, his voice dropping to a low, intense whisper. "Because all I see is how fucking beautiful you are."

"I don't recognise myself anymore."

His grip on my shoulders tightened. "Open your eyes, love. Please. For me."

There was something in his voice, a plea that I couldn't ignore.

Slowly, reluctantly, I did as told, but I didn't focus on myself. No, instead I stared at him, taking in how his tall frame dwarfed mine, how his chest brushed against my back with each breath. His gaze bore into mine through the reflection and my breath caught at the intensity in his eyes. He was the gorgeous one, not me.

For a moment, I thought I saw something more there, a flicker of desire perhaps? But it was gone so quickly, I must have imagined it.

"Now, tell me what you see," he said, his breath warm against my ear.

I forced myself to lower my gaze, taking in my reflection. The dress I wore clung to my curves, accentuating the swell of my belly and the fullness of my breasts. My hair, usually so carefully styled, was slightly mussed from trying on clothes. My cheeks were flushed, my eyes wide and uncertain.

My brain couldn't stop there. It zeroed in on the flaws beneath the fabric. The stretch marks, the cellulite on my thighs, the dark line running from navel to pubic bone, slight discolouration at my hairline from melasma. Then there was the swelling… all of the swelling. I couldn't remember what I'd looked like before all of this.

I swallowed hard. "I see someone who doesn't look like me anymore. Someone who's getting fat. Who's changing in ways I can't control. I see stretch marks and swollen ankles and..."

"Stop." His fingers brushed across my shoulders, teasing the strap of the dress. "Let me tell you what I see."

His hands moved from my shoulders, leaving the straps in place. They slid down my arms, leaving goosebumps in their wake. "I see a woman who's more beautiful than ever, who's absolutely breathtaking. Every curve, every inch of you is perfect."

I shook my head, tears pricking at my eyes. "You don't have to say that, Charlie. I know I'm not—"

"Let me finish." His hands came to rest on my hips, his touch warm even through the fabric of my dress. I couldn't help but lean into him, enjoying his touch even if I shouldn't. "I see curves that turn heads. You don't even notice the way men look at you when we're out."

Tears pricked at my eyes, threatening to spill over. "Charlie..."

"I see beauty in the softness of your skin, in the fullness of your figure. You're creating life, Em. How could that be anything but breathtaking?"

His words washed over me, making it impossible for me to look away from our reflection. His eyes blazed with sincerity, his face a mask of determination.

"But it's not just your body," he continued. "It's everything about you. I see strength and courage. A formidable woman who uprooted her entire life, moved across the country, and is facing all of this with such grace. The way you light up when you talk about the baby. The determination you show every day, facing this unexpected challenge head-on. How could anyone not be in awe of you?"

A tear escaped, rolling down my cheek. His hand came up, gently wiping it away. "You're incredible. Every inch of you, inside and out. I wish you could see yourself the way I see you."

The dam broke. Tears flowed freely now. "I don't feel incredible," I choked out between sobs. "I feel scared and over-whelmed and... and so alone."

"You're not alone. I'm right here. I've always been here."

I turned into him, burying my face in his chest. His arms wrapped around me, strong and secure, as sobs wracked my body. His shirt grew damp with my tears, but he didn't seem to mind. One of his hands came up to stroke my hair, the gentle motion soothing me.

"Shh, it's okay," he murmured, one hand rubbing soothing circles on my back. "Let it out. I've got you."

"I'm sorry," I mumbled into his chest. "You have nothing to be sorry for," Charlie murmured. "I should have been clearer about how amazing you are. I was so afraid of making you uncomfortable that I ended up making you feel invisible. That's the last thing I ever wanted."

I pulled back slightly, looking up at him. His eyes were soft, filled with an emotion I was afraid to name. "So you really don't think I'm... unattractive?"

His laugh was low and warm. "You're stunning. Pregnancy has only enhanced your beauty."

"Thank you," I whispered.

He smiled, giving my shoulders a gentle squeeze. "No need to thank me for telling the truth. Now, why don't you try on that green dress? I have a feeling it's going to look amazing on you."

Charlie left me alone in the cubicle with a barrage of thoughts. Everything he'd said was about how other men looked at me. Not him.

Clearly, he was just trying to boost my confidence, nothing more.

CHAPTER TWENTY-THREE

CHARLIE

"Hey, Em, did you want to order in for dinner tonight?" I called out, hearing footsteps on the stairs. "I was thinking maybe—"

The words died in my throat as I stepped into the hallway and caught sight of Emma, a vision in emerald green. The dress we'd bought earlier hugged her curves perfectly, accentuating the swell of her belly and the fullness of her breasts. Her dark hair cascaded in soft waves around her shoulders, and her makeup emphasised her already glowing features.

I swallowed hard, trying to school my features before she noticed me drooling. "Wow. You look... incredible."

Her lips curved into a smile, a calculated glint in her eye. "Thank you. I'm glad you approve."

Something about her tone set me on edge. "So, uh, where are you headed? Meeting Mona for dinner?"

She paused at the bottom of the stairs, studying me intently. "Actually, I have a date."

Had the world tilted on its axis?

"A date?" I repeated, certain I'd misheard.

"Yes, a date." She lifted her chin slightly, a defiant glint in her brown eyes. "Is there a problem with that?"

Who could she be going on a date with? When did this happen? How had I missed it?

"I... no, of course not." I struggled to keep my voice even. "I guess I'm surprised. You didn't mention anything earlier."

Emma shrugged, adjusting her purse strap. "It came up rather suddenly. I didn't think it required a formal announcement."

The casual way she dismissed my concern only fuelled the fire building inside me. I clenched my fists, trying to rein in the emotions threatening to spill over.

"So, who's the lucky guy?" I asked, aiming for nonchalance and missing by a mile.

"Does it matter?"

"Of course, it matters," I snapped, my control slipping. "You're pregnant, Emma. With my child. I think I have a right to know who you're spending time with."

Her eyes flashed dangerously. "A right? I wasn't aware my personal life required your approval, Charlie."

"That's not what I meant."

Only that's exactly what I'd meant. Fuck.

I ran a hand through my hair in frustration. "I'm just concerned. Dating during pregnancy can be complicated. There are risks to consider, potential complications—"

"Spare me the lecture," Emma said, her voice sharp. "I'm well aware of my condition and the risks involved. I'm not some helpless damsel who needs you to make decisions for me."

Her words stung, but I pressed on. "I never said you were helpless. I'm trying to look out for you and the baby. Is that so wrong?"

Her laugh lacked any trace of humour. "If you really

wanted to look out for me, you wouldn't have spent the last month avoiding me like I had the plague."

Her accusation hit me like a physical blow. "Avoiding you? I haven't been—"

Only I had.

"Oh, please," she scoffed. "One minute you're all attentive and caring, telling me how beautiful I am, and the next, you can barely stand to be in the same room with me. Do you have any idea how confusing that is?"

I opened and closed my mouth, searching for a response. Had I really been that transparent?

"I don't understand," I finally managed. "If you've been feeling this way, why didn't you say something?"

Emma's eyes blazed. "Why should I have to? We're both adults, Charlie. We're living together, about to have a child together. I shouldn't have to spell out the obvious attraction and chemistry between us."

My breath caught. She'd felt it too? All this time, I thought I'd been hiding my growing feelings, but apparently, I'd done a piss-poor job of it.

"Em, I—"

"No," she cut me off, taking a step closer. "You don't get to make excuses. You've been sending mixed signals for weeks, and I'm tired of it. I have every right to see whoever I want."

The implication behind her words hit me hard. My mind conjured images of Emma with another man, touching her, kissing her. Rage and possessiveness surged through me.

"So that's what this is about?" I growled, closing the distance between us. "You're that desperate to get laid?"

"How dare you!" I laughed, the sound harsh and bitter. "Jesus, Emma, do you have any idea how hard it's been to keep my hands off you? Every day, watching you walk around in those skin tight yoga leggings, stealing my shirts and parading yourself around the house, flaunting a body I'm not allowed to touch." I ground my teeth. "It takes every ounce of self-control

I have not to pin you against the nearest wall and show you exactly how interested I am."

Her breath hitched, her chest rising and falling rapidly. "Then why didn't you? Why have you been pushing me away?"

"Because I'm trying to do the right thing!" I exploded.

We stood there, chests heaving, the air between us crackling with tension.

"What if we could satisfy our physical needs without any new strings?" Emma asked.

I swallowed hard. "Meaning what?"

"We could try a friends-with-benefits agreement of sorts.

"You're suggesting we sleep together... casually?"

She nodded. "It would allow us to deal with this tension between us while still maintaining our focus on the baby."

"Are you sure that's what you really want? I... I want you to feel comfortable here," I said carefully. "Not like you owe me anything or have to do things just because I want them."

"I do. Plus this way, we can both get what we clearly need without pressure." Emma studied me, her eyes narrowing slightly. "Do you think you could handle that? Just sex, no strings attached?"

I nodded, trying to project confidence I didn't entirely feel. "I think it's worth a try. It's got to be better than this constant push and pull between us, right?"

A slow grin stretched her lips. "Exactly."

"Okay."

"So we're doing this?" she asked, a glint of triumph flickering in her eyes.

"Yes."

My brain short-circuited. What the fuck had I just agreed to and why did I feel like it was going to backfire on me?

"Are you sure?" I asked, giving her one last chance to back out. "We don't have to—"

Emma cut me off by closing the distance between us and

pressing her lips to mine. The kiss was hard, desperate, months of pent-up desire pouring out in a single moment of contact. My hands found her waist, pulling her as close as her pregnant belly would allow as I deepened the kiss, tasting the sweet gloss on her lips.

When we finally broke apart, both breathing heavily, her eyes were dark with desire.

A low growl escaped me as I bent and captured her lips again, walking her backwards until her back hit the wall. My hands roamed her body, savouring the curves I'd been admiring from afar for so long. Her fingers tangled in my hair, tugging lightly in a way that sent shivers down my spine.

I trailed kisses along her jaw, down her neck, revelling in the soft sighs and gasps she made. When I reached the sensitive spot just below her ear, she sighed happily. Her belly brushed against my abdomen, reminding me that this time wouldn't be like New York. It sobered me slightly. I pulled back, meeting her gaze.

"Are you absolutely sure about this?" I asked, my voice husky with desire. "We can stop if you want. No pressure."

She cupped my face in her hands, her eyes soft but determined. "If you stop, I might murder you in your sleep. So get fucking on with it!"

Those words broke the last of my restraint. I scooped her up in my arms, earning a surprised squeak, and carried her towards the stairs.

"What are you doing?" Emma laughed, her arms looping around my neck.

"Taking you to bed." My lips found hers again as I carefully ascended the stairs. "Unless you have any objections?"

She shook her head, nipping at my bottom lip. "None whatsoever."

CHAPTER TWENTY-FOUR

EMMA

Charlie kicked my bedroom door open and strode in. He set me on my feet at the bottom of the bed before stepping around me. My eyes instantly zeroed in on the mirror. I'd never thought anything of it before now. It was just a mirror. But as his fingers grazed my spine and tugged at the zipper on my dress, its positioning bothered me.

I pressed a hand to my chest, stopping the dress from sliding from my body, and turned to face him. "Can we cover the mirror?"

His brow wrinkled as he considered my request. "No, I want you to see yourself the way I do."

"But, I—"

"Shh, love. Trust me." He turned me gently to face the mirror. He stood behind me, his chest pressed against my back, bending so that his chin rested on my shoulder. "Remember what I said in the store?"

He pressed a kiss to my shoulder, just above the neckline of the dress. My eyes fluttered at the caress.

"Remember?" His teeth grazed my neck, prompting me to focus.

His words from earlier echoed in my mind, taking on new meaning. When he'd talked about men noticing me, he hadn't been speaking hypothetically. He'd been describing himself.

I nodded, my breath catching as his lips trailed along my neck. "You really see me that way?" I whispered, meeting his eyes in the mirror.

"God, yes," he breathed, his gaze intense. "You were irresistible in New York, love." His hands moved to my hips, fingers splaying across my belly. "Carrying my baby didn't change that."

I swallowed hard, trying to see myself through his eyes. The woman in the mirror stared back at me, her cheeks flushed, eyes bright with desire. Charlie stood behind her — behind me — his tall frame dwarfing mine, his hands possessive on my body.

He tucked his fingers beneath the neckline of my dress and dragged it off my shoulders. I fought it for a second, but then I focused on the desire burning in his eyes, shining back at me through the mirror. I let go, and my dress fell to the floor, leaving me in just a pretty bra and underwear that didn't hurt my skin.

"Beautiful," Charlie murmured, his hands skimming my sides. "Absolutely beautiful."

His touch felt like electricity against my skin, chasing away my insecurities. I leaned back against him, revelling in the warmth of his body. I turned into him, my head tilting back, lips searching for his. He kissed me deeply, one hand cupping my face while the other splayed across my belly.

It quickly turned desperate, needy. His tongue slipped into my mouth, dancing with mine, heightening the desperation. Each touch sent sparks of anticipation spiralling through my veins.

I whimpered into his mouth, my hands clinging to his hair

while his hands roamed my naked body. The touch of his fingers on my bare skin made me shiver, reminding me of how much I'd missed this.

With a desperate moan, I deepened our kiss, my hands clawing at his chest, tugging his t-shirt up until my hands could splay across his abs. He groaned against my lips before pulling back to reach behind his head and tear the t-shirt off. He flung it away from us.

"Better?" He lowered his head again with a tiny smirk twisting his lips.

I nodded, busy ogling his naked torso. My hands caressed him while he claimed my lips again, trailing lower and lower until I hit his waistband and decided that patience was not a virtue I currently possessed. I popped the button on his jeans.

"Slow down, darling," Charlie said, chuckling. "We've got all night."

"I don't want all night. I want you now." I opened the zipper and shoved the jeans off his hips with very little grace. I just needed them gone.

"Okay, love." He kicked them off, abandoning them on the floor with my dress. "Have it your way."

My gaze wandered down his chest, to the obvious outline of his arousal straining against his boxers. His eyes never left mine as my fingers hooked into the waistband and pushed them down, freeing his cock. It stood at attention, long and thick, glistening with pre-cum. I couldn't help but stroke it, enjoying the way it felt in my hand. I might have also enjoyed watching him strain for control, his neck taut and the vein in there popping.

I loved the weight of him in my hand, the velvety texture of his skin against my fingertips. His hand came to rest on my shoulder, squeezing as I continued to stroke him, building a slow rhythm.

But it wasn't enough.

I needed to taste him.

"Are you sure about this?" Charlie asked, his voice laced with concern as he watched me lower myself to the floor. My pregnancy had made a few tasks more challenging, but I refused to let it stop me now.

"I'm fine."

I wanted this. Needed it.

Once settled on my knees before him, I leaned forward, my hand still wrapped around him. When I finally closed my lips around the head of his cock, he let out a low groan. That guttural sound urged me on and I sucked him harder, my lips sliding up and down his length. I teased him with my tongue, flicking it over the head and then tracing the vein that ran along the underside.

I took him deeper, gagging slightly as I pushed my limits. He moaned, panting, his hips jerking against my face.

"Emma, stop," he grunted, sounding strained and desperate.

I took him deeper again, using my hands to massage his balls.

"If you keep doing that, I'm going to come." His hands tangled in my hair, gently tugging but not forcing.

I smiled around his girth, enjoying the power I held over him. "That's kind of the plan."

"Well, it's not my plan."

He pulled away with a strength I couldn't resist. As I panted for breath, staring up at him with wet, glazed eyes, he swept me up in his arms, lifting me easily off the floor. I wrapped my arms around his neck, feeling delicate but powerful at the same time.

"Perfect," he whispered against my ear as he placed me on the edge of the bed. "Someone was looking out for me when I knocked over your champagne stack."

"Pyramid."

"Hmm." He pressed a kiss to my jaw. "Can't say I care

what it was right now, darling." Another to my neck. "I'm otherwise preoccupied." One to my shoulder.

He kept going, pressing soft kisses against my skin, his breath hot as it freed the butterflies in my stomach. He moved slowly, almost reverently, from my collarbone to my breasts. He inched closer, drawing circles around my nipples with his tongue, never touching, just driving me insane. My breaths quickened and my heart raced while my fingers dove into his hair and tugged hard.

"Charlie," I panted.

He hummed, the tone vaguely questioning.

"Can we speed this up?"

He chuckled but then his warm lips finally captured my nipple. A low moan escaped me as a bolt of pleasure shot straight to my core.

"Oh, fuck, like that, yes!" I hissed, my voice trembling with pleasure.

As he alternated between my nipples, using his lips and teeth to tease me, I let my head fall back, my eyes growing heavy with need.

His hand snaked down my side, gently nudging my thigh. "Lean back on your elbows, Em," he said, his voice rough and his Canadian accent thickening.

I did as he asked, shifting my weight so that I was propped up on my elbows, my breasts thrusting forward for his eager lips. He kissed his way down my stomach and I bit back the demand for him to return to my nipples. It helped that each tender touch of his lips anywhere on my body sent a jolt of electricity that intensified my need for him.

He nudged my legs wider on the mattress while his fingers encircled my ankles. I protested as he lifted them, forcing me to spread even wider before he placed my feet on the edge of the bed besides me. One panicked glance at the mirror confirmed my fears. Every intimate inch of me was on display.

He made a satisfied sound, his hazel eyes sparkling with desire as they raked over me.

"Can we cover the mirror?"

Charlie shook his head, pressing two fingers against my clit and kissing the protests away. Once I'd melted against him, he dragged his lips along my jaw again and let his fingers reduce me to a quivering mess.

"Watch yourself in the mirror," he whispered, his voice full of passion and intent. "I need you to see how beautiful you are, how much I worship your body."

The gravelly edge of his voice and his teasing fingers made it next to impossible to deny him. I didn't want to look, but I was helpless against the sight of Charlie's large hands on my body, his fingers parting my thighs and stroking through my folds. My unease about my body faded away under the relentless dance of his fingers.

"Alright," I said, though the bitter edge of self-consciousness lingered, gnawing at the edges of my pleasure.

Charlie stared up at me, his eyes focused on mine with an intensity that stole my breath.

That wasn't the look of a man taunting me or trying to make me uncomfortable. He truly wanted me to understand, to see what he saw when he looked at me.

His pace increased, his thumb pressing down on my clit as he slid two fingers into my pussy. My response was instantaneous, my hips jerking forward, seeking more friction.

And he gave it to me, adding his mouth to the mix.

His stubble tickled my sensitive skin and his tongue lapped at my clit while his fingers thrust in and out of me.

In the mirror, all I could see was his taut body kneeling before me while he clutched my shaking thighs, holding me open at all costs. One of my hands threaded into his hair, locking him to me as my eyes glazed over with need.

Watching myself lose control of my body to the waves of pleasure he invoked would never be normal. But I could acknowledge that there was a certain erotic quality to watching his head bobbing between my legs with such rapt attention.

My moans filled the room and staying upright quickly became a problem. I collapsed onto the mattress shaking as he drove me higher and higher. My pussy clenched around his fingers as the coil tightened inside of me.

He didn't let up, he merely picked up the pace until my body convulsed at the first wave of the orgasm washing over me.

Because that wasn't good enough apparently, Charlie's lips engulfed my clit, sucking hard and catapulting me higher.

Another rush of pleasure washed over me. I bucked against his face, my fingers digging into the sheets. When he finally released me, I was nothing more than a contented, quivering puddle on the bed.

Seriously. I couldn't even keep my eyes open.

"Fuck," I panted.

He shifted around but I didn't bother opening my eyes. The bed dipped beside me and he stroked my cheek. I turned my head, enjoying the soft sensation.

"Look at me, love."

I forced my eyes open and found him hovering over me with a smug look of satisfaction plastered across his face.

"You like that?" he asked, grinning.

His fingers drifted from my face, caressing the swell of my breasts with a barely there touch that made my nipples harden even more.

"Yes," I moaned, gripping the sheets tighter.

"You've got that satisfied look on your face that only I can give you." He leaned in, whispering in my ear. "I'm the only one who knows how to make you feel this way."

"Fuck, Charlie," I groaned, my body still trembling from the aftershocks of my orgasm.

"You're so eager." He brushed a stray strand of hair from my face.

I raised an eyebrow, my protest dying on my lips as he yanked me into a sitting position.

"What are you doing?"

"I'm going to fuck you long and hard from behind," he said, his voice hoarse and his eyes dark with lust. "And when you're screaming for me to stop, I'm going to turn you around, throw your legs over my shoulders, and fuck you until you can't form words."

The very thought of it sent a wave of lust crashing over me, rendering me speechless.

"How does that sound?"

"Yes," I said, my tone far too eager. "To all of that. Yes."

"Good."

But instead of doing just that, he got up and walked around the bed.

"What are you doing?" I asked as he started collecting pillows.

"Making sure I don't hurt you."

He arranged them in a pile in the middle of the bed. Once satisfied with the arrangement, he instructed me to get on all fours over the pillows. I did as told and tried to ignore the fact that if I glanced to my left, I'd see myself in the mirror with my ass in the air.

But again, he didn't take me like I desperately wanted. Somewhere behind me, he opened a drawer and started rifling through it. What he could possibly need from my dresser, I couldn't say.

"What are you doing?"

"It's a surprise," he said, his tone cryptic. "Don't move."

Curiosity burned through me. Somehow I did as told.

When he returned, he pressed a soft kiss to my lower back. "Good girl."

His fingers brushed against my clit, making me jump. Only it wasn't just his fingers. He attached something cool and smooth to the sensitive nub. It suctioned to me and I tensed.

"What is that?"

"You'll love it," he said, pressing a kiss to my lower back before straightening up.

Then he leaned over me, his hard cock nudging my entrance until my pussy clenched with need. Instead of slamming into me, he wrapped his arm around my waist and tapped the thing between my legs. The sudden hum of a vibrator sent me cross-eyed, a choked cry tearing from my throat.

"Fuck!" I screamed, bucking against the relentless stimulation, my body shuddering with an instant orgasm.

"See?" He gathered my hair back from my face and used it to turn my head, forcing me to meet his lust-filled gaze in the mirror. "I said you'd love it."

"You're insane."

He chuckled, but didn't comment. He straightened up and nudged the tip of his cock against my entrance. Before my brain could string two thoughts together, he thrust into me, filling me to the brim.

I groaned and Charlie swore.

"It's been too fucking long."

My eyelids fluttered as he filled me completely; the sensation of him inside me after so long was almost too much to handle. My back arched, my breasts grazing against the mattress as I let out a needy whimper. He leaned over me, his grip on my hips tight as he began to thrust. Each movement of his hips sent a wave of pleasure through me, my muscles clenching around his cock.

"Fuck, you're so tight," he grunted, his face twisted with lust.

"Yes, Charlie," I moaned, my voice strained.

As he began to fuck me in earnest, the intense pleasure of his thrusts mingled with the mind-numbing sensations of the vibrator, pushing me to the edge of sanity. I was incoherent, cursing him, pleading for mercy, but also more. The tension within me coiled tighter with each passing second.

"You feel so good," he groaned. His fingers tightened on my hips, pulling me back with more and more force. "It's been too long. Don't know how I resisted you all this time."

"Me. Either," I panted.

He reached around and grabbed the vibrator, pressing it harder against my clit as he continued to fuck me. The intense stimulation was almost too much to handle, my body tensing as the orgasm began to build inside of me.

"You're going to come for me, aren't you?" Charlie growled, his rhythm increasing.

"Yes," I moaned.

And then the coil snapped and I lost control of my body. It hit me so hard my vision blurred and my body shook. I couldn't move as he pulled out of me. He released the vibrator and set it aside while his fingers caressed my lower back with soothing circles.

"That was incredible," I said, still catching my breath.

"I'm glad you liked it." He helped me turn over until I lay on my back. I stared up at him, taking in all the tiny details I'd missed. Like the look of pure need that claimed his expression or the way his pupils blew so far the black almost consumed the hazel. "We're not done yet."

Charlie propped my hips up with a pillow or two. "Is this okay?" he asked, his tone serious.

CHAPTER TWENTY-FIVE

*C*harlie

"Yes," she said, swallowing hard.

"Fuck, you look good enough to eat right now," I said, staring at her as she lay there with her hips propped up. The toy I'd bought her sat beside her, glistening with her arousal. She turned her head, probably wondering why I was grinning at the sheets. Her cheeks flushed when she spotted it.

"You didn't have to buy me that."

"Yes, I did." I leaned over and placed a tender kiss on her stomach. "The books said you'd get unbearably horny. I needed to be prepared." I pulled back and our gazes locked. Purposefully holding eye contact, I added, "Plus, I kinda liked watching you react to it."

Her face flushed a deeper shade of red, and she bit her lip. "Why do you always have to be so..."

"Perfect?" My brows rose at her snort of laughter.

"Not the word I was looking for."

"Ah." I shifted, positioning myself between her thighs again. "You must mean thoughtful then."

She shook her head at me and my grin widened. My heart ached at the tiny curl of her lips and the satisfied glaze in her eyes. From now on, putting that expression on her face was my one goal for as long as she'd have me.

I reached for her legs and tucked them in the crook of my arms, pulled her closer to me. "Comfortable?"

"Yes," she said again, her voice slightly strained as I repositioned her.

I tucked more pillows under her to make sure she was propped up comfortably. I wanted her to feel as good as possible, and the satisfaction of taking care of her was indescribable. I stared at her for a moment, trying to commit the image of her pregnant and glowing to memory.

"You're sure?"

Her eyes narrowed. "Will you just shut up and fuck me already?"

I chuckled. "I thought you'd never ask."

I gently placed her legs over my shoulder, trying not to scoff at myself for being so careful with her. I'd just been pounding into her from behind. Where was the overbearing protectiveness then?

Her mouth opened and I thrust before she could form the words. My hips pulsed in slow, short bursts while I sank deeper, savouring every inch.

She moaned, the sound low and throaty, her eyes locked on mine. I couldn't have looked away even if I'd wanted to. If only she knew how deeply she owned me. The thought of her experiencing this with anyone else made my heart ache. I didn't want to share her with anyone else. Didn't want to lose her.

I slowly withdrew, my cock slick with her arousal, before thrusting back in with a groan. Her lips parted with pleasure and her eyelids fluttered. The idea of another man being inside her, claiming her, made me grit my teeth. It was irrational, I knew that. But it still unleashed a possessive streak I didn't know I had.

"I want to fill you up with my cum." I pounded into her,

muttering my unhinged thoughts, my voice low and filled with need, unable to keep them to myself. "I want to watch you work my cock, milking me and taking everything I've got."

Her eyes widened in surprise, but then a spark of heat flared in them and her pussy clenched tight around my cock. She nodded eagerly.

"Yes. I want that too."

Her response sent a rush of excitement through me, and I fucked her harder, releasing one of her legs to tease her clit with my thumb.

"Good girl," I whispered, my voice a growl. "Milk me good, Emma. Take every last drop from me."

Her moans grew louder, her body tensing as she chanted my name. The only name I ever wanted to hear fall from her lips. Her inner walls clamped down on me as an orgasm ripped through her, robbing me of the ability to resist.

My thrusts grew harder, faster as I chased my own release. It claimed me quickly, making me curse as my cock pulsed and I emptied myself inside of her.

CHAPTER TWENTY-SIX

CHARLIE

*W*here the fuck did that come from?

I lay on my back, staring up at the ceiling, my chest heaving from round… I didn't even know. I'd lost count. My mind spun as I tried to make sense of the unexpected turn of the night. And I didn't mean the fact we were now friends with benefits.

I'd never wanted kids, and the thought of going bare inside a woman had always freaked me out. Yeah, I'd expected it to feel incredible, but that?

I'd do it again. Right now if she'd let me.

Something about removing that fear had unlocked a kink I didn't know I had.

Emma's head rested on my chest, her hair fanned out across my skin like silk. I couldn't stop myself from tracing lazy patterns on her bare shoulder.

After the last time, we'd showered and I'd finally let the spent cum seep out of her. Watching it run down her leg and into the drain had made me want to scoop her up and start all over.

It made no sense.

She was already pregnant. I couldn't put another baby in her, so why was I now fixated on it?

I kept waiting for her to question it, but she never did. Just chuckled each time I propped her hips up and stopped my cum from escaping. She definitely hadn't seemed put off, so maybe she liked it too.

"I have to say, I'm impressed."

I tensed. "About what?"

"For someone who's been out of practice for so long, you certainly haven't lost your touch."

I laughed, some of the tension draining from me. "Are you implying that I could ever be rusty in the bedroom?"

She propped herself up on an elbow, her eyes dancing with mischief. I stared at her, drinking in the sight of her flushed cheeks, her tousled hair, the sparkle in her eyes. She'd never looked more beautiful, and the knowledge that I was the cause of that glow sent a surge of male pride through me.

"Well, you did say it had been a while. I was half expecting you to fumble around like a teenager at prom."

"I'll have you know I'm always on top form," I said, pulling her closer. "Especially when it comes to a particular beautiful, pregnant woman who drives me crazy."

She burst out laughing, the sound filling the room and warming me from the inside out. Fuck, I loved her laugh. I made a mental note to make her laugh like that as often as possible.

"Lucky me, then."

I pressed a kiss to her forehead, inhaling the scent of her shampoo, mixed with the lingering aroma of our passion. "No, I'm the lucky one."

I grinned, unable to resist pulling her closer for a kiss. When we parted, I found myself lost in her eyes. How had this happened? How had this woman snuck past all my defences and made me want more than just a casual arrangement?

"So... what happens now?" She snuggled closer to me, her tone softening.

The question hung in the air between us, laden with possibility and a hint of uncertainty. "Now," I said slowly, choosing my words with care, "we figure out how to make this work. Because I don't want to go back to pretending I'm not incredibly attracted to you."

She tensed in my arms. "Are you sure? I mean, this is a lot to take on. A baby, a... whatever this is... it's not exactly the carefree bachelor life you're used to."

I tilted her chin up, meeting her gaze with a smile. "I wouldn't have it any other way."

She bit her lip, a flicker of vulnerability passing across her face. "Really?"

"I want you. I want to be there for our baby. I want us to figure this out together."

Tears welled up in her eyes, and for a moment, I feared I'd said too much too soon. But then she smiled, a radiant, beautiful smile that took my breath away.

"I want that too," she whispered. "So much."

I pulled her in for a kiss, pouring all my emotions into it. When we broke apart, both breathless, I rested my forehead against hers.

"It's not going to be easy," I whispered. "We're both stubborn and set in our ways. And we're going to need to figure out how this whole parenting thing works, as well as what our arrangement looks like with a baby in the mix." I lifted a hand and caressed her cheek. "But I'm willing to put in the work if you are."

Emma's smile grew, her eyes shining with unshed tears. "I am, but I'm still scared."

My hand stilled. "Scared of what?"

What could she possibly be afraid of? Didn't she know she had me wrapped around her little finger?

She took a deep breath, her gaze dropping to my chest. "Afraid that you're only doing this out of a sense of duty. That you wanted me but not the baby. That I was destroying your life." She grimaced. "Then you started avoiding me, and I worried you wanted the baby and not me."

Her words hit me like a punch to the gut. How could she think that? Had I really been so closed off, so guarded, that she couldn't see how much she meant to me? How much they both meant to me?

"Look at me," I said, my voice hoarse with emotion. When she raised her eyes to meet mine, I continued, pouring every ounce of sincerity I possessed into my words. "I want you *and* our baby. You're not destroying my life, you're making it better. Fuller. More meaningful than I ever thought possible. Before you, my life was all about the next big deal, the next... whatever. But now? Now I have something real to look forward to. Something that matters."

A tear slipped down her cheek, and I brushed it away.

"I've been attracted to you since that night at the wedding. The baby... it just gave me a chance to realise how much I want this, want us to try and make something work."

"Oh, Charlie." Her lip trembled, and she buried her face in my chest.

I held her close, stroking her back as she shook against me, muttering apologises about baby hormones while she cried. The vulnerability of the moment struck me. It was petrifying, laying my heart bare. But it also felt incredibly right.

"I'm scared too, you know," I murmured into her hair, the confession slipping out before I could stop it. "I've never done anything like this before. And being a father... it terrifies me. What if I'm no good at it? What if I turn out like my old man?"

The fear that had been lurking in the back of my mind

since I found out about the baby bubbled to the surface. But I forced myself to continue. "It also excites me. Because it's with you. You're going to be an incredible mother. If I fuck up, you'll be there to set me straight. And somehow, that makes all the difference."

She lifted her head, her eyes red-rimmed but full of love. The sight of it stole my breath.

"We're quite a pair, aren't we?" she said with a watery chuckle. "Both scared out of our minds but willing to jump in anyway."

I laughed, the tension breaking. "That's what makes us perfect for each other. Two damaged halves make a whole."

Emma rolled her eyes, but she was smiling. "Fairly sure that's not what the saying means."

"Ah, but it suits my purposes so I'm rolling with it." I shrugged, my amusement draining. "My old man was the worst role model and I'm going to make mistakes, but I hope," I caressed her cheek, brushing away a tear, "we can give each other a little grace to learn from them."

"Okay. I can do that." She bit her lip, her curious gaze fixed on me. "Did he hurt you?" Anger flickered in her gaze and I fell a little harder for her.

"Not physically, no." I smiled at her, brushing my thumb across the lines of anger furrowing her brow. "He cheated on my mother, and started throwing it in her face. He said horrible things to both of us. I'd never thought of him as a great dad before, but watching how he treated my mother and by exten- sion me…" I shrugged. "I don't know, it just never felt like he wanted me, like in his mind he'd been trapped in a situation that had destroyed his life and he resented us."

I blew out a breath, willing away the pressure that always developed in my throat when I talked about him, to go away.

"Charlie," Emma whispered, her voice hoarse. "That's awful."

"It's in the past, love." I wrapped my arm around her and

pulled her tighter against me. "Until you, I didn't realise he'd affected me so much, but I'm working on it, okay?" I smoothed her hair back.

"I'm sorry. That must have been hard."

"It was a long time ago." I shrugged, trying to play it off. "But it's part of why I was so hesitant about all this at first. I don't want to be like him."

"You're not," she said, tone fierce. She smiled. "Come on, Hollywood Hotshot, you're nothing like him. You've been here for me, for us, from the beginning. You could have paid me off and turned your back on us. You didn't. Instead, you cooked for me, bought me gifts, got me the best doctors, read every book you could get your hands on. That's more than he would have ever done."

Her words wrapped around me like a warm blanket. "Thank you," I murmured, pressing a kiss to her temple.

We lay in comfortable silence for a while, just enjoying the closeness, the intimacy of the moment. My hand drifted to rest on her swollen belly. Our child. The thought still boggled my mind, fuelled a warmth inside of me that I couldn't attribute to anything other than joy.

"Have you thought about names for the baby?" I asked, curiosity getting the better of me.

Emma hummed thoughtfully. "I've always liked the name Prue for a girl."

"Really?" My breath caught, happy memories flooding back for once. "That was my grandmother's name. She practically raised me."

When my father was doing fuck knows what and my mother had sunk into yet another of her depressive episodes, Nan was the only consistent figure in my life.

Her eyes widened in surprise. "What a coincidence."

"I'd say." A smile tugged at my lips as I thought about my grandmother. "She was amazing. Strong, kind, with a wicked sense of humour that could cut through any bullshit. Always had time to listen, no matter how busy she was. She's the one who taught me to cook, who came to all my hockey games, who encouraged me to be better every day. After my dad left, she moved in with us to help my mom."

"She sounds wonderful."

"She was. I think she would have loved you." I grinned. "Probably would have told me I was punching above my weight class."

Emma smiled, the gesture gentle but sad at once. "I wish I could have met her."

"Me too." I pressed a kiss to her forehead. "But maybe we can honour her memory by giving our daughter her name. If it's a girl, of course."

"I think that's a great idea."

I stared at Emma, my mind conjuring an image of a little girl with her features and my eyes. The thought filled my chest with warmth, a feeling I couldn't quite name but knew I wanted to hold onto forever.

"What about for a boy?" Emma asked a few moments later.

"Well, we're definitely not naming him after my father."

She snorted. "Agreed. And my dad's name was Herbert, so that's out too."

I laughed, shaking my head. "Yeah, let's not saddle the poor kid with that. What about... Liam?"

"Why Liam?"

"I just like the sound of it." I toyed with her hair, circling it around my finger and releasing it to start all over again. I couldn't stop touching her now I was allowed to. "It means 'resolute protection'. I like the idea of our son being strong, protective."

A slow smile spread across Emma's face. "I like it."

Then I remembered my conversation with Jesse and groaned.

"What is it?" She laughed, propping herself up again to stare into my eyes.

"You're meeting my friends in a few weeks." I sighed. "So you should probably be prepared for the song and dance they'll pull trying to get you to agree to using one of their names in some way."

"They wouldn't?" she asked.

"Oh you think so?" My brows arched. "Jesse's already convinced he has dibs on the middle name. He's been texting me baby name suggestions for weeks."

Emma's eyes widened, a mix of amusement and disbelief dancing across her face. "You're kidding."

I shook my head, chuckling. "I wish I was. He's even offered to babysit for a month straight if we name the kid after him." I winced, considering how traumatised our baby would be after a night with his wild triplets.

I hadn't even told Emma about his offer for us to babysit for practice. She'd agree without thinking, and I'd seen those kids when they thought their parents weren't looking. The memories alone made me shudder.

"And don't get me started on Lukas. He's threatened to teach him or her German swear words if we don't at least consider Lukas as a middle name."

She laughed. "I'm sure they're not serious." Her amusement trailed off. "Right?"

"I'll let you be the judge of that when you meet them." I grinned, pulling her back down to tuck into my side. "They're a handful, but they're good people. They'll love you."

"Well, they'll have to get in line." She nestled into my side, her fingers tracing lazy patterns on my chest. "Lila would be pissed if she didn't get a look in on the name game."

I groaned. "Great, now we'll have a bidding war on our hands. Maybe we should just give the kid five middle names and be done with it."

Emma swatted my chest lightly. "Our child is not going to

need a separate page for their full name on official documents."

Our child.

The words sent a thrill through me. I glanced down at her, her head resting on my chest, her body curved against mine, and I was struck by how right this felt. How comfortable. It was a feeling I'd never experienced with any other woman.

In that moment, the reality of what I'd said earlier hit me full force. I meant every word about wanting to explore this with her, about being there for her and the baby. But the depth of my feelings caught me off guard. The realisation should have terrified me. In the past, it would have sent me running for the hills.

But with Emma? Talking about our future, our child... it filled me with a joy I'd never known before.

That didn't mean I wasn't worried or scared. The thought of being responsible for another human life, of opening myself up to the possibility of heartbreak... it was downright terrifying.

But for the first time in my life, the potential reward far outweighed the risk. Still, I knew I couldn't tell her the full extent of my feelings. Not yet. Friends with benefits was a start. It would keep her satisfied and only me in her bed. I'd have to be patient if I wanted more.

There was, however, one thing eating at me still.

"So are we just going to pretend that I didn't turn into a caveman before?" I asked, unable to keep my silence any longer.

Her lips curved into a teasing smile. "Oh, your newfound obsession with making sure not a drop of cum escapes?"

Heat crept up my neck, but I couldn't deny it. "Yeah, that."

She laughed, the sound warm and free from judgement. "I think someone's discovered a breeding kink."

I groaned, covering my face with my hand. "That sounds so..."

"Hot?" Her voice dropped, turning hoarse and sultry.

I peeked at her through my fingers. "You're not freaked out?"

"Not at all." She shook her head, a small smile tugged at her lips. "Actually, I found it sexy. The way you looked at me, the intensity in your eyes... it was a huge turn-on."

Relief washed over me, followed quickly by a renewed spark of desire. "Oh really?"

"Really." She trailed her fingers down my chest. "And it's not like you can get me any more pregnant right now. So why not enjoy it?"

I caught her hand, bringing it to my lips for a kiss. "You're amazing, you know that?"

She grinned. "I have my moments. Now, are you going to keep talking, or are you going to show me that caveman side again?"

I didn't need to be asked twice. In one swift motion, I rolled us over, hovering above her so I wouldn't crush the bump. I captured her lips in a searing kiss, all the while marvelling at how lucky I'd gotten finding someone who accepted all of me — even the parts I was just discovering myself.

CHAPTER TWENTY-SEVEN

EMMA

"Oh come on," Charlie muttered, gesturing at the TV. "That's not how hostage negotiations work at all. Where did they get their technical advisor, a B-movie from the 80s?"

I hummed in agreement, only half-listening. I shifted on the couch for the hundredth time, trying to find a position that didn't make me acutely aware of the throbbing ache between my thighs. Charlie sat next to me, his arm draped casually over the back of the sofa and his thigh pressed against mine. Every inch of my skin tingled with awareness of his proximity.

On screen, the movie played on — some action flick Charlie had picked. The plot eluded me entirely.

It had only been a couple of days since Charlie and I had embarked on our new friends with benefits agreement. We'd settled into it with ease. The fact the morning sickness had finally let up probably helped.

My body had replaced all the energy I'd wasted trying not

to throw up with an insatiable appetite for... well, everything. Food. Charlie. Especially Charlie.

In the bedroom. Bathroom. On the stairs. On the couch. In his office.

We'd pretty much christened every room of the house at this point.

My thighs clenched involuntarily at the thought. The ache intensified, a pulsing need I couldn't ignore. I squirmed again, crossing and uncrossing my legs in a futile attempt to alleviate the pressure.

"You okay there, Em?" Charlie asked, his voice cut through my hormone-addled thoughts. "You're fidgeting more than Jesse's triplets on a normal day."

"Fine," I lied, forcing a smile I hoped didn't look as strained as it felt. "Just can't get comfortable. This couch must be conspiring against me."

He nodded, a flicker of concern crossing his features before he turned his attention back to the movie. I stared at his profile, admiring the strong line of his jaw, the curve of his lips.

The ache throbbed again, more insistent this time. I bit my lip, eyeing Charlie from beneath my lashes. Did he have a limit? How many times could I ask before he got tired of me?

You're being ridiculous. This is exactly what you agreed to. He's not going to suddenly decide you're too much trouble.

But my body refused to listen to reason. Every cell screamed for his touch, his kiss, his-

"Okay, seriously." Charlie turned to face me fully, concern etched across his features. "What's going on? You're squirming like you've got ants in your pants and a bee in your bonnet. Talk to me, Em."

"It's just... you know. Hormones. They're kind of driving me crazy right now."

"Ah. Need a little help with that?"

"You don't have to. We already... earlier... I don't want to be a bother."

"Hey." He tucked a strand of hair behind my ear, his touch sending shivers cascading down my spine. "Look at me, Em."

Reluctantly, I met his gaze. The tenderness I saw there nearly undid me.

"The whole point of this arrangement is to help you, remember?" He smiled. "To make sure you're comfortable and taken care of. I can't do that if you don't tell me what you need."

"I know, I just…" Embarrassment and desire warred within me, leaving me flushed and breathless. "I worried it might get to be too much. That you'd get sick of me always... wanting."

Charlie laughed, the sound warm and rich and full of promise.

He leaned in, his lips brushing against the shell of my ear as he spoke. "Trust me. I could never get enough of you. We could keep this up for a decade, and I'd still want more."

My heart skipped a beat, then started racing double-time.

Did he mean that?

The idea of a decade with Charlie... my mind raced with possibilities. "So?" His hand cupped my cheek, thumb stroking gently across my skin. "What do you say? Want me to take care of you?"

I swallowed hard.

I nodded, the motion subtle, shy, and so not me. What had happened to the badass business owner who made impossible things happen? Somehow, moving to LA, I'd lost track of her.

"Yes," I whispered. "Please."

Charlie's lips curved into a wicked grin that sent liquid heat pooling low in my belly. In one swift motion, he pulled me onto his lap, his hands sliding under my oversized t-shirt.

"You're wearing far too many clothes for what I have in mind."

I shivered as his fingers trailed up my sides, leaving goose-bumps in their wake.

"Oh?" I asked, my voice breathy and uneven. "And what exactly do you have in mind?"

"Let me show you." He captured my lips in a searing kiss, stealing my breath and scattering my thoughts to the four corners of the earth.

His hands roamed my body, igniting sparks of pleasure everywhere he touched, I lost myself in the moment. But a tiny voice in the back of my mind whispered, *Is this enough? Or will you always crave more?*

I pushed the thought aside, focusing on the heat building between us. For now, this would have to be enough. I couldn't risk losing what we had by asking for more.

My t-shirt and bra went flying across the room and he kissed me. Long, drugging kisses that made my head spin and those pesky thoughts quiet.

While he stole my breath, he cupped my breast, causing my nipple to pebble against his palm. I gasped into his mouth at the jolt of pleasure radiating down to my core.

One day soon, I'd stop being shocked at how much he could turn me on. Just a look and I was soaked for the man.

"These are so perfect," Charlie said, admiring my breasts. He leaned in, lips hovering over my left nipple. "Do you know how hot it is to think about sucking on your nipples when you start lactating?"

His sudden breeding kink fascination had caught us both off guard, but it only made me more aroused. I couldn't deny that the thought was strangely exciting, but I couldn't quite pinpoint why. Maybe it was the added element of intimacy, or the sense of newfound power in my sexuality. Whatever the reason, it made my nipples ache with anticipation.

"Is that a deal-breaker?" I asked playfully, not wanting to burst our pleasure bubble. "I read that it won't stop until I stop breastfeeding so… if it makes you happy…"

Charlie chuckled, nipping my nipple lightly. "Don't worry. I just can't resist the thought of it." He rolled his eyes as if embarrassed by his newfound fascination. "And just so we're clear, I'm already plenty happy."

His mouth enveloped my right nipple, and he began to suck. Each pulse of his lips sent ripples of pleasure through my body, making my core clench with desire. My head fell back and my eyes closed in bliss, a soft moaning escaping me. The movie droned on in the background, forgotten.

He switched between my nipples, giving each one equal attention. His hands massaged my breasts, making my sensitivity even more pronounced. It felt as if my entire body was concentrated in those two small points of contact. I couldn't believe that something so simple could bring me to the brink of orgasm.

"I... I'm close," I whispered, my voice trembling with anticipation.

He released my nipple with a small pop and looked up at me, his eyes full of desire and surprise. "From just that?"

I nodded, chewing my lip.

"Then I guess I'd better hurry up."

I protested as Charlie lifted me. He settled me back in my seat with a confident smirk.

He chuckled. "I'm not done with you yet so get rid of the disappointment."

Then he hooked his fingers into my leggings and panties and tore them off me. With a firm grip, he opened my legs wide enough to make room for his broad shoulders.

His gaze dropped from my eyes to my aching core. "Is this all mine?" he asked, a possessive glint in his eye. "Are you this wet because of me?"

He ran a single finger through my lower lips, dragging a desperate moan from deep in my throat. I needed him to finish what he'd started.

"Yes." I reached for him, my fingers threading through his hair. "I need to come. Now."

Chuckling, he let me guide his head to where I needed him.

His soft breaths hit my sensitised clit first and I shivered. Then his beard tickled my thigh and he sealed his lips around my clit, applying an intense pressure that almost pulled me from the couch.

My eyes fell shut on a happy sigh as I fell straight over the edge. I arched my back as waves of absolute bliss flooded through me.

"Yes," I hissed, my grip on his hair growing fierce. "Don't stop."

Charlie kept the pressure going as he added in shallow thrusts with his tongue and deeper ones with his fingers. The exquisite torture pushed me over the edge again. I grasped his hair, pulling him closer as I rode out my second orgasm of the night.

He didn't stop there. He kept the pressure going to drag out my orgasm, turning it into a never ending rush of pleasure.

"Oh fuck," I groaned, the film on the screen becoming nothing more than a blur of colours and noise.

My words turned into pleas, my nails digging into the couch as he continued his relentless pleasure attack.

"Charlie, please... stop," I begged, my voice lost to panting breaths.

Instead of stopping, he slowed down, the sensation ebbing only slightly, prolonging my state of orgasmic bliss. Sweat trickled down my neck.

Finally, mercifully, he released me, panting slightly as he rested back on his haunches.

As the intensity faded, I slumped back against the sofa, panting and spent. My breasts still ached from his attention, but in the best possible way.

"That good?" he asked, his voice husky.

All I could do was hum an agreement. I could barely remember my own name and he wanted to have a conversation? What even were words?

While he basked in the satisfaction of rendering me mute,

Charlie traced circles on my belly. I glanced down at him, still kneeling between my legs. His gaze was fixed on my stomach, that male satisfaction I'd expected replaced by a teasing quirk of his lips.

He leaned in, his nose almost touching my stomach and whispered, "Thanks for messing with your mama's appetites."

He pressed a soft kiss to my stomach and my ovaries just about exploded. Did this man need to be any more attractive to me? Absolutely not.

CHAPTER TWENTY-EIGHT

CHARLIE

*A*s my lips touched her skin, something extraordinary happened. A tiny flutter, barely perceptible, brushed against my mouth. I froze, my heart skipping a beat.

"Did you..." I trailed off, my eyes wide as I stared at Emma's belly.

"I think someone wants to say hello."

I placed my hand gently on her stomach, holding my breath. For a moment, nothing happened. Then, like a butterfly's wing against my palm: a kick. Our baby's kick.

A tidal wave of emotion crashed over me. Joy, wonder, and an overwhelming sense of love flooded my system.

He was real before, of course, but now? I don't know, this was more solid than an ultrasound image or hearing his heartbeat somehow.

"Hey there, little one," I murmured, my voice thick with emotion. "I'm your dad."

The word felt foreign on my tongue. Dad. Father. A title I never thought I'd claim, let alone embrace.

As the reality of it sank in, a cold tendril of fear snaked its way through my chest. Images of my own father flashed through my mind — his perpetual disappointment, the horrible things he used to say to my mother, the sound of the front door slamming as he walked out on us for the last time, the years of silence that followed.

What if I screwed this up? I knew I was a better person than he would ever be, but I still couldn't shake the worry.

"You okay?" Emma's hand covered mine on her belly, warm and reassuring.

I swallowed hard, forcing a smile. "Yeah, I'm fine. It's just... a lot, you know?"

She nodded, her eyes full of understanding. "It's overwhelming, isn't it? Feeling her move for the first time."

My brows rose. Did she know something I didn't? "How long have you been feeling the baby move?"

Emma bit her lip, a flicker of guilt crossing her features. "A few weeks now. At first, it was only small flutters, but lately, it's been getting stronger."

"Why didn't you tell me?"

"I didn't think you'd want to…" She averted her gaze, her fingers fidgeting with the tassels on one of the new pillows. "You know, touch me. Not until this week, at least."

For a second, it felt like I'd been sucker punched. Had I really been so distant? So caught up in my own fears and insecurities that I'd made her think I didn't want to be involved?

"Emma, love, look at me," I said, gently tilting her chin up. Her eyes met mine, hesitant and vulnerable. "I always wanted to touch you. To be there for you and our baby. Feeling them move... it makes it all so real. I want to be there for every moment."

I stroked her cheek, staring into her hesitant gaze and willing her to believe me.

"I've said it a lot and I'll probably never stop, but I'm sorry I made you feel like that. It wasn't my intention, okay?"

Relief flooded her features, and she leaned into my touch. "Really?"

"Really." I pressed a soft kiss to her forehead. "This is all new territory for me, and I guess I've been fumbling my way through it."

As if on cue, another kick pressed against my palm. A small laugh escaped me, joy bubbling up again.

"I can't believe we're having a baby," I marvelled, shaking my head in wonder. "A tiny person who's half you and half me."

Emma smiled, her eyes shining. "Yeah, it gets me sometimes too."

I grinned. "We need to start planning the nursery. I've got some ideas sketched out, but I want to run them by you. What do you think about a space theme? Or maybe something more nautical?"

I started to stand, eager to retrieve my sketchbook, but Emma's hand on my arm stopped me.

"Hold on there, Picasso." She raised a brow, but it was the heated glint in her brown eyes that really froze me to the spot. "Weren't you in the middle of something before our peanut decided to join the party?"

I smirked, instantly catching onto her meaning.

"You're right." I tugged my t-shirt over my head. "How could I forget?" My joggers and boxers hit the floor. "Where were we?"

"About to let me ride you." Her voice dropped, turning all gravelly and lust-filled.

My cock hardened and her gaze lowered, a hungry expression claiming her face.

It was my turn to chuckle. "Was I?" I stroked myself, enjoying the way her pupils dilated with need. "Or do you want something else first?"

Without a word, she eagerly sat forward and opened her

mouth. Her hands landed on my hips, tugging me forward until the tip touched her lips.

Without hesitation, she sucked me deep, tearing a groan from my throat.

As I lost myself in Emma once more, the fears and doubts that had plagued me moments ago faded into the background. This — Emma needing me as fiercely as I needed her, our baby growing strong and healthy — this was what mattered. And I'd be damned if I let my past dictate our future.

I may not have had the best example of fatherhood growing up, but I'd learn. I'd stumble and make mistakes, sure, but I'd never stop trying. Never stop showing up. Because this little family we were creating? It was everything.

CHAPTER TWENTY-NINE

EMMA

I flopped onto the bed in my room and stared up at the ceiling, a giddy smile plastered across my face. Charlie had just left for work wearing an almost identical blissful expression.

My phone buzzed on the nightstand, startling me out of my reverie. Lila's name flashed on the screen. I picked up, trying to school my voice into something resembling normal.

"Hey, Lee. What's up?"

"Hey," she said, dragging out the word with clear hesitation. "I've got some bad news." Her voice crackled through the speaker, the background noise suggesting she was in the middle of event preparations. "The Tanner wedding just dropped us. They're postponing indefinitely due to family issues."

"Oh." I tried to muster up the appropriate level of concern. But I couldn't seem to wipe the smile off my face or inject the right amount of disappointment into my voice. "That's too bad." I paused, a fleeting moment of worry breaking through my blissful haze. "Wait, do you think it's really family reasons? Or is it because of... you know, my situation? The fact that I can't be there to run the show myself?"

Lila sighed. "Honestly? I'm not sure. They didn't say anything specific, but you know how people talk in this industry. Your absence has been noticed."

I chewed my lip, a pang of guilt cutting through my happiness. "Maybe I should call them, explain the situation better—"

"No, don't do that. I'll handle it. You focus on taking care of yourself and the baby. Speaking of which, why do you sound so chipper? This is kind of a big deal, and you're practically giggling over there."

I bit my lip, torn between addressing the work issue and sharing my news. "It's nothing, really. I'm just... in a good mood today."

"A good mood?" Lila's tone was incredulous. "You just lost a major client, and you sound like you've won the lottery. What happened?"

I sighed, knowing I couldn't keep it from her even if I wanted to. "Charlie and I... we kind of came to an arrangement."

"What kind of arrangement are we talking about here?"

My cheeks burned. "The kind where we stop pretending we're not attracted to each other and do something about it."

"Emma Sullivan!" Lila squealed, causing me to pull the phone away from my ear. "You little minx! I want details. Now."

I laughed. "Calm down. It's not that big of a deal."

"Not that big of a deal?" She scoffed. "This is huge! Wait a minute, why aren't we FaceTiming right now? I need to see your face for this conversation."

"Um, because you called me, remember? You're supposed to be working."

"Screw work," Lila said dismissively. "This is major news.

I'm calling you right back on FaceTime, and you better answer."

The line went dead, and seconds later, my phone lit up with her video call. I swiped to answer, and her face filled the screen, flushed with excitement.

"Okay, spill." Her eyes sparkled. "I want every single detail. How did this happen? When? And why didn't you call me the second it did?"

I couldn't help but grin at her enthusiasm. "It's literally been two weeks, and we were kind of busy afterwards," I said, my voice going weirdly squeaky as I tried to communicate my meaning with a raised brow.

No way would I be uttering the words when I had no idea if someone would overhear us.

Her eyes widened, her mouth forming a perfect 'O' as understanding dawned. "Emma Sullivan! You naughty minx!" She leaned closer to the screen, her voice dropping to a conspiratorial whisper. "So, how was it? Did he rock your world? Again? Because girl, if he didn't, I'll fly out there myself and give him a piece of my mind."

Heat rushed to my cheeks, and I buried my face in my hands, peeking through my fingers at the screen. "Lila! I'm not giving you a play-by-play of my sex life."

"Oh, please. I'm your best friend. I've earned the right to ask about your sex life, especially when it involves a hot Holly-wood agent who's knocked you up." Then she pouted. "I didn't even get the details after the first time."

I groaned, flopping back onto the pillows. "Fine. If you must know, it was incredible." My mind drifted back to the previous night, a shiver running down my spine. "The best I've ever had."

Lila sniggered. "Good thing you seem to be stuck with him then."

I covered my face, my cheeks burning with mortification.

"Please don't say that to him when you meet him. This is just casual, remember?"

"Right, 'casual'," Lila said, air quotes evident in her tone. "Tell me how it happened. Last time we talked, you were still convinced he saw you as nothing more than a baby incubator."

"I know." I sighed, sitting up and propping myself with pillows. "I was so wrong. We had this moment at the maternity store, and then—"

"Hold up." Her expression tightened as her tone sharpened. "Please tell me you didn't christen a changing room."

"Of course not!" I gasped, feeling my cheeks heat up. "We talked, okay? He told me how attracted he's been to me this whole time."

"Aw, Em. That's so sweet. But wait…" She sobered slightly. "Wasn't there a reason you didn't want this to begin with? What changed?"

I bit my lip, thinking back on the past few months.

"Lee, I've been so blind," I breathed, running a hand through my hair. "He's been amazing this whole time, and I just... I couldn't see it."

"What do you mean?"

"It's everything," I said, my voice thick with emotion. "The flowers he'd leave in my room 'just because.' The pregnancy pillow he researched for hours to find the perfect one. He didn't just hire a nutritionist; he learned to cook all these special pregnancy-friendly meals. He'd leave little notes with my prenatal vitamins, reminding me I was doing great."

I paused, overwhelmed by the flood of memories. "He even started learning to give me prenatal massages, Lila. And last week, I found him asleep on the couch, surrounded by baby books and a notepad full of questions for our next doctor's appointment. He's having the glass stair railing and bannister replaced with a child-proof-able one."

"Oh, Em," Lila said softly.

"I know." I sighed, wonder and guilt consuming me. "And

it's not just the big things. It's the little gestures too. He always makes sure my water bottle is full. He installed a handrail in the shower because he noticed I was getting unsteady."

I shook my head, marvelling at my own obliviousness.

"How did I miss all of this?"

Lila shrugged, her smile sympathetic. "You've been going through a lot. Pregnancy isn't easy, especially under these circumstances."

"I know, but still. My mood swings, my insecurities... they've been clouding my judgement for months. I convinced myself he was just fulfilling his duty, that he couldn't possibly care about me beyond the baby. But looking back now, it's so clear. Every action, every gesture... they were all his choices to support me, not mindless obligation."

"It sounds like he really cares about you." She wiggled her brows at me, grinning suggestively. "Maybe more than just a friend with benefits."

"Maybe... I don't know. It's complicated."

"Complicated how? The man is clearly head over heels for you."

"I don't know about that. We're having a baby together, but we barely know each other. I'm trying not to get ahead of myself."

"Honey, I think you're way past that point," Lila said. "You're living together, he's taking care of you, you're sleeping together... sounds like a relationship to me."

"But we agreed to keep it casual. Friends with benefits, remember?"

Lila snorted. "Right, because that always works out so well. Especially when there's a baby involved." Lila's expression softened. "I get that you're scared. But we need to talk about the practical stuff too. What's your plan after the baby comes? Are you thinking of staying in LA?"

I sighed, running a hand through my hair. "I don't know. I

guess I'll have to stay here, right? I mean, Charlie's here, and he'll want to be involved with the baby…"

"Okay, so if you're staying in LA, what about your business? Have you thought about setting up shop there?"

"A little. But it feels incredibly daunting right now. Starting over in a new city, building a client base from scratch…"

Her eyes lit up. "But think about it! LA is full of celebrities and rich people who throw lavish parties. It could be amazing for your business!"

I chewed my lip, considering. "Maybe… but I wouldn't even know where to start."

"Well, doesn't Charlie know like everyone in Hollywood? I'm sure he could introduce you to some potential clients."

My stomach clenched at the suggestion. "He's actually offered to do that already. But it feels weird. I don't know if I want to mix business with our relationship, you know? It's all so new, and I don't want to make things any more complicated than they already are."

"Honey, things are already complicated. You're having a baby with the man and sharing his bed. I'd say that ship has sailed."

I groaned, covering my face with my free hand. "I know, I know. But letting him hook me up with business contacts… it feels like using him."

"Or you'd be letting him support you in your career, just like you're supporting him by carrying his child. It's called partnership."

She had a point, but the thought of relying on Charlie's connections made me uncomfortable. I'd built my business from the ground up in New York. The idea of starting over, of potentially being seen as Charlie's pregnant fuck buddy rather than a successful businesswoman in my own right, terrified me.

"Stop overthinking this." Lila rolled her eyes. "That man is the father of your child. He clearly cares about you. It's not using him, it's accepting support from someone who wants to see you succeed. If he's offering to help, why wouldn't you let him?"

I squirmed, uncomfortable with the idea. "I've always done everything on my own."

"Okay, let's break this down," Lila said, her tone softening. "Forget about the business for a second. How do you feel about Charlie? Really feel?"

I took a deep breath, trying to sort through the jumble of emotions. "He's amazing, Lila. Kind, thoughtful, supportive. And the way he looks at me sometimes... it makes me feel like I'm the only woman in the world."

"Still sounds like more than just a friends-with-benefits situation to me."

"I'll think about it. But enough about me and my crisis. How's everything going with you? How's the wedding prep coming along?"

Her eyes widened comically. "Oh shit, the wedding! I completely forgot!" She glanced off-screen, presumably at the venue around her. "Everything's fine. Well, as fine as it can be when the mother of the bride is insisting on neon pink table runners at the last minute."

I winced in sympathy. "Ouch. Need any advice?"

"From the woman who just admitted she has no idea what she's doing with her own life? I think I'll pass," Lila said, amusement softening the harsh words.

I stuck my tongue out at her. "Hey, I may be a mess personally, but I'm still a damn good wedding planner."

"True. Okay, hit me with your wisdom, oh great one."

We spent the next half hour strategising ways to tackle the table runner crisis, falling easily into our familiar professional rhythm. As we talked, a pang of nostalgia for my old life in New York hit me. But at the same time, a new excitement bubbled up inside me. Maybe starting fresh in LA wouldn't be so bad after all.

CHAPTER THIRTY

EMMA

"Why did I have to go for a six-foot-four giant?" I muttered mostly to myself.

I shifted on the couch, trying to find a comfortable position. My swollen ankles protested and my back ached no matter how I sat. A sigh escaped my lips as I rubbed my belly, marvelling at how much it had grown in the past few weeks.

"Because you have excellent taste in men, obviously."

Charlie smiled at me from the other end of the couch, my feet in his lap. His strong hands worked magic on my swollen ankles, kneading away the aches and pains.

I rolled my eyes, not bothering to hide my exasperation. "Oh yes, clearly. My taste is so refined I managed to get knocked up by a stranger at a wedding."

His thumbs dug into a particularly sore spot, eliciting a groan of relief from me. "A stranger? Is that all I am to you now, Sullivan?"

"You know what I mean," I grumbled, shifting slightly as he moved to my other foot. "I swear this kid's going to be a linebacker or something. How am I supposed to push out a baby with your genes?"

Charlie's eyes sparkled with mischief as he continued his ministrations. "I'll have you know my genes are top-notch. You should consider yourself lucky to be carrying such a prime specimen."

I snorted.

"Oh yes, I'm so blessed. Truly, I wake up every day thanking my lucky stars for your 'prime specimen' genes that are currently turning me into a human incubator for what feels like a future NBA player."

"Now, now." His hands moved up to massage my calves, his touch sending shivers through me. "Don't go giving our little one a complex before they're even born. Besides, my money's on NHL, not NBA."

I nudged him with my foot, but there was no real heat behind the gesture. "Your obsession with hockey is going to be the death of me, I swear."

He smiled, but his focus remained on a particularly tight knot in my calf. "What's really bothering you? You seem more uncomfortable than usual today."

I sighed, letting my head fall back against the cushions. "I don't know. I guess I'm just feeling... sluggish? Like I can't move properly anymore. Everything's an effort, and I miss being able to do simple things without feeling like I've run a marathon."

Charlie nodded, his brow furrowing in thought. Then, his eyes lit up and I bit back a groan. Here we go again. The last time he got that look, I ended up with a new wardrobe.

"You know, I was reading in one of those pregnancy books—"

"Oh god. Here we go again with the books."

"Swimming! It's supposed to be great for pregnant women. Low-impact exercise, helps with back pain, reduces swelling, improves circulation — all that good stuff."

I eyed him sceptically. "Swimming? In case you haven't noticed, I'm not exactly in bikini shape right now."

"Nonsense. You're beautiful, pregnant or not. Besides, who's going to see you but me? We have a perfectly good pool in the backyard."

"I don't know..."

"It'll make you feel better, I promise," he said, his voice soft and encouraging. "And if you're really that worried about the bikini, you could always skinny dip."

I gasped, smacking his arm. "Charlie!"

He laughed, holding up his hands in surrender. "Kidding, kidding! But seriously, give it a try. What have you got to lose?"

I chewed my lip, considering. The idea of feeling weightless, of escaping the constant pull of gravity on my expanding body, did sound appealing. But still...

"What about the neighbours? I don't want them seeing me like this."

"We have a privacy fence. Unless the neighbours have suddenly developed x-ray vision or a penchant for peeping, no one's going to see you but me."

I hesitated, my resolve wavering. "Okay," I relented finally. "But if I hate it, I'm blaming you."

His face split into a triumphant grin, and I couldn't help but mirror his smile. "Deal. Now go get changed, and I'll meet you by the pool."

Twenty minutes later, I stood at the edge of the pool, clutching my robe tightly around me. The water looked inviting, shimmering in the late afternoon sun, but I couldn't shake the feeling of vulnerability.

"Ready?" Charlie called as he stepped through the patio door wearing swim trunks.

My breath caught as I took in his toned physique. It wasn't

fair that he could look like that while I felt like a beached whale.

He approached me with a gentle smile, holding out his hand. I glanced nervously at the fence, double-checking for any gaps or low spots.

"Are you sure no one can see in?"

He chuckled, squeezing my hand reassuringly. "Positive. It's just you and me, Em. No judgement, remember?"

I took a deep breath, steeling myself. "Okay. Here goes nothing."

Slowly, I untied my robe, letting it fall open. Charlie's eyes roamed over me, a spark of appreciation lighting them up. I fought the urge to cover myself, feeling exposed despite knowing that he'd given me the most intense orgasms of my life.

"You know," he said, his voice low and warm, "I've seen you naked plenty of times now, but there's something about you in that bikini..." He trailed off, shaking his head with a soft chuckle. "You're gorgeous, Em. Pregnancy suits you."

"You don't have to say that." My fingers twitched, desperately wanting to take the robe back and cover my body.

"I'm not just saying it." He stepped closer. His hand came to rest on my belly, warm and comforting. "You're carrying our child. How could that be anything but beautiful?" His eyes met mine, sincerity shining in them. "Besides, you know I can't resist you in any state of dress... or undress."

My heart fluttered at his words, and I couldn't stop myself leaning into his touch. The way he looked at me, like I was the most beautiful thing he'd ever seen, chipped away at my insecurities. Maybe this wouldn't be so bad after all.

"You're ridiculous," I murmured, but I couldn't keep the smile from my face.

"Maybe. But I'm also right." Charlie grinned, his hand sliding to my lower back. "Now, are you ready to get in this pool, or do I need to throw you in myself?"

I let him guide me to the steps and down to the first level. The water lapped at my ankles, cool and inviting. I hesitated, unable to forget how exposed I was. My stretch marks seemed to glow in the afternoon sun, announcing themselves with glee.

Charlie's hand remained steady on my back, a warm anchor. "Take your time, love. No rush."

I nodded, taking a deep breath. One step, then another. The water rose to my knees, then my thighs as I made my way down the steps. With each inch, I felt a little of the weight lift from my body.

"Oh," I breathed, surprised by the sensation.

"Good, right?"

I nodded, unable to form words as I waded deeper. The water cradled my swollen belly, supporting its weight in a way I hadn't experienced in weeks. My feet left the bottom of the pool, and I gasped at the sudden weightlessness.

"I've got you." Charlie's arm wrapped around my waist to steady me.

For a moment, I froze, hyper-aware of his touch on my bare skin. But just as quickly, I relaxed into his hold, relishing the buoyancy.

"This is..." I trailed off, searching for the right word.

"Amazing?"

I laughed, the sound lighter than it had been in weeks. "Yeah, amazing works."

We floated together, his arm a steady presence around me. The tension in my lower back eased, and I sighed in relief.

"Feeling better?" Charlie asked, his voice low and intimate.

I nodded, closing my eyes and tilting my face towards the sun. "I forgot what it felt like to not ache."

His thumb traced circles on my hip, sending little shivers through me despite the warm water. "I'm glad. You deserve to feel good at all times."

I opened my eyes, catching his gaze. The tenderness there made my breath catch. For a moment, I let myself imagine this wasn't just about the baby — that his care, his touch, meant something more.

"Thank you," I whispered, meaning it for more than just the swim.

His smile softened. "Anytime, love. Now, how about we do a few laps? Get that circulation going?"

I groaned. "And here I thought this was just about relaxation."

Charlie laughed, the sound echoing across the water. "Can't let you get too comfortable. Come on, I'll race you."

"Oh, you're on," I said, surprising myself with my enthusiasm. "But don't think I'll go easy on you just because I'm carrying precious cargo."

His eyebrows shot up. "Wouldn't dream of it. On three?"

We counted down together, and then we were off. The water parted around me as I swam, my body feeling lighter and more agile than it had in months. He kept pace beside me, his powerful strokes creating small waves that lapped against my skin.

By the time we reached the other end of the pool, I was breathless and laughing. The lap had no effect Charlie, but then he hadn't exactly raced me, more kept pace.

"Tie?" he asked, his hair plastered to his forehead.

I grinned, affection rushing through me for this ridiculous man. "Tie. But only because I'm being generous." And you let me win.

He clutched his chest in mock offence. "Generous? I'll have you know I was holding back."

"Sure you were." I splashed him.

His eyes narrowed. "Oh, it's on now, Sullivan."

Before I could react, he sent a wave of water crashing over me. I squealed, the sound echoing off the fence.

"Charlie!" I sputtered, wiping water from my eyes. "You're dead."

What followed could only be described as an all-out water

war. We chased each other around the pool, splashing and laughing like kids. For those moments, I forgot about my swollen ankles, my aching back, and all the worries that had plagued me. I felt light, carefree — happy in a way I hadn't been in too long.

Eventually, we called a truce, both of us breathless and grinning. Charlie swam closer, his hand finding mine under the water.

"See? Told you swimming would be good for you."

I rolled my eyes, but I couldn't keep the smile from my face. "Alright, alright. You were right. Happy now?"

"Ecstatic." He tugged me towards the shallow end. "Come on, let's cool down a bit. Don't want you overdoing it."

We settled on the steps, the water lapping at our chests. Charlie's arm draped casually over my shoulders, and I leaned into him, savouring his warmth.

"So," he said after a moment, his fingers tracing patterns on my arm. "I've been meaning to talk to you about something."

My heart skipped a beat. Those words never preceded anything good. "Oh?"

He nodded. "I may have gotten a bit ahead of myself, but..." His eyes lit up, a smile tugging at his lips. "I might have secured a spot for our little guy at Celestial Heights Preschool."

"Isn't that one of the top private preschools in LA?"

He nodded, looking a bit sheepish. "It is. I know it's early, but their waitlist is insane. I figured it couldn't hurt to get our foot in the door."

"That's... wow."

His grin widened. "I know, I know. I'm getting ahead of myself. But I want our kid to have the best, you know?"

Our kid. The words echoed in my mind, filling me with a longing I hadn't allowed myself to feel before. I placed a hand on my belly, imagining a little boy or girl with Charlie's eyes and my stubborn chin.

"You keep saying he," I said, trying to keep my voice light. "What if it's a girl?"

Charlie shrugged, his eyes twinkling. "Then she'll be the best damn hockey player LA's ever seen."

I laughed, shaking my head. "You and your hockey obsession. What if our child wants to be a ballerina? Or a scientist?"

"Then she'll be the most graceful ballerina on the ice," he said without missing a beat. "Or the scientist who invents rocket-powered skates."

The image made me chuckle.

"Seriously, though, whatever our child wants to be, I'll support them. I just... I want them to have every opportunity, you know?"

I nodded, my throat tight with emotion. "I know. Me too."

We fell silent for a moment, the only sound the gentle lapping of water against the pool's edge.

"You know," he said after a while, a hint of mischief in his voice. "I may have also been eyeing some baby skates."

I groaned, but I couldn't keep the smile from my face. "Charlie, no. Our child is not going to be on the ice before they can walk."

"But think of the head start they'll have!" His eyes sparkled with enthusiasm, his grin widening as excitement radiated from him. "By the time they're in kindergarten, they could be the next Gretzky!"

"The next who?" I asked, raising an eyebrow.

He gasped, pressing a hand to his chest in mock horror. "Wayne Gretzky? The Great One? Only the greatest hockey player to ever live?"

I shrugged, biting back a grin at his scandalised expression. "Sorry, not all of us grew up worshipping at the altar of ice and pucks."

"Well, that settles it." He pulled me closer. "We're going to have to educate you on the finer points of hockey. Can't have our kid growing up with a mother who doesn't know Gretzky from Gandhi."

Our kid. There it was again, that causal assumption of a shared future that made my heart race.

I stared up at him, studying his profile as he launched into an impassioned speech about the importance of knowing hockey history. His eyes lit up as he spoke, and he gestured animatedly with his hands. It was captivating. Not the words, but the man himself. The way his brow wrinkled in concentration, the curve of his smile, the enthusiasm that radiated from every pore.

This wonderful, ridiculous man who secured preschool spots before we even knew the sex, who bought baby skates, who looked at me like I hung the moon even when I felt like a beached whale would be the father of my child.

But it wasn't enough. I wanted more.

More than just co-parents, more than friends with benefits. I wanted lazy Sunday mornings and heated debates over whose turn it was to change diapers. I wanted a future where our child grew up with two parents who loved each other as much as they loved them.

But did Charlie want the same thing?

CHAPTER THIRTY-ONE

CHARLIE

"This is heaven."

I couldn't help but grin. "Told you swimming would help."

She cracked one eye open, fixing me with a playful glare. "Don't get cocky, Delacroix. I still haven't forgiven you for the baby skates."

I chuckled, about to retort when the shrill sound of the doorbell cut through the tranquil atmosphere. Emma's eyes flew open, a flicker of panic crossing her face.

"Relax," I said, standing up. "I'll get it."

I headed into the house, begrudgingly leaving her floating peacefully. Her eyes closed, and a contented smile played on her lips.

A delivery guy handed me a large box covered in Canadian postage stamps.

"What did you order now?" Emma asked as I made my way back to the pool, grinning like a kid on Christmas morning.

"I didn't order anything." I set the box down on a nearby table. "It's from my sister."

"Oh, is this one of those care packages you mentioned?" She swam to the edge of the pool, propping her arms on the ledge.

I nodded, reaching for the box cutter. "Yep, right on schedule. V's never missed a quarter since I moved to LA."

"And why exactly do you need care packages? Isn't everything better in LA?"

"Oh, Em," I sighed dramatically, reaching for the box cutter. "There are some things even Hollywood can't improve upon. Like proper maple syrup, ketchup chips, nanaimo bars and..." I paused for effect, pulling out a familiar, purple-wrapped bar, "Canadian chocolate."

Her brows shot up. "You can't be serious. What's so wrong with American chocolate?"

"Everything," I muttered, unwrapping the bar. The rich, sweet scent of cocoa filled the air, and I couldn't help but close my eyes and inhale deeply. "Fuck, I've missed this."

When I opened my eyes, Emma stared at me, a mix of amusement and curiosity on her face. "You're ridiculous, you know that?"

"Maybe," I conceded, breaking off a square. "But I'm also right. Here, try this." I crouched beside the pool, holding out the piece of chocolate. "Open up."

Emma hesitated for a moment, eyeing the chocolate suspiciously. Then, with a resigned sigh, she opened her mouth. I placed the square on her tongue, my fingers brushing against her lips for the briefest moment. The touch sent a jolt of electricity through me, and I had to resist the urge to lean in and taste the chocolate myself — straight from her mouth.

Her eyes widened as the chocolate melted on her tongue. A soft moan escaped her, and I had to shift uncomfortably, my mind instantly going to places it shouldn't.

"Okay, I'll give you this one. It's pretty good."

I grinned triumphantly. "Only pretty good? You can do better than that."

She laughed, the sound light and carefree. "Fine, it's amazing. Happy now?"

"Ecstatic." I broke off another piece for myself. As the rich flavour burst on my tongue, a wave of nostalgia washed over me. Memories of cold winter nights, hot cocoa, and Veronica's laughter.

"You okay there?" Emma's voice pulled me from my reverie. "You looked a million miles away for a second."

I nodded, offering her a small smile. "Yeah, just... remembering. This stuff reminds me of home."

She reached out, placing a wet hand on my knee. "Tell me more about it? Your home, I mean."

The gesture, so simple and yet so intimate, made my heart skip a beat. I covered her hand with mine, marvelling at how natural it felt.

"Well, it's nothing like LA, that's for sure." I shuffled around until my feet dipped in the water and Emma rested her chin against my knee. "Huntsville, Ontario. Small town, lots of trees, lakes everywhere you look. Winters that make you question why humans ever settled there in the first place."

She chuckled, her thumb absently tracing circles on my thigh. "Sounds beautiful."

"It is. Especially in the fall when all the leaves change colour." I shook my head, a sweet ache in my chest from missing a place and a time that could never exist again. "There's this place where they make a skating trail that winds through the forest. V and I used to spend hours there, racing each other, pretending we were Olympic speed skaters."

"That sounds magical."

I nodded, a wistful smile tugging at my lips. "It really was. Especially at night when they'd light it up with torches. The way the flames would flicker off the ice, casting shadows through the trees... it was like stepping into another world."

"I can't even imagine," Emma said, her voice tinged with a hint of longing.

"I'll take you there someday," I said before I could stop myself. The words hung in the air between us, loaded with implications neither of us were ready to address.

Clearing my throat, I quickly changed the subject. "Anyway, want to see what else V sent?"

Emma nodded, pushing herself up to get a better view of the box. I started pulling out items, explaining each one.

"Ketchup chips — don't knock 'em till you've tried 'em. Coffee Crisp bars — the best chocolate bar you've never heard of. Oh, and these," I held up a small container, "are butter tarts. They're like tiny pecan pies, but a million times better."

As I continued to unpack the box, my hand brushed against something soft. Curious, I pulled it out, revealing a worn, slightly faded stuffed moose.

"No way," I breathed, staring at the toy in disbelief.

Emma tilted her head, studying my reaction. "What is it?"

I held up the moose, a lump forming in my throat. "This is Mr Antlers. He was my favourite toy when I was a kid. I thought I'd lost him years ago."

"He's cute," Emma said, reaching out to touch one of the moose's fuzzy antlers. "But how did your sister get him?"

I shook my head, still in shock. "I have no idea. Last I remember, he disappeared during one of our moves. I was devastated."

As I turned the toy over in my hands, a small piece of paper fell out. I picked it up, immediately recognising Veronica's handwriting.

"Found this little guy while helping Mom clean out the attic," I read aloud. "Thought you might want him for old times' sake. Maybe he'll keep you company in that big, empty house of yours. Love, V."

I looked up from the note to find Emma watching me, her

expression open and understanding. "That's really sweet of her."

"Yeah," I said, my voice thick with emotion. "V always did have a knack for sentimental gestures."

Her hand found mine. "Tell me about Mr Antlers."

I ran my thumb over the moose's worn fur. "Well, I got him on a camping trip when I was about five. Dad had promised to take us fishing, but it rained the entire weekend. We ended up spending most of the time in this tiny gift shop near the camp-ground. I saw Mr Antlers and fell in love instantly."

"Let me guess," Emma said, a teasing note in her voice. "You named him yourself?"

"Hey, don't mock my five-year-old naming skills. I'll have you know he was the envy of all the other stuffed animals."

Her eyes sparkled with amusement. "Oh, I'm sure. The most popular moose in all of Ontario, no doubt."

"Damn straight," I said, puffing out my chest in mock pride. "He was the king of the toy box."

Her laughter echoed across the water, light and carefree. It amazed me how quickly she'd gone from self-conscious and hesitant to relaxed and playful. The pool had worked its magic, easing her aches and lightening her mood.

"Want another piece?" I asked, breaking off another square of chocolate.

Emma's eyes lit up. "Oh, go on then. Since you're twisting my arm."

I placed the square on her tongue and she moaned again as if it were the first piece. The sound went straight to my groin, and I shifted uncomfortably.

"You know, this reminds me a bit of the chocolate I used to have back in England."

"Oh yeah? Tell me more."

She smiled, a wistful look crossing her face. "Well, we had Cadbury Flakes, but they tasted nothing like the ones you can get here. They were crumbly milk chocolate bars that melt in your mouth with just the right amount of sweetness. I used to beg my mum to buy them every time we went to the shop."

"What other British treats did you like?" I asked, genuinely intrigued. Emma rarely talked about her childhood, and when she did, it was almost never with that happy twist of her lips.

"Oh, there were so many." A faraway look settled over her features, a gentle smile playing on her mouth. "Jaffa Cakes — these little cake-biscuit things with orange jelly and chocolate on top. But I haven't had them since my aunt moved me. I remember being disgusted when I first tried the American versions." She shuddered.

I grinned, enjoying this glimpse into her past. "We'll have to see if we can find some of those here. I bet there's a British import store somewhere in LA."

"You don't have to do that." Then she smirked. "I will say, though, your Canadian chocolate is pretty damn good. But don't tell anyone I admitted that."

"Your secret's safe with me," I promised, winking at her. An idea struck me, and before I could think better of it, I reached for my phone on the nearby lounge chair. "Hey, speaking of Canadian things, want to meet my sister?"

Emma's eyes widened in alarm. "What? Now?"

"Yeah, why not?" I nodded, already pulling up Veronica's contact. "It'll be fun, and I should let her know the package arrived."

"Charlie, wait—"

The familiar beeping of the video call filled the air. Emma glared at me, her cheeks flushing. "Charlie," she hissed through gritted teeth, "I'm in a bikini. In a pool. This is not how I imagined meeting your family."

I paused, realising the awkwardness of the situation. "Oh, right. Sorry, I didn't think—"

But before I could finish, the call connected, and Veronica's face appeared on the screen.

"Hey, brother!" Veronica's smiling face filled the screen, her dark hair pulled back in a messy bun. "To what do I owe the pleasure?"

"Hey, V." I angled the phone so she couldn't see Emma yet. "Got your care package today. Perfect timing, as always."

She beamed. "Glad to hear it. Did you like the surprise?"

"Mr Antlers? Are you kidding? I love it. But how did you find him?"

She laughed. "Found him tucked away in a box in Mom's attic. Thought you might like to know he lives."

I chuckled. "You were right about that."

I watched Emma as she ran a hand through her damp hair, trying to make herself look presentable. The sight of her fussing over her appearance to meet my sister made my heart skip a beat.

"So, I might have been keeping a secret too."

Veronica's brows shot up. "Oh?"

"Yeah. There's someone I want you to meet." I turned my body, pulling my feet from the pool and shifting until Emma fit into the screen behind me. "V, this is Emma. Emma, meet my sister, Veronica."

Emma waved shyly from the pool, a nervous smile on her face. "Hi, Veronica. Nice to meet you."

Veronica's eyes widened, a grin spreading across her face. "Oh! Hi! I didn't realise Charlie had company."

Emma blushed. "I've heard a lot about you."

"Really?" Veronica's brows shot up, her gaze darting between Emma and me. "That's funny, because Charlie here hasn't mentioned a word about you." She fixed me with a pointed look. "Care to explain?"

I cleared my throat, feeling like I was in the hot seat. "Well, uh, Emma and I... we met at a wedding a few months ago. She's staying with me for a bit."

Her eyes narrowed suspiciously. "Staying with you? That's new. You've never had a girl stay over for more than a night or two."

"V," I warned, feeling my cheeks heat up.

Emma laughed nervously. "It's not quite like that. I'm actually—"

"Pregnant," I blurted out, unable to hold it back any longer. "We're expecting a baby."

Veronica's jaw dropped, her eyes widening in shock. For a moment, she just stared at us, speechless. Then, all at once, her face lit up with excitement.

"Oh my god!" she squealed, her voice so loud I had to turn down the volume on my phone. "Are you serious? I'm going to be an aunt?"

I nodded, a grin spreading across my face despite my nerves.

"This is amazing!" A wide smile stretched her lips. "How far along are you? Do you know if it's a boy or a girl yet? Have you picked out names?"

Emma laughed, her earlier nervousness seeming to melt away in the face of Veronica's enthusiasm. "We're about twenty-four weeks along. We don't know the sex yet — we're keeping it a surprise."

"Twenty-four weeks?" Veronica's happiness tapered off and she grimaced. "Why didn't you tell me sooner? Have you told Mom?"

I winced, rubbing the back of my neck. "Not yet. I'm working up to it."

She rolled her eyes. "You better do it soon, or I might let it slip next time we talk."

"You wouldn't dare," I growled, but there was no real heat behind it.

"Try me." She smirked. Then her eyes crinkled at the corners, softening as she turned her attention back to Emma. "You know, it's really nice to finally meet one of Charlie's girl-friends. He's always been so private about his love life."

The words hung in the air. Emma's smile faltered, and I glanced at her, noting the flush creeping up her neck.

"We're not actually... I mean, Emma and I aren't..."

Emma's gaze met mine, a mixture of emotions I couldn't quite decipher swirling in her eyes. I cleared my throat, trying to find the right words.

"V, Emma and I aren't together," I finally managed. "We're co-parenting."

Veronica's eyebrows shot up. "Oh! I'm sorry, I assumed... I mean, you've never introduced me to any of your girlfriends before, so I thought..."

"Yeah, well." I rubbed the back of my neck, my face burning. "I never introduced you to any of them because they weren't... you know, serious. Or future-worthy."

The words left my mouth before I could fully process them, and I froze, realising what I'd implied. I glanced at Emma, trying to gauge her reaction. Her eyes widened, a flicker of surprise — and something else I couldn't quite read — passing across her face.

An awkward silence settled over us, broken only by the gentle lapping of water against the pool's edge. I scrambled to change the subject, my mind racing.

"When are you planning to visit?" I asked, my voice a little too loud in the quiet. "You know, to meet the baby and spoil him rotten?"

"Or her." Emma scoffed.

"Oh, I'm already planning my trip." Veronica picked up on my desperation and ran with it. "The second we're off the phone I'll have flights pulled up and an order started for baby gifts."

Emma laughed, but it sounded a bit forced. "You really don't need to buy anything."

"Nonsense." Veronica waved her off. "It's my duty as an aunt to spoil this child. Besides, someone needs to make sure they grow up with proper Canadian values."

I rolled my eyes. "And what values would those be? An unhealthy obsession with hockey and maple syrup?"

"Exactly." Veronica nodded solemnly. "I'm glad you understand the importance of our cultural heritage."

I watched her as she laughed at another of Veronica's embarrassing stories about our childhood, her hand absently tracing circles on her swollen belly. The sight made my chest tighten with a mixture of emotions I hadn't quite prepared to name.

As much as I appreciated our friends-with-benefits arrangement, it wasn't enough. Not for me. But how could I tell her that without scaring her away? Emma valued her independence fiercely. The last thing I wanted was for her to feel trapped or like she'd lost any more control of her life.

CHAPTER THIRTY-TWO

EMMA

I stiffened, my eyes darting to the door. Any second now, Charlie would burst in, full of apologies and explanations. He had to.

The clock on the wall ticked away, each second amplifying my growing unease. Where was he? He'd never missed an appointment before.

I pulled out my phone, tapping out another message.

EMMA

Where are you?

The message joined a string of increasingly frantic texts I'd sent over the past hour. No response. I hit the call button, listening to the rings with bated breath.

"Hey, this is Charlie. Leave a message, and I'll get back to you as soon as I can."

I hung up, frustration bubbling in my chest. "Come on, Charlie," I muttered, glancing at the clock again. "Don't do this to me."

"The doctor is ready for you now, Ms Sullivan."

"Can we wait a few minutes?" I asked, hating the pleading note in my voice. "My... partner should be here soon."

The receptionist's lips thinned. "I'm sorry, but we're already running behind schedule. If you'd prefer to reschedule—"

"No." I heaved myself up from the chair, my thirty-week belly making the simple action a chore. "No, I'll go in now."

My phone buzzed as I waddled towards the examination room. Hope flared in my chest, only to be extinguished when I saw it was a work email.

"Hello, Emma. How are you feeling today?" The doctor asked as I entered.

"Great." I plastered on a smile, hoping she wouldn't notice the lie. "Just a little tired."

She glanced at the door as I shut it, surprise flickering across her face. "Is Charlie not joining us today?"

The question hit me like a sucker punch. "He's... stuck in traffic," I mumbled, the lie tasting bitter on my tongue.

She nodded, but I caught the flicker of concern in her eyes. As she began the examination, asking routine questions about my symptoms and diet, my mind wandered.

Why hadn't Charlie shown up? Had something happened? Or had he simply... forgotten?

The thought sent a chill through me. Charlie forgetting about us seemed impossible, yet here I sat, alone in a doctor's office while he was god knows where.

"How is the morning sickness?" the doctor's voice snapped me back to reality. "Any progress?"

I blinked, refocusing on the doctor's question. "Oh, the morning sickness? It's... actually much better. I haven't thrown up in over a week."

The doctor's eyebrows shot up, a smile spreading across her face. "That's excellent news, Emma! How are you feeling overall?"

"Less like death warmed over." I smiled, though it was weak. "I can keep food down now, which is a nice change."

"I'm glad to hear it." The doctor scribbled in my file. "Let's hope it stays that way for the rest of your pregnancy. Alright, let's do a quick scan to check on the baby. If you could lie back and lift your shirt, please." She gestured to the examination table.

I did as told, shuffling up onto the table. I winced as the cool gel hit my skin. My eyes fixed on the screen as the doctor moved the wand over my stomach, but I barely saw it, too busy sifting through the last few months. I'd had to swallow my pride to accept Charlie's help and move in with him, but that shouldn't have made me dependent on him.

Was it when he'd insisted on installing that handrail in the shower? I'd brushed it off as unnecessary at the time, but now I used it every day. Or maybe it was earlier, when he'd started stocking the fridge with my favourite snacks without me asking.

"The baby's measuring right on track," the doctor said, oblivious to my internal struggle.

While she continued to inspect the baby, images flashed through my mind. Charlie bringing me ginger tea in bed when the morning sickness hit hard. His hand on my back, steadying me as I wobbled out of the shower. The way he'd rearranged the kitchen when I refused to ask him for help to reach the higher shelves, putting everything I needed within easy reach.

When had I started expecting these things?

Should I have put up more of a fight the first day I moved in and insisted on carrying my own suitcase? Or told him not to bother when he'd stayed up all night researching pregnancy-safe foods when I couldn't keep anything down? He'd shown up the next morning with a grocery bag full of bland crackers and herbal teas, a triumphant grin on his face.

The list grew longer with each passing second. Charlie scheduling my appointments and adding them to his calendar. Him rubbing my swollen feet without me having to ask. The way he'd started making decisions about the nursery, picking out paint colours and furniture.

My stomach churned, and not from morning sickness. How had I let this happen? I'd always prided myself on my independence, on never needing anyone. Yet I was pregnant and reliant on a man I barely knew.

I'd given up control, piece by piece, without even noticing. My life, my choices, my body — they all seemed to revolve around Charlie now.

"Everything looks good," the doctor's voice cut through my spiralling thoughts. "The baby's growing right on schedule. Do you have any questions?"

I shook my head, unable to trust my voice. She handed me a wad of paper towels and chatted about my next appointment, explaining what I should expect now that I was in my third trimester. My hands trembled as I wiped the gel off. I focused on my breathing, forcing air into my lungs while my body tried to seize up in panic.

What had I done? How had I let myself become so dependent? And more importantly, how could I claw back some semblance of control? How could I even allow this to happen?

I mean I knew *why* it had happened. At some point I'd started to believe in the stupid man because…

A sweet ache developed in my chest and the backs of my eyes burned. I frowned at the clinical walls. I couldn't possibly…

Love him? Could I?

The realisation hit me like a punch to the gut, leaving me breathless because yes, I did. I hadn't just become dependent on Charlie — I'd fallen for him. Hard.

But it didn't matter if he loved me back or not. Because I loved him. The thought was terrifying and exhilarating all at once.

We'd fallen into an easy routine: sharing meals, laughing over my latest weird craving, me reading while he binge watched the latest TV show, Charlie talking to the baby every night. I'd even braved one of his premieres so he'd stop nagging me about it.

I'd always prided myself on my independence, on never needing anyone. Yet I was alone in a new city, pinning my hopes on a man I'd known for less than a year. A man I loved, who might not love me back.

A few hours later, I jumped at the scrape of a key in the lock. Charlie burst through the door, his hair dishevelled and his tie askew.

"Hey, Em!" He called out, barely glancing my way as he rushed towards the stairs. "Sorry I missed your calls. Work was crazy today. Everything okay?"

I stared at him. Could he tell? Was I looking at him differently than I normally did?

"Everything okay?" I repeated, my voice carefully controlled. "You missed the appointment."

He froze, one foot on the stairs. Slowly, he turned to face me, confusion etched across his features. "Appointment?"

The word hung in the air between us, heavy with implications. Charlie's eyes widened as realisation dawned.

"Shit. Emma, I'm so sorry. I completely forgot." He rushed back down the stairs, his face a mask of guilt and remorse. "I can't believe I forgot. I'm such an idiot. There was this crisis with one of my clients, and I just... I have no excuse. I should have been there."

I chewed my lip, torn between the urge to forgive him instantly and the need to protect my heart. If I forgave him too fast, he'd know something was up.

"It's fine," I said, my voice carefully neutral. "These things happen."

"No, it's not okay." He ran an agitated hand through his hair. "This was important. I should have been there for both of you." He moved closer, his eyes pleading. "I'll make it up to you, I promise. I'll be at every appointment from now on. I'll take the whole day off if I have to."

One look at that earnest face and my resolve weakened. But I couldn't let him see how much his words affected me. How much he affected me. I could handle knowing he didn't love me, but hearing the words from his lips would break my heart.

"Really, Charlie, it's fine," I said, injecting a hint of coolness into my tone. I unconsciously placed a protective hand on my belly. "The baby's fine. Growing right on schedule. And my morning sickness seems to be done."

"That's great news!" A genuine smile lit up his face. Then his expression turned serious again. "But I still feel terrible. Is there anything I can do? Anything at all?"

I shook my head, afraid that if I spoke, I'd reveal too much. That I'd tell him how much I needed him. How much I loved him.

He glanced at his watch, panic gripping him. "Shit, we're going to be late. I need to shower before we meet Jesse and Lukas." He started up the stairs, taking them two at a time.

CHAPTER THIRTY-THREE

EMMA

"If they start being too obnoxious, just nudge me, okay?" Charlie said as he guided me towards the entrance of one of Los Angeles's trendiest restaurants. "I'll set them straight for you."

I smiled, but it felt as brittle as sunbaked plastic. My heart raced, a mix of anticipation and dread churning in my stomach.

What if they hate me? What if I say something stupid?

I shook my head, trying to dispel the thoughts. "You okay?" Charlie asked when we stepped into the restaurant. His hand pressed against my lower back, guiding me through the bustling crowd.

I nodded, forcing another smile. "Fine. Just a bit overwhelmed."

The truth? I was still hurt that he missed the appointment, still reeling from the realisation that I loved him. And the clusterfuck of a day. On top of all that, I'd never felt more out of place.

The restaurant oozed wealth and sophistication, from the crystal chandeliers to the impeccably dressed patrons. My simple maternity dress seemed woefully inadequate.

The scent of sizzling steaks and spices wafted through the air, making my mouth water. After weeks of battling morning sickness, the mere thought of a full meal without nausea seemed like a miracle. Thankfully, my body had decided it was time to stop torturing me.

A waiter brushed past us, carrying a tray of colourful cocktails. My fingers twitched with longing. Just a few more months. Then I could indulge in all the fancy drinks I wanted. For now, I'd settle for sparkling water and mocktails.

"Charlie! Over here!" A booming voice cut through the chatter.

My stomach clenched as I spotted a group waving enthusiastically from a corner table.

"Remember what I said," Charlie murmured before he led me towards them. "Just nudge me."

"About time you showed up." A tall, athletic man with an easy grin stood up. "We were starting to think you'd chickened out."

Charlie raised an eyebrow, smirking. "Keeping you on your toes, Jesse. Can't have you getting complacent."

The guys laughed and exchanged those typical half-embrace, half back-pat man hugs. I bit back a smile at the ridiculousness of it all. But then four pairs of eyes settled on me, and my amusement evaporated. Their curious gazes made me hyper-aware of my swollen belly and the way my maternity dress clung to my new curves.

"Everyone, this is Emma," Charlie said, his hand resting reassuringly on my lower back. "Emma, meet the gang. Jesse and Lukas are my idiot friends." He pointed to the guys grinning at me. "And their far too patient wives, Zoey and Celina."

"Nice to meet you all," I managed, my voice steadier than I expected.

"Nice to finally meet you, Emma." Jesse, the one who'd called out to us, extended his hand. His tall frame towered over me as he leaned in for a handshake. "Charlie's been keeping you all to himself."

"I hope he's only told you the good things." I shook his hand, willing my palm not to sweat.

"Oh, he's told us plenty." Jesse winked, his warm brown eyes crinkling with amusement, earning him an elbow in the ribs from his wife.

Zoey, a petite brunette with kind eyes, smiled warmly at me. "Don't mind him. We're just excited to meet you." She enveloped me in a hug, catching me off guard. But as she squeezed me gently, some of the tension gripping me dissolved. "How are you feeling? Charlie mentioned you'd been having a rough time with morning sickness."

"Better, actually," I said, surprised by her genuine concern. "That's partly why we agreed to dinner. It's nice to be able to eat without seeing it again five minutes later."

Celina, a statuesque redhead who I recognised as a former Olympic British gymnast, laughed. "Oh, I remember those days. Pregnancy is no joke."

"So, Emma." Zoey rested her elbow on the table and propped her chin on it, her eyes sparkling with interest. "How did you and Charlie meet? I'm dying to know the full story."

Jesse grinned, brushing back a lock of sandy hair from his forehead. "Oh, I already know this one, but I want to hear it from your perspective. See if Charlie was exaggerating."

I glanced at Charlie. He shrugged, directing a small smile at me. "Go ahead. Tell them how I swept you off your feet."

I snorted, unable to help myself. "Is that what you've been telling people? As I recall, you swept my champagne tower off its feet."

The table erupted in laughter. More of the tension drained from my shoulders as a result. I told them how he'd stared at the mess of broken glass like a deer caught in headlights, how he'd apologised, but still hadn't learned his lesson since I regularly caught him walking around the house with his gaze fixed on his phone and not his surroundings.

Charlie groaned. "I maintain that champagne tower was out to get me."

"Sure it was."

"Hey, I offered to help clean up," Charlie said, but his eyes danced with amusement.

Lukas, who'd been quiet until now, leaned forward, his broad shoulders hunching as he rested his elbows on the table. "And that led to... you know?" He waggled his eyebrows suggestively.

My face burned. "Well, not immediately. But yes, eventually."

"I can't believe you left out the part where you destroyed her display," Jesse said, shaking his head at Charlie.

"Typical. Always trying to make yourself look good."

"In my defence, I was trying to preserve some dignity." Charlie held up his hands in mock surrender.

"Wait." Zoey held up her hand, her brow furrowed. "So this was just a one-night stand? That doesn't sound like you, Charlie."

I shifted uncomfortably in my seat, the easy atmosphere taking a nosedive. Here we go. The judgement. The questions I didn't have answers to. Charlie cleared his throat, his hand finding mine under the table.

"It wasn't exactly planned," he said, his voice soft. "But sometimes the best things in life aren't."

Celina grinned. "Right answer." She jabbed Lukas in the side with her elbow. "You should take some lessons from him, Lucky."

Lukas groaned, running a hand through his short blond hair. "I'd rather not."

"Of course you wouldn't." Celina rolled her eyes, a fond exasperation in her voice. "Remember our anniversary?"

Lukas paled, his blue eyes widening. "Oh, come on. Not this again."

"Oh, do tell." Jesse rubbed his hands together gleefully.

"He forgot," Celina said, glowering at Lukas. "And when I reminded him, he said, and I quote, 'Babe, every day with you is like an anniversary.'"

Charlie choked on his drink, coughing and sputtering. "Smooth, Weber. Real smooth."

I glanced between them, feeling like I was watching a well-rehearsed play. There was clearly a history here, layers of inside jokes and shared experiences I couldn't quite grasp.

"Hey!" Lukas threw his hands up in exasperation. "I thought it was romantic!"

"It would have been," Celina said, "if you hadn't followed it up with 'So, can we just order pizza and watch the game?'"

Jesse wiped his eyes, his face red from laughter. "Oh man, Lukas. You really need to work on your game. Maybe Charlie can give you some pointers on how to sweet-talk your way out of trouble."

"Please, don't encourage him." Zoey shook her head, amusement and exasperation dripping from her words. "The last thing we need is Lukas trying to be smooth. Remember the rose petal incident?"

A collective groan went around the table. I raised a brow, equal parts confused and curious.

Charlie leaned in close. "Trust me, you don't want to know. Let's just say it involved a lot of rose petals, a faulty air conditioning unit, and an impromptu visit from the fire department."

I laughed. These people were crazy, but in the best possible way.

Lukas buried his face in his hands, his ears turning red. "Can we please talk about literally anything else?"

"Nope," Jesse said, popping the p. "This is too much fun.

Come on, Lukas, give us your best romantic line. Show Charlie how it's done."

Lukas sighed dramatically, then straightened up, puffing out his chest. He turned to Celina with an exaggerated flutter of his eyelashes. "Baby, you must be a hockey puck, because you've got me chasing you all over the ice."

There was a moment of silence before the table dissolved into laughter once again.

"Oh god," Celina gasped, clutching her sides. "That was terrible. Please, never say that again."

Charlie shook his head, a grin tugging at his lips. "Thanks for making me look good, man."

"Okay, enough ribbing on me. I'd rather learn more about Emma." Lukas leaned forward, his curious gaze fixed on me. "What made you decide to keep the baby and move across the country? That's a pretty big decision."

The question caught me off guard, and I fumbled for a moment. He made it sound like I'd just jumped at the chance for a cross-country trip, but I hadn't meant to move in. I'd needed help.

"I guess... it didn't feel like I had much of a choice at first. I had some health issues that complicated things, and my business in New York was struggling. Charlie offered to help, and... well, here I am."

I paused, trying to find the right words to explain the whirlwind of emotions and decisions that had led me to this moment.

It took a concerted effort not to think the L word.

If I thought it, maybe they'd read something on my face and call me out. They'd tell Charlie and then our lives would become even more complicated than they already were.

"It wasn't an easy decision. I mean, I barely knew Charlie, and the idea of moving across the country, away from everything and everyone I knew... it was terrifying. But something just felt... right. Like this was where I was meant to be, as crazy as that sounds."

As the words tripped off my tongue, the enormity of the change washed over me. As much as I was meant to be here and I would have struggled without him, I had completely upended my life for this pregnancy, for Charlie. Maybe this was why he'd been so hesitant to start a real relationship. Had he been trying to protect me from even more upheaval?

"It doesn't sound crazy at all." Celina reached out, patting my hand. "Sometimes you just have to trust your gut, even when your head is telling you it's insane."

Charlie squeezed my hand under the table, and I glanced at him, absorbing the concern in his eyes. I gave him a small nod, trying to reassure him I was okay.

"Well, we're certainly glad you're here now," Zoey said, her voice warm.

A server interrupted us to take our order. I scanned the menu, the pregnancy cravings coming in handy for once. I hadn't been able to get the smell of that steak out of my mind since we walked in the door. Once we'd all ordered, Zoey asked me how I liked LA so far.

"It's... different. Definitely a change of pace from New York. I'm still getting used to all the sunshine and palm trees."

"And the traffic," Charlie added with an exaggerated shudder. "Don't forget the traffic."

The table collectively groaned.

"Thankfully, I don't have to deal with that. One benefit of bed rest I guess."

"Yes, that's definitely a positive." Celina shook her head, her ponytail swinging. "If you thought New York was bad, just wait. LA takes it to a whole new level."

"Welcome to LA," Jesse said with a theatrical wave of his hand. "Where your commute time is directly proportional to how important your meeting is."

The conversation flowed more easily after that and I found

myself actually enjoying the way they all bantered back and forth. I'd always craved the big friend group with lots of people who got you. I had Lila, of course, but this was something else.

If Charlie was into me, too, this could really be my life...

But I shook off the thought as quickly as it came. It was just the love-buzz talking. Maybe. Just because I'd fallen for him didn't mean he felt the same way. Still, I couldn't quite squash the tiny spark of hope that flickered in my chest as I watched Charlie laugh with his friends, fitting so seamlessly into this world that part of me longed to be a part of.

"I thought he was just another smooth-talking agent." Zoey smirked at her husband. "But he wore me down eventually."

Jesse grinned, pulling her close. "More like I annoyed you into submission. I think you finally agreed to go out with me just to shut me up."

"That's not entirely inaccurate." Zoey tapped her chin thoughtfully. "But I have to admit, once I gave him a chance, I was pleasantly surprised. Turns out there's more to him than designer suits and a silver tongue."

"Aww, babe." Jesse pressed a hand to his chest. "That might be the nicest thing you've ever said about me."

"Don't let it go to your head."

Lukas snorted into his drink. "That's hardly challenging."

"Yeah, did you and Zoey barely see each other in your first year because of clashing schedules?" Celina asked, her tone suggesting she knew the answer and she wasn't impressed. "Nope."

"Exactly," Lukas said, his German accent breaking through in his excitement. "Our schedules were insane, and between hockey games and competitions, we were constantly travelling to different parts of the world. It wasn't until the Olympics when I finally got to nail her down."

Celina smacked Lukas's arm, her eyes narrowing. "Nail me down? You make it sound so romantic."

"What? It's true!" Lukas rubbed his arm, feigning hurt. "It

was fate. Both of us at the Olympics, when I'd spent a year trying to get a date out of you."

"Fate had nothing to do with it," Celina said, her own German accent becoming more pronounced. "You practically stalked me in the Olympic Village and the British team almost filed a complaint against you."

Lukas brushed that allegation away with his wine glass. "Nothing could have stopped me from winning my love."

"Wait." I leaned forward, intrigued. "How did you two actually meet? Before the Olympics."

The restaurant hummed with the clinking of silverware and the low murmur of conversation. Soft jazz played in the background, nearly drowned out by the laughter from nearby tables. Our waiter approached, balancing a tray laden with our appetisers.

"It was in the university dining hall at Cardiff Met. I'd gone in for a late-night snack after training, and this *Riesenbaby* comes stumbling in, still in his hockey gear." Celina rolled her eyes, but a fond smile played on her lips.

"Riesenbaby?"

The waiter placed our dishes on the table while our conversation continued.

"It means 'giant baby' in German." Lukas grinned, utter pride in his eyes as he threw back his shoulders and his massive frame seemed to expand even further. "Because I'm so adorably large."

Celina had learned German for him? Wow, talk about commitment.

Jesse nearly choked on his drink, coughing and sputtering. "More like because you act like a toddler."

Zoey jabbed her elbow into her husband's ribs. "Shh, let them tell the story."

"Anyway." Celina shook her head at him, shooting him a look that was equal parts exasperation and fondness. "He comes up to me, all sweaty and gross, and says in the worst attempt at a pickup line I've ever heard—"

"Excuse me, love, but I think you dropped something," Lukas said, adopting an exaggerated German accent that made his voice boom across the table.

"And do you know what this idiot did?" Celina asked, her lips pursed.

I shook my head.

"He bent down, picked up a sugar packet from the floor, and said, 'You dropped your nametag, Sweetener.'"

The table erupted in laughter and groans. Even I could concede that that was a terrible pick up line.

Charlie wiped tears from his eyes. "Oh man, Lukas, that's terrible. Even I could do better than that."

I raised a brow at Charlie. "Oh really? Because I seem to remember a certain someone using some pretty cheesy lines at a wedding not too long ago."

He had the grace to look sheepish. "Hey, they worked, didn't they?"

"So what happened next?" I asked, turning back to Celina and Lukas. "Clearly, you didn't fall for that line."

Celina shook her head. "No, definitely not. I told him to get lost in no uncertain terms. I was completely focused on qualifying for the Olympics. Gymnastics was all that mattered to me then. I had no time for distractions, especially not hockey-playing Riesenbabys." She smirked. "Which by the way, is my favourite German word."

Lukas chuckled, but then his amusement faded and he stared at his wife. "But I didn't give up," Lukas said, his voice softening with the memory. "I kept seeing her around campus, and I knew I had to keep trying."

"And how did that go?" Jesse asked, smirking.

Lukas's cheeks reddened. "Let's just say I made a fool of myself more than once. But eventually, I wore her down."

Celina snorted, her fork pausing halfway to her mouth.

"More like he made a nuisance of himself in the Olympic Village until I agreed out of pure exasperation. Warning off any athlete who so much as looked at me with a hint of interest." She crossed her arms and fixed Lukas with a stern glare. "He cut off my stress relief and made sure he was the only person I could turn to."

"And here we are, years later." Lukas smirked, draping his arm over Celina's chair.

"It wasn't all smooth sailing though," Celina added, her expression growing more serious. "After graduation, I stayed in Wales for Olympic training while Lukas got drafted by the Stingers. That's when the real challenge began."

"How did you manage?" I asked, my hand unconsciously resting on my belly. "The distance, I mean. It must have been incredibly difficult."

"It sucked, plain and simple." Lukas nodded, his jaw tightening at the memory. "We'd go months without seeing each other in person. Different time zones, crazy schedules... there were days when I wondered if we'd make it."

"But we did." A soft smile claimed Celina's lips. "We had to get creative. Lots of late-night Skype calls, care packages..."

"And some pretty steamy phone conversations." Lukas waggled his brows suggestively.

"Lukas!" Celina swatted his arm, her cheeks flushing.

The table erupted in laughter once again, and I joined in, caught up in the warmth of their shared experience. For a moment, my earlier insecurities faded, replaced by a sense of belonging.

We finished off our appetisers just in time for our main course to arrive. The waiter placed my plate of perfectly cooked steak in front of me and I held myself back until the others had received their meals. Once the waiter left, all bets were off. So maybe the baby was still influencing my tastebuds but right then I couldn't care less. I dug in, savouring each bite.

Once the initial craving had been satisfied, I refocused on

the conversation flowing around me and turned to Celina. "So, what finally brought you to LA?"

She tilted her head thoughtfully, her eyes meeting Lukas's. "Love, I suppose. After the Olympics, I had to make a choice. My gymnastics career or a life with Lukas here. It wasn't easy, but..." She trailed off, her gaze softening as she looked at her husband.

"But she chose me," Lukas said, his voice filled with a mixture of pride and awe. "Still can't believe my luck sometimes."

I glanced at Charlie, a question forming in my mind: Would we ever have that kind of connection?

CHAPTER THIRTY-FOUR

EMMA

"What about you two?" Zoey asked, cutting into her salmon. "Any plans for after the baby comes? Will you stay in LA, Emma?"

I opened my mouth, then closed it again. I had no idea how to answer.

"We haven't really talked about it," Charlie said. "But I hope Emma will stay. LA's grown on her, right, Em?"

I glanced at him sharply, searching his face for any hint of deeper meaning. Did he really want me to stay?

I nodded, forcing a smile. "Yeah, it's... different from New York, but I'm starting to see the appeal."

The appeal being Charlie.

"Oh, you have to stay!" Celina clapped her hands together excitedly. "There's so much to explore in LA. Have you had a chance to do any sightseeing yet?"

I shook my head, my hand unconsciously resting on my belly. "Not really. Between the morning sickness and doctor's appointments, I haven't ventured out much."

"Well, we'll have to change that," Zoey said. "You mentioned earlier that you love romantic comedies, right? We should totally take you on a studio tour! It's fascinating to see where all the movie magic happens."

Charlie perked up at this. "That's a great idea. Emma's been cooped up in the house for too long. A tour could be fun."

"And we could do lunch at that cute little café on Melrose afterwards." Celina pulled out her phone and started typing away. "You know, the one where they filmed that scene from *La La Land*? I'll check when they have availability."

"Oh, speaking of movies," Jesse said, gesturing around the table with his fork, "did you hear about the premiere at the Chinese Theatre next month? It's supposed to be the event of the season."

Zoey's eyes lit up. "I've already started looking for the perfect dress. Emma, you should come with us! I know the most amazing stylist who could hook you up with a gorgeous maternity gown."

"Oh, while I remember." A mischievous look overtook Jesse's face. "How's Saturday for your trial run?"

Charlie's eyes widened, and he shook his head almost imperceptibly. But Jesse either didn't notice or chose to ignore the warning.

"I have a work thing and Zoey is desperate to join me."

"Please say yes." Zoey leaned forward, a desperate manic glint in her eyes. "He's going to an event with all of the Hemsworth brothers. You can't make me miss that, Charlie."

"What trial run?" I asked, curiosity piqued despite my growing unease.

Jesse grinned at Charlie. "You didn't tell her?"

Charlie glared at Jesse and his amusement only deepened.

"I told Charlie you two could babysit our triplets for a night. You know, get some hands-on experience before your little one arrives."

My brows shot up. "That's…"

Words failed me. The thought of one child scared me. How the fuck were they handling three?

"Intense," Charlie answered for me. I glanced at him and he rubbed the back of his neck, looking uncomfortable. "I wasn't sure you'd be up for it. Jesse's kids can be a bit of a handful."

"Oh, come on." Jesse laughed. "They're not that bad. They're just... energetic."

Zoey snorted. "Honey, don't undersell it. We bred delinquents."

"No we didn't."

She stared at him, absolutely deadpan. "So they didn't redecorate our living room with permanent markers last night while I made dinner?"

"It was abstract art. Very avant-garde. We could sell it for millions."

"It was vandalism," Zoey said, her tone exasperated. "And you just encouraged the little monsters."

As Jesse launched into a spirited defence of his children's artistic talents, my mind whirled. Why hadn't Charlie told me? Did he not want me to meet his friends' kids? Or did he not trust me to handle it?

"I think it's a great idea," I said, surprising even myself. "We should definitely take you up on that offer, Jesse."

Charlie's head snapped towards me, his eyes wide. "Are you sure? I mean, triplets are a lot to handle, especially when you're..."

"Pregnant?" I finished for him, a hint of challenge in my voice. "I'm pregnant, Charlie, not incapacitated. Besides, it'll be good practice, right?"

An awkward silence fell over the table. I could sense Charlie's discomfort, but a part of me relished it. Let him squirm a little. Maybe it would prompt him to actually talk to me about these things instead of making decisions on my behalf.

"Well, that's settled then!" Jesse clapped his hands together, oblivious to the tension.

"So, Emma," Zoey said, her voice cutting through my spiralling thoughts. "Have you and Charlie started thinking about names yet?"

"We've discussed a few options," I said, pushing a stray piece of asparagus around my plate. "But we haven't made a final decision yet."

"Oh, I remember that phase," Celina said, her fork paused halfway to her mouth. "Lukas and I must have gone through a hundred names before we settled on ours."

Celina's fork clinked against her plate as she set it down, her eyes sparkling with amusement. "We had a whole system, didn't we, Lucky? Spreadsheets, pro-con lists, even a bracket tournament."

Lukas groaned, rubbing his temple. "Don't remind me. I still have nightmares about that bracket."

"It worked, didn't it?" Celina nudged him playfully. "We ended up with the perfect name for our little Maximilian."

Jesse sniggered. "That poor kid."

Celina's eyes narrowed, her relaxed demeanour shifting to defensive in an instant. "And what exactly is wrong with Maximilian?"

"Nothing, if you're naming a 19th-century Bavarian prince." Jesse shook his head.

Lukas straightened in his chair. "It's a strong name with a rich history. It means 'greatest' in Latin."

"Yeah, greatest target on the playground," Jesse muttered under his breath.

Zoey elbowed her husband sharply. "Be nice," she hissed.

I glanced at Charlie, unsure how to navigate this sudden tension. He just shook his head, an amused smile tugging at his lips.

"I think it's a lovely name," I said, trying to smooth things over.

Celina beamed at me. "Thank you, Emma. At least someone here has good taste."

"Oh come on." Jesse held up his hands in mock surrender. "I'm just saying, don't call him anything but Max in front of other kids."

"That might have crossed our minds before we named him." Lukas threw a sheepish glance at Jesse.

The tension around the table dissipated, replaced by chuckles and eye rolls.

"So you went to all that trouble," Charlie said, amusement colouring his tone, "just to end up calling him by a nickname?"

Celina shrugged, a small smile playing on her lips. "It gives him options. He can be Maximilian for formal occasions, Max for everyday use. It's versatile."

"Plus," Lukas added, grinning, "it drives my mother crazy when we use the nickname. She insists on using his full name every single time."

I couldn't help but laugh at that. "Sounds like you've got all your bases covered."

"Do you at least have some frontrunners?" Zoey asked.

Jesse snorted, nearly choking on his drink. "Oh, come on. Don't play coy with us, Charlie-boy. I know for a fact you've been considering my suggestions."

"Man, I appreciate the effort, but we're not using your ridiculous names."

"My names are not ridiculous."

My brows shot up. "Oh yes, how could I forget. Rocket and Hashtag sound like very serious names." I shook my head as everyone else sniggered. "Thanks for that."

"I'll have you know that Rocket is a perfectly acceptable name for a future Hollywood mogul."

"Hold up." A line formed between Lukas's brows. "Why does Jesse get name privileges and I don't? I thought we were all friends here."

"Trust me," Charlie said, rolling his eyes, "you're not

missing out on much. Unless you think Hashtag is a viable option for our child's future."

Lukas leaned back in his chair, a mischievous glint in his eye. "Hashtag Delacroix has a certain ring to it."

Charlie groaned, dragging a hand down his face. "Please, for the love of all that's holy, don't encourage him."

"What?" Jesse spread his hands innocently. "I'm just trying to help you stay ahead of the curve. In a few years, everyone will be naming their kids after social media trends."

"Over my dead body," I muttered, stabbing a piece of asparagus with perhaps a bit more force than necessary.

Zoey caught my eye and winked. "Don't worry, Emma. We'll make sure these idiots don't corrupt your baby-naming process."

"Speaking of babies," Celina piped up, her eyes sparkling with interest, "have you started thinking about the nursery yet? I know it's still early, but time flies when you're preparing for a little one."

I froze, my fork hovering midair. The nursery. Another thing we hadn't started. Another reminder of how unprepared we were, how fragile this whole situation felt. Of course, Charlie had ideas, but we hadn't gotten any further and really, did I want us to? It would be yet another thing he had to pay for because my savings were quickly dwindling.

"We've been... a bit preoccupied," Charlie answered smoothly, saving me from fumbling for a response. "But we'll get to it soon, right, Em?"

I nodded, forcing a smile. "Of course. We've just been taking things one step at a time."

"Oh, you have to let me help!" Celina said, immediately reaching for her phone. "I know the most amazing interior designer who specialises in nurseries. She did Max's room, and it's absolutely gorgeous. I'll send Charlie her number right now."

"That's... very kind of you."

A nursery designer? What happened to a simple crib and a changing table?

"And don't forget the baby shower," Zoey said. "We should start planning that soon. I'm thinking a Gatsby-themed extravaganza. What do you say, Emma?"

"That sounds... interesting," I said, trying to keep the uncertainty out of my voice. "But maybe something a bit more low-key?"

Zoey's face fell for a moment before she brightened again. "Of course! We can do whatever you're comfortable with. Maybe a nice brunch at the Beverly Hills Hotel? Or a spa day at Shutters on the Beach?"

"Hey, speaking of celebrations." Charlie jumped in, steering the conversation in a different direction. "Didn't you guys just get back from the Maldives? How was it?"

Jesse's eyes lit up. "Oh man, it was incredible. Crystal clear water, white sand beaches, and the most amazing seafood you've ever tasted."

"The sunsets were to die for," Zoey added, a dreamy look in her eyes. "We're already planning our next trip."

As they launched into a detailed account of their tropical getaway, I found myself drifting. My hand unconsciously moved to my belly, using our baby's gentle kicks to ground myself. I studied Charlie from the corner of my eye, taking in his rapt expression.

Did he resent me for tying him down? For keeping him from jetting off to exotic locales on a whim?

The waiter appeared, clearing away our dinner plates with practised efficiency. The clink of silverware against china punctuated the conversation, a stark contrast to the whirlwind of thoughts in my head.

"Would anyone care for dessert?" the waiter asked, his voice pulling me back to the present.

A chorus of enthusiastic agreement went around the table and the waiter handed out dessert menus. While everyone deliberated, Charlie's attention shifted to me and his brow creased in concern.

"You okay, Em?" he asked, his voice low, for my ears only. "You've been quiet."

I plastered on a smile, hoping it didn't look as forced as it felt. "I'm fine. Just a bit tired, I guess."

He nodded, but I could tell he didn't believe me. "Let's skip dessert and head out now."

"No, no, I'm okay, really."

The last thing I wanted to do was add pulling him away from his friends early to my list of reasons he might one day resent me.

Everyone ordered and the waiter left us to collect our desserts.

"You know, I still can't believe it sometimes." Lukas leaned back in his chair, his expression thoughtful. "I never thought I'd see the day when Charlie Delacroix would be a dad," he said, his voice tinged with amusement. "He always said he never wanted kids."

The words hit me like a physical blow. The chatter around the table faded to a dull roar as I struggled to process what I'd just heard. Charlie... never wanted kids? But then why...?

I turned to look at Charlie, hoping to see denial or at least discomfort on his face. Instead, he wore a look of resigned amusement, as if Lukas had just revealed an embarrassing childhood story rather than dropped a bombshell on our relationship.

"Things change." Charlie shrugged, reaching for his glass of wine. "Another round of drinks, anyone?"

Charlie never wanted kids? How had I not known this? And if he'd never wanted children, what did that mean for us, for our relationship afterwards?

And 'things change'? What kind of bullshit response was that?

I forced myself to smile and nod as the conversation picked

up again, but I felt like I'd been punched in the gut. Every casual touch, every shared laugh now seemed tainted by this new knowledge.

Their conversations floated around me, going in one ear and out the other.

Charlie never wanted kids.

The phrase echoed in my mind, a relentless drumbeat of doubt.

At some point the waiter returned with an array of decadent desserts, setting them down with a flourish. The sweet aroma of chocolate and caramel wafted through the air, doing nothing for my mood.

Had I trapped him in a life he never wanted? Was I dooming us to the same fate as his parents — resentment, obligation, a loveless marriage held together by duty and a child?

Not that I'd marry him. At least not now.

I glanced around the table, taking in the easy camaraderie, the shared experiences, the casual mentions of exclusive events and luxury vacations. This was Charlie's world.

And where did I fit? A pregnant wedding planner from New York, thrust into a life I'd never imagined, with a man who might not even want me here.

The baby kicked, a sharp reminder of the life growing inside me. A life that tied Charlie and me together, for better or worse. But was that enough? Could we build a real relationship, a family, on such a shaky foundation?

CHAPTER THIRTY-FIVE

CHARLIE

"Did you have fun tonight?" I asked as we pulled into the driveway and killed the engine. "I think my friends might actually like you more than me now."

Emma just hummed noncommittally, her gaze fixed on the house beyond the windshield. The silence stretched between us, heavy and uncomfortable. It was a far cry from the easy banter we'd shared over breakfast this morning. I just had to go and ruin it by missing the doctor's appointment.

"You okay?"

She shifted in her seat, still not meeting my eyes. "I'm fine."

"Come on, I may not be a mind reader, but even I can tell something's bothering you." I reached out to brush a strand of hair from her face. She flinched. "Is it the baby?"

"It's not the baby." She finally met my gaze, a humourless laugh escaping her. Her eyes were stormy, filled with emotions I couldn't quite decipher. "It's you. You're making me uncomfortable."

Her words hit me like an arrow through the heart. "Me? What did I do?"

Other than missing *one* appointment in five months.

"If you don't know, there's no hope for you." Emma fumbled with her seatbelt, trying to get out of the car. In her haste, she struggled with the clasp, growing more frustrated by the second.

"Here, let me help—"

She cut me off with a growl that, despite the situation, I found adorable.

"I don't need your help!" she snapped.

She finally freed herself from the seatbelt and I watched, helpless, as she attempted to heave herself out of the car. Under different circumstances, I might have found her determined waddle endearing. Right now, it just made my chest ache with worry and confusion.

Unable to stand by and do nothing, I quickly got out and rushed around to her side. "Just let me—"

She batted my hands away.

With a huff, Emma stormed off towards the house — well, as much as one can storm while seven months pregnant. I followed behind, utterly bewildered. What the hell had happened between the restaurant and now?

"Can we talk about this?" I asked while she fumbled with her keys at the front door.

She whirled around to face me. "Oh, *now* you want to talk? That's rich, coming from you."

I blinked, taken aback by the venom in her voice. "What's that supposed to mean?"

She just shook her head, finally managing to unlock the door, leaving me to trail after her like a lost puppy. Which wasn't far off how I felt.

I followed her into the living room but this time I didn't try to approach her. Instead, I watched as she paced back and forth, one hand on her lower back, the other gesticulating wildly as she muttered under her breath.

"Talk to me. What's going on?"

Emma stopped abruptly, fixing me with a look that was equal parts hurt and anger. "Why didn't you tell me you never wanted children? It seems like something I should have known when I first got here."

Shit. I thought she got it. It's not like I'd kept my family history secret.

"It's not that simple."

"Really?" She crossed her arms, brows raised in challenge. "Because it seems pretty straightforward to me. You never wanted kids, and now you're stuck with one. With me."

She might as well have slapped me. I stared at her, momentarily shocked.

Is that really what she thought? That she was some kind of burden I'd been saddled with?

"Whoa, hold on a second." I took a step towards her and she immediately backed away. "That's not—"

"Don't 'whoa' me right now, Charlie," she snapped. "I want answers. Why did you insist I move in with you? Why are you going through all the motions of being a father if it's not what you want?"

I took a deep breath, trying to calm the whirlwind of emotions in my chest. How could I make her understand when I was still trying to figure it out myself?

"Did you hear the part where I told Lukas things had changed?"

"Yes, but—"

"Well I meant it." I took a careful step towards her. She didn't react, too busy staring at me with narrowed eyes. "Yes, before you, I would have said I didn't want kids. But—"

"But what? You had a change of heart? Just like that? What, did the ghost of Christmas future visit you in your sleep?"

Despite the tension, I couldn't help but chuckle at her sarcasm. "I'm more of a Grinch than a Scrooge."

She didn't laugh. Tough crowd.

I moved closer, desperate to gather her in my arms and force her to listen to me. "It's not just like that. You have to understand—"

"Understand what?" She threw her hands up in exasperation, nearly knocking over a vase in the process. I made a mental note to move any breakables out of arm's reach. "That you've been feeding me hollow reassurances for months? That you've been playing the role of the supportive partner because you thought you had to?"

"That's not—"

"No, let me finish," she cut me off, her voice rising. "Do you have any idea what it's like to have your life completely upended? To have control ripped away from you? I won't do that to another person. I won't trap someone in a life they never wanted."

I flinched at her words. Did she mean her aunt moving her to the US or the baby? Maybe both. The pain in her voice was palpable, and it tore at my heart.

"What was your plan?" she asked, her tone bitter. "Play happy families until the baby comes, then what? Slowly distance yourself? Weekend visits and child support checks?"

"Jesus, Emma, no!" I ran an agitated hand through my hair. "Is that really what you think of me?"

She deflated slightly, her anger giving way to exhaustion. "I don't know what to think anymore. And yes, I know some of this is the hormones talking, but you know what? That's your fault too. You put this baby in me with your expired condoms."

I wanted to argue, to defend myself, but I knew she needed to get this out. So I bit my tongue and let her continue.

"Do you have any idea how terrifying this is?" Her voice cracked. "To feel like your body isn't your own anymore? To know that every decision you make affects not just you, but this tiny person growing inside you? And now to find out that the one person I thought I could rely on never even wanted this in the first place?"

Tears welled in her eyes, gutting me.

"How long before you start to resent me, Charlie? How long before you look at me and this baby and see nothing but the life you never wanted?"

Her words hit me like a physical blow. I took another careful step towards her, my heart aching.

"Emma, please. You have to believe me when I say that's not true."

She stared at me with narrowed eyes, unmoved by my plea.

"I could never resent you, love. Can't you see that?"

Her lower lip trembled, and she glanced away.

I wanted nothing more than to pull her into my arms, to kiss away her doubts and fears. But I knew she needed more than that. She needed the truth.

"You know me better than almost anyone. You know I can't function without my morning coffee, that I talk in my sleep, and that I have an irrational fear of pigeons."

Emma's lips twitched slightly at that last one, and I pressed on.

"You've seen me at my best and my worst. Hell, you've watched me negotiate million-dollar deals in my underwear because I forgot about the time difference."

That earned me a small chuckle, and hope took root inside of me.

"You know I secretly love those cheesy Hallmark movies you watch, even though I pretend to hate them."

Her features softened, but she still looked guarded. "Charlie..."

"You know about my dad, Em. You know how he left, how it affected my family. How could you think that wouldn't shape my views on having a family of my own?"

Memories of my father flooded my mind. The missed

birthdays, the broken promises, the day he walked out on us for good. It was like watching a greatest hits reel of disappointment. A lump formed in my throat, threatening to choke me. I could almost smell the stale beer on his breath, and hear the slam of the door as he left for the last time.

I swallowed hard, pushing back the tide of emotions. I focused on Emma's face, her eyes wide with concern despite her anger. This woman, who had stumbled into my life and turned everything upside down, made me believe I could be better than my old man ever was.

"Before I met you, the idea of having kids terrified me. That's true. I was afraid of turning into him."

She chewed her lip. "Why didn't you tell me when I first arrived?"

I ran a hand through my hair, frustration evident in my voice. "Because by then, things had already changed. *You* have changed everything. When you showed up, telling me you were pregnant... I should have been terrified. And part of me was. But mostly, I was... excited." I stared into her eyes, willing her to see the truth in mine. "For the first time in my life, the idea of being a father didn't *only* scare me shitless. Because it wasn't just any kid. It was *our* kid. Yours and mine."

"But how can you be sure?" Emma's eyes glistened with unshed tears. "How do you know you won't change your mind down the line?"

"Because I have you."

She blinked, confusion evident in her eyes. "Me?"

I nodded, a soft smile tugging at my lips. "I'm not gonna lie. I'm still scared witless. But it's not just fear. It's excitement, hope, anticipation. When you walked into my office and dropped that bomb, I only needed a couple of seconds to realise I'd do anything for you. For both of you."

Emma shook her head, her disbelief plain to read.

"You make me want to be better," I said, rushing on before she could find the words to deny me. "To face those fears head-on. To be the kind of man, the kind of father, that you and our child deserve." I grimaced, the weight of my words settling on my shoulders. I'd rather die than disappoint my kid. "I look at you, at how strong and brave you are, facing all of this. How can I not step up and be just as brave?"

"But I'm not brave."

"Yes, you are, love."

She shook her head. "No. I'm terrified!" Her voice rose, panic edging into her tone. "I have no idea what I'm doing. My body's a stranger to me. One day I'm craving pickles and ice cream, the next I can't stand the smell of my favourite perfume. I can't sleep, I can't work, I can't even tie my own shoes!"

Emma's breath came in short gasps, her words tumbling out faster and faster.

"And you! You're just sailing through this like it's no big deal. Planning nurseries and talking about the future like it's all set in stone. How can you be so calm when our entire lives are about to implode? And why the hell haven't you told your mother yet? Are you ashamed of us?"

"Of course not!" I exclaimed, frustration seeping into my voice.

She let out a bitter laugh, tears welling in her eyes. "Then why haven't you told her about the baby? About us? It's been four months, Charlie!" Emma's voice cracked. "Four months, and your mother still doesn't know she's going to be a grandma. You only told Veronica because I was right there. Why is that?"

That wasn't remotely true. I was always going to tell Veronica, but my mother? My father had scarred her in ways no therapist could heal.

"Why haven't you told your aunt?"

Emma scoffed. "That's different. I'm not close to Ginny like you are to your mother and sister."

"Fair point." I blew out a breath and studied her. "But there's more going on here than just my family, isn't there?"

She nodded, tears now flowing freely. "I feel like I'm losing control of everything. My body, my emotions, my finances. I'm peeing constantly, I cry at commercials, and I'm completely dependent on you. This isn't me, Charlie. I don't know who I am anymore."

My heart ached seeing her like this. I took a tentative step forward, relieved when she didn't back away. "Emma..."

"And what if we're making a huge mistake?" she continued, her words tumbling out in a rush. "Should we even be doing this? Maybe we should consider adoption. Or maybe I should just leave now, before—"

"No!" The word tore from my throat, raw and desperate.

Before I could think, I closed the distance between us, wrapping my arms around her and pulling her close. She struggled against me, her fists beating weakly against my chest.

"Let me go!" she sobbed, her whole body shaking. "We're not a good fit. If we were, things would have worked out by now. I wouldn't feel like I'm walking on eggshells, trying to figure out how you feel about me!"

I held her tighter, one hand cradling the back of her head as she cried into my shirt. "Shh, Em, please," I murmured, my own voice thick with emotion. "Don't say that. We are a good fit. The best fit."

Gradually, her struggles subsided, her sobs quieting to hiccupping breaths. I stroked her hair, pressing my lips to the top of her head.

"I'm so sorry," I whispered. "I hate seeing you in pain. I hate seeing you cry. I love you so much."

She stilled in my arms, then slowly pulled back to look at me, her eyes wide and searching. "What did you say?"

"I love you," I said again, softer this time. "I'm in love with you. I have been for months, probably since you walked into my office honestly." I cupped her face in my hands, brushing away her tears with my thumbs. "I've been driving myself crazy trying to maintain boundaries. I was afraid I'd be taking advantage of you while you're dependent on me. I couldn't be certain your thoughts were your own due to the pregnancy hormones."

Emma's hand covered mine, her touch tentative but warm.

"I didn't want to dive headfirst into the relationship I wanted with you for fear that you'd change your mind and destroy my heart after the baby came. That you'd realise you didn't want me."

Emma's lips trembled. "Charlie, I—"

"Let me finish," I said softly. "I know I screwed up by not telling you about my past feelings on having kids. But you've changed everything for me. Can't you see that? I can't wait to meet our baby, to build a life with you both."

Emma's eyes shimmered with fresh tears, but this time, a glimmer of hope shone in their depths. "You really mean that?" she whispered.

I pressed my forehead against hers. "I want it all, Em. The good, the bad, the three AM feedings, the first steps, the tantrums. I want to argue about whose turn it is to change diapers and who gets to choose the movie for date night. I want you. All of you."

For a moment, she stared at me, saying nothing and my world crawled to a halt. Fear gripped my heart while I waited for her to say something, do something. Could she ever love me too?

Then, she let out a watery laugh and my lungs expanded with relief. That sounded like a happy laugh, right?

"You idiot," she whispered, her hands gripping my wrists. "I love you too. That's what scares me the most."

Relief washed over me like a tidal wave. "Yeah?"

She nodded, a small smile breaking through her tears. "Yeah. I've fallen in love with you, Charlie Delacroix, and it scares the hell out of me. Because what if I'm not enough? What if I'm a terrible mother? What if—"

I silenced her with a kiss, pouring all my love and reassurance into it. When we broke apart, both breathless, I rested my forehead against hers again.

"You're more than enough. You're perfect, control freak tendencies included."

She chuckled and I grinned.

"You're also going to be an amazing mother, but we'll figure this out together, okay? No more holding back, no more silence. Just you and me. Just us."

Emma let out a shaky breath. "Promise?"

I smiled, brushing my nose against hers. "Promise."

She laughed, the sound like music to my ears. "Okay."

I pulled her into as tight a hug as I could. I cupped her face in my hands and kissed her, pouring all the love and longing I'd been holding back into it. Emma responded immediately, her lips soft and eager against mine.

When we finally broke apart, both breathing heavily, I rested my forehead against hers again. "So," I said, my voice husky, "what do you say we call my mom tomorrow and give her the shock of her life?"

Emma's lips curved into a smile. "Sounds like a plan."

"Good." I leaned in to kiss her again, but as our lips met, a groan escaped me. "Because I have plans for you right now," I murmured against her mouth.

"What?" She let out a surprised squeak as I scooped her up into my arms. "What are you doing?"

I grinned, already heading for the stairs. "I think we need to christen our new relationship, don't you? After all, we've got a lot of lost time to make up for."

Emma's laughter echoed through the house as I carried her upstairs, my heart lighter than it had been in months.

CHAPTER THIRTY-SIX

EMMA

I never thought this could happen.

Never in my wildest dreams did I imagine Charlie could want me, want us, the way I wanted him. For months, I'd been preparing myself for heartbreak, convincing myself that this was temporary, that he'd eventually tire of playing house.

But now... now everything had changed.

He loved me.

He wanted our baby.

He wanted a future with us.

How could I have been so blind to miss the signs?

His fingers traced my skin as he tugged my panties off, leaving goosebumps in their wake. He stared down at my naked body with a look of pure need painted across his gorgeous face. I'd get to wake up to that face for the rest of my life. It barely felt real. I couldn't wipe the stupid, happy grin from my face even as my body clenched with desire.

We were going to be a real family. The thought brought tears to my eyes, happy ones this time.

I reached up, cupping Charlie's face in my hands. His hazel eyes met mine, brimming with love and desire.

"I hope you never stop looking at me like that," he whispered before capturing my lips with his.

His kiss was gentle but desperate, long and drugging. It consumed my thoughts, leaving me glowing with the absolute certainty that he was mine.

He trailed kisses along my jaw and down my neck. I shivered and the empty ache in my core intensified. Maybe it was the hormones, or maybe it was the newfound certainty of our relationship, but every caress felt electric.

"Charlie," I breathed, running my fingers through his hair as he lavished attention on my collarbone.

He paused and my fingers dove into his hair, trying to pull him back. He resisted.

"You okay, love? Is this too much?"

I shook my head, smiling at his concern. "No, it's perfect. You're perfect."

His answering grin was breathtaking. He moved lower, pressing soft kisses to my swollen belly. The tenderness of the gesture brought fresh tears to my eyes. This man, who I'd convinced myself couldn't possibly want this life, was worshipping the very evidence of our shared future.

"I love you," he murmured against my skin. "Both of you."

His hands skimmed up my sides, cupping my breasts gently. I gasped at the sensation; my body had become so much more sensitive lately. He seemed to understand without me saying a word, his touch becoming feather-light as he explored.

"You're so beautiful," Charlie said, his voice filled with awe. "I can't believe you're finally all mine."

I pulled him up for another kiss, pouring all my love and newfound certainty into it. "I am yours," I whispered against his lips. "And you're mine. Always."

As Charlie's hands continued their exploration, I lost myself in the sensation, in the love and desire coursing through me. His touch trailed lower until his fingers danced just above my aching clit. "Yes," I hissed, my hips thrusting upwards in search of relief.

Charlie chuckled darkly. "You want it, darling? Beg for it."

"Please," I moaned.

"Please what?"

"Make me come."

His finger brushed against my clit, and my entire body shuddered. While he continued to stroke me, he lowered himself to kneel at my feet. I choked on a moan as he added his tongue to the mix. He teased me, varying the pressure while his fingers thrust inside of me.

"Oh, Charlie," I whimpered, already hovering on the edge of orgasm.

"Come for me, Emma," he whispered, his breath hot against my ear.

Between his skillful touch and wicked tongue, I flew over the edge before I was ready. I cried out, my body convulsing.

"Yes, fuck yes," I moaned, riding his hand unashamedly, chasing the intense waves of pleasure.

"Fuck, you're gorgeous when you come." Charlie straightened up and buried his face in my neck, pressing a soft kiss below my jaw, then licking a soft kiss to my earlobe. "I'll never get enough of putting that blissed-out expression on your face."

I chuckled. "Good, because my needs have not changed."

His face lit up with a sly smile. He stood up and shoved his boxers down, revealing his thick, hard cock. He climbed onto the bed and lay down, patting his lap.

"Get over here and ride me."

I crawled towards him without hesitation, threw my leg over his waist and straddled him. My fingers curled around his cock and he bit his lip, like he was seconds away from losing control. The idea made my pussy clench. His hands roamed my body, caressing my curves and teasing my sensitive nipples. I dragged the tip through my folds, my eyes fluttering shut at the delicious but light pressure.

"If the plan is to torture me, it's working."

"Just making sure you want it bad enough." I opened my eyes and grinned down at him.

He snorted. "If you don't give me that pussy right now, I'm going to return the favour with some of my new toys."

I sank down slowly. Not because I didn't want to play, I definitely did. But I only had so much restraint. I groaned as I bottomed out, overwhelmingly full.

"Oh fuck, yes," he hissed, his hands gripping my hips.

I began to ride him, my movements slow and measured, enjoying the feeling of him sliding in and out of me. Each time I bottomed out, he tilted my hips, grazing my clit against his cock. Mindless with pleasure, my movements quickly developed into erratic rocks.

"You're mine," he muttered as he took control, pounding into me from below. "I'm going to fill you up with my cum, make sure you remember it. Every single day."

My inner walls clenched at his words. Why was that hot? It was fucking unhinged, yet my body loved it. Would it stop being hot once the baby arrived? When his new obsession gained real consequences?

I couldn't say, but I wasn't sure I wanted it to.

This was a piece of him reserved only for me.

But beneath the dirty talk, there was an undertone of love and devotion I couldn't miss. Even in the reverent way he gripped me, the soft glint in his eyes, his love shone through.

Had it always been there?

As I continued to ride him, my orgasm built inside of me, a relentless force that could not be denied. I moaned, "Oh god, Charlie, I'm going to…"

I couldn't get the words out before my body locked up and pleasure rushed through me.

Charlie let out a triumphant roar, following me over the edge. His body bucked beneath me as he came inside of me, filling me to the brim. It was an intense, soul-baring moment, one that left me feeling both drained and yet somehow fuller than before.

Still wracked with aftershocks, I slid off him and laid on my back, completely spent and sleepy.

"If you keep satisfying me like this, we'll never have another argument again."

"I like that idea." He chuckled and curled around me, his hand sliding down to my belly. "Next time, I'll just bend you over the nearest surface and make love to you until you forget why you were pissed at me."

He pressed a soft kiss to my lips. His fingers caressed my entrance, making me moan. I realised what he was doing. One glance in that frustratingly well-positioned mirror and I confirmed my suspicions.

Charlie was scooping up his cum and pushing it back inside of me. I moaned as he unintentionally stoked the aftershocks, teasing me with slow, deliberate strokes. I stretched languidly, my body still humming with satisfaction. Five minutes went by and still his fingers continued their gentle exploration, sending little sparks of pleasure through me. I couldn't help but chuckle at his focused expression.

The doorbell rang, echoing through the house and with a dramatic sigh, Charlie rolled out of bed. I admired the view until he pulled on a pair of sweatpants. He left, grumbling something about disabling the doorbell and I reached for my robe.

My question still circled in my mind. If he kept up like this, I'd end up pregnant again as soon as it was medically possible.

Do I want that?

He could always get a vasectomy or I could get the implant. The idea of him indulging in his quirks without consequences held a certain appeal. But then again...

I padded barefoot down the hallway, consumed with the image of another baby, a sibling for our peanut. A real family unit, complete with a ring on my finger and Charlie by my side. The thought warmed me from the inside out.

When I reached the landing above the stairs, I stopped, staring down at the mess of our entryway with confusion. Charlie stood amongst a maze of boxes.

"What's all this?" I asked.

Charlie glanced up at me, panic flickering across his face. "Oh, you know. Just... stuff." He ran a hand through his hair. "Go back to bed, I'll be up before you know it."

I descended the stairs, my narrowed eyes fixed on him, unconvinced.

"Oh really? It's nothing?"

He nodded but his eyes widened when I reached for the nearest box. I pried it open to reveal a tiny onesie covered in cartoon dinosaurs.

"'Just stuff,' huh?" I held up the onesie, smirking. "I didn't realise you'd taken up doll collecting."

Charlie's ears turned pink. "Okay, so I might have gone a little overboard with the baby shopping."

I laughed, digging through more boxes. Each one revealed more adorable baby items — clothes, toys, even a state-of-the-art baby monitor.

"A little overboard?" I shook my head, unable to keep the amusement out of my voice. "Charlie, you've bought enough for a small army of babies. Should I be worried you're planning on starting a daycare?"

He chuckled, wrapping an arm around my waist. "Can you blame me for being excited?"

I leaned into him, my heart swelling with affection. "Buying so much stuff, anyone would think you want more kids."

Charlie stiffened behind me, his arm tightening. "Do you?" he asked, his tone serious. "Want more kids, I mean."

I studied him. Hope and uncertainty warred in his eyes, reminding me of our earlier conversation. How could I have ever doubted this man's commitment?

"Well," I said, letting a coy smile play on my lips, "I wouldn't be opposed to the idea. You know, hypothetically speaking."

The grin that spread across his face could have lit up the entire city of Los Angeles. "Yeah?"

I nodded, my own smile growing. "Yeah. But let's get through this one first, shall we?"

Charlie pulled me closer, his eyes sparkling with excitement. "Absolutely. But just for future reference, how many are we talking? Because I'm thinking six would be a good, round number."

"Six?" I burst out laughing, shaking my head in disbelief. "Are you insane? Three, tops."

"Four?" he negotiated, waggling his eyebrows.

"Three," I insisted, still giggling. "And that's my final offer."

He pretended to consider this, tapping his chin thoughtfully. "Well, I suppose I can work with three. For now."

Surrounded by baby paraphernalia, my chest aching with more love than I knew what to do with, I couldn't help but wonder how we'd gotten here.

Wonderful, clumsy but thoughtful Charlie. Who would have thought that the man who once claimed he didn't want kids would now be haggling over how many we should have?

"What?" He asked at my chuckle.

I shook my head, smiling up at him. "Nothing. I'm just... happy. Really, really happy."

He leaned down, pressing a soft kiss to my lips. "Me too, Em. Me too."

EPILOGUE

CHARLIE

"I swear to god, if you don't find a way to make this baby teleport out of me right now, I'm going to shove your entire hockey stick collection up your nose!"

I should have been prepared for it but every time a contraction hit I flinched. Her face was flushed, hair plastered to her forehead with sweat as she gripped my hand so tightly I thought my bones might snap.

"I don't think that's physically possible, love." I immediately regretted my words as her grip on my hand tightened to bone-crushing levels.

"Don't you dare 'love' me, you overgrown maple syrup guzzler!"

I took a deep breath, trying to steady my nerves as the beeping of the monitors filled the room. Emma's face contorted in pain again, and I felt utterly helpless.

"I'm sorry, I'm so sorry." There were breathing techniques for this, weren't there? Wasn't that what we'd spent weeks practising in those annoying birthing classes? "Just breathe, Em. In through your nose, out through your mouth."

She fixed me with a glare that could melt steel. "Don't you dare tell me to breathe, you overgrown tree of a man. This is all your fault!"

"You're right, it's all my fault." I nodded frantically, agreeing with everything she said. "I'm a terrible person. Just focus on your breathing, okay? Just breathe."

"Breathe? Breathe?!" Emma's voice rose an octave. "I'm trying to push a watermelon out of my vagina because of your stupid, giant genes!"

"Okay, okay!" I held up my free hand in surrender. "No more breathing. Got it."

Behind me, my sister and Emma's best friend both failed to suppress their laughter. I glanced over my shoulder, levelling my own glare at the pair of them. They stared back at me, both red-faced and shaking with mirth.

"You're so screwed," Veronica mouthed.

"This isn't funny," I snapped at them.

"Oh, but it is." Veronica wiped tears from her eyes.

I opened my mouth to snap at her, but Emma's scream cut me off. Another contraction hit, and her grip on my hand tightened impossibly further.

"Oh god," she moaned. "Why did I let you talk me into a natural birth? I hate you. I hate you and your stupidly tall genes."

"I know, I know," I soothed, wiping her forehead with a damp cloth. The smell of antiseptic mixed with sweat filled my nostrils. "You can have all the drugs you want next time, I promise."

Emma's eyes flashed dangerously. "Next time? You think there's going to be a next time after this? You're delusional!"

I loved her.

Emma flopped back against the pillows, exhausted. "I can't do this. It's too much."

My heart clenched at the defeat in her voice. I leaned in close, pressing my forehead to hers. "Yes, you can. You're the strongest person I know."

"That's utter bullshit. I could be Iron Woman and I'd still struggle to get your kid out of me." She glared at me. "Your mother told me you were a ten-pound baby. Why didn't you warn me I was in for a giant?"

I chuckled nervously. "Hey, maybe our kid will take after your side of the family. Nice and petite."

Another contraction hit, and Emma's face contorted in pain. "I swear to god, Charlie, if this baby is over eight pounds, I'm never letting you touch me again!"

Lila snorted from her position by Emma's other side. "Yeah, right. Like you two can keep your hands off each other for more than five minutes."

"Shut up, Lila." Emma directed her glare at her best friend. "You could have stopped this too."

"As if." Lila scoffed. "You were set in your ways before you even called me, bitch. Direct all of that energy at your baby daddy."

"Thanks, Lila. Appreciate the support," I muttered sardonically.

"Any time," she threw back with a sunny smile.

I ignored her and focused on Emma. She was breathing hard, but the contraction had passed, for the moment.

Staring into her eyes, the room faded away, and it was just us. I whispered praises to her, encouraging her. All the while I cursed my mother. I'd known going to see her instead of calling would be a bad idea, but I'd let Emma talk me into a trip to Ontario.

The damn woman had broken out the baby albums, albums I was shocked to learn she still had. I'd always assumed the maternal bone had skipped her and in the end I'd kind of wished it had.

Emma had taken one look at newborn me and freaked the

fuck out. And understandably so when my mother backed the pictures up with a gruesome account of my birth and the number of stitches she'd needed afterwards.

She'd taken to Emma with ease though, falling in love with her almost as fast as I had.

Another contraction hit, and her grip on my hand tightened again. I swore I heard something crack.

"Jesus Christ on a hockey stick!" I yelped, trying to pry my fingers loose. "Em, love, I need that hand."

"Oh, you need that hand?" Emma's eyes narrowed, her voice dripping with sarcasm. "I'm sorry, am I inconveniencing you?"

I opened my mouth to respond but thought better of it. Veronica and Lila burst into another fit of giggles.

"Some support you two are," I muttered.

"Oh, we're supporting," Lila said, wiping tears from her eyes. "We're supporting our own entertainment. This is better than any reality TV show."

I turned back to Emma, whose face was flushed and damp with sweat. Her hair clung to her forehead in dark tendrils, and I brushed them away gently.

"You're doing great, love," I said, trying to keep my voice steady. "Remember what the instructor said about visualising? Picture yourself on a beach or something."

Her grip on my hand loosened slightly as the contraction passed. Her eyes flashed with a mix of pain and irritation. "Are you kidding me? The only thing I'm visualising is punting you into the Pacific Ocean."

I chuckled, the sound thready with nerves. "Okay, no beaches. How about this — it'll all be over soon, and we'll get to meet our baby. Don't you want to know if it's Prue or Liam?"

Her eyes softened for a moment, a flicker of excitement breaking through the pain. "Hell, yes."

Utter pride welled inside of me. How someone as flaky and

selfish as her aunt Ginny could raise someone like Emma, I had no clue.

I'd spent weeks convincing her to introduce us and break the news and I'd ended up wishing I'd never bothered. My blood boiled just remembering it.

We'd video called her to break the news about the baby. Ginny had barely reacted, just shook her head and lamented that she thought she'd taught her better. She'd gone on about how Emma's parents' genes must have been too strong for her to influence Emma towards a "childfree and carefree life." The whole interaction had amused Emma, but it had left me fuming.

The next few hours passed in a blur of contractions, encouragement, and more creative insults than I thought possible. Just when I thought I couldn't take any more, the doctor announced it was time to push.

With one final, ear-splitting scream from Emma, our child entered the world. The room filled with the most beautiful sound I'd ever heard — our baby's first cry.

"Congratulations," the doctor beamed, holding up our squalling, squirming infant. "It's a girl!"

My jaw dropped. A girl. We had a daughter.

The nurses quickly cleaned her up and wrapped her in a soft blanket before placing her in my arms. My world shifted on its axis as I took in her tiny, scrunched-up face. She was perfect — all red and wrinkly and absolutely beautiful.

"Hi Prue," I whispered, my voice choked with emotion. "I'm your dad."

Tears blurred my vision as I gazed at our daughter. I was overwhelmed with love, fear, and a fierce protectiveness I'd never experienced before. I'd do anything for this tiny human.

I caught Emma's tired but joyful gaze and smiled. "Em, she's perfect."

As I placed our daughter in Emma's arms, I couldn't help but think how wrong I'd been about everything. All my fears about fatherhood, about not being ready, about messing things up — they seemed to melt away as I watched Emma cradle our little girl.

EMMA

"Welcome to the world, Prue Delacroix," I murmured, pressing a soft kiss to our daughter's forehead.

I cradled Prue against my chest, marvelling at her tiny features. Her button nose, her rosebud lips, her impossibly small fingers. How had Charlie and I created something so perfect?

Just nine months ago, we'd been strangers.

Now, here we were, a family.

The thought made me chuckle. If someone had told me at Abi's wedding that the clumsy guy who knocked over my champagne tower would end up being the father of my child, I'd have laughed in their face.

But life has a funny way of surprising you.

"She's absolutely beautiful, Em." Lila leaned in for a closer look. "Can I hold her?"

I hesitated for a moment, surprised by how reluctant I was to let Prue go. But I nodded, carefully transferring her into Lila's arms.

"Support her head," I said.

Lila rolled her eyes but complied. "I've held babies before, you know. I won't break her."

"She's not just any baby. She's my baby. And she's perfect."

Veronica laughed, peering over Lila's shoulder. "She really is. Good job, you two. You make cute kids."

Lila carefully handed the newborn over to Veronica. "Hey there, little niece," she cooed. "I'm your Aunt V. When you want to kick ass and take names, you come to me, okay, kid?

I've got you." She leaned closer, her voice dropping to a whisper while she smirked at Charlie. "And when you want to wrap your daddy around your little finger, I'm all ears."

Lila snorted. "Please, this kid's already got Charlie whipped. Did you see his face when she was born? Total goner."

"Like you're any better." I crossed my arms and stared at Lila with a raised brow. "I saw those tears."

"Allergies," Lila said dismissively, but her voice was thick with emotion. She took Prue back from Veronica. "Oh, sweetie. Aunt Lila's going to make sure you know how to wrap all the boys around your little finger. Unlike your mom, who needed your dad to literally knock her up before she made a move."

"Lila!" I gasped, torn between laughter and outrage. "She's only an hour old!"

"Never too early to start learning the important things in life," Lila winked.

I shook my head, amused that Prue already had a fan club.

Charlie cleared his throat, looking sheepish. "Hey, V, Lila... I'm sorry for snapping at you earlier. I was just stressed and—"

"Don't sweat it, big guy." Lila waved him off. "It was a tense experience. We get it."

Veronica, however, grinned. "Oh no, you're not getting off that easy. I'm holding this over your head for at least a year. Maybe two."

As they bickered good-naturedly, I caught Charlie's eye. "Don't think you're getting an apology from me, mister. You deserved every word."

To my surprise, he just laughed. "I know, love. I'd expect nothing less."

He knew? What the fuck?

Before I could question that declaration, the door swung open, and a familiar figure strode in. My jaw dropped.

"Aunt Ginny?"

Charlie tensed, his expression darkening. "What are you doing here?"

Ginny raised an eyebrow, unfazed by his hostility. "I was invited, wasn't I? I got Emma's message."

"Yeah, but—" Charlie sputtered, caught off guard. "We didn't think you'd actually come."

I squeezed his hand, silently urging him to calm down. "It's okay, handsome."

Ginny approached the bed, her eyes fixed on Prue. For a moment, she just stood there, studying our daughter's face. Then, to my utter shock, she smiled.

"She's beautiful, Em," she said, her voice gruff but sincere. "You did good, kid."

I blinked back tears, overwhelmed by the unexpected praise. "Thanks. Do you want to hold her?"

Ginny hesitated, a flicker of uncertainty crossing her face. "Are you sure?"

"I'm sure," I said firmly.

I glanced up at Charlie, silently pleading with him to understand. This was important to me, even if I couldn't fully explain why.

He hesitated, but after a moment, he nodded, squeezing my hand in support.

Ginny looked between us, then back at Prue. "If you're certain..."

"I am," I insisted, even as a small voice in the back of my mind questioned why I needed this so badly.

But as Lila carefully transferred Prue into Ginny's arms, I pushed those doubts aside. This was about family, however complicated and messy it might be. And maybe, just maybe, it was about second chances, too.

I watched in amazement as Ginny held Prue with a mixture of awe and trepidation on her face. This was the woman who had always kept me at arm's length, who had dismissed my pregnancy like it was nothing more than an inconvenience. Yet she cradled my daughter like she was the most precious thing in the world.

The room fell silent. Charlie stood tense beside me, his jaw clenched tight enough to crack walnuts. I knew that look — it was his 'about to go into full protective mode' face. Sure enough, he cleared his throat, breaking the spell.

"So, Ginny," he said, his voice deceptively calm. "Care to explain your sudden interest in our family? Last I checked, you weren't exactly thrilled about this whole situation."

Oh boy. Here we go.

I braced myself for the fireworks.

"You're right," she said quietly. "I wasn't thrilled. But I was wrong."

She looked up at me, her eyes shining with unexpected emotion. "I'm proud of you, Emma. You're stronger than I ever was. You've built a life for yourself, found love, created this beautiful little person. You've done everything I was too scared to do."

I blinked, stunned. Was this really happening? Or was I hallucinating from the post-birth hormones?

"I love you," Ginny continued, her voice thick. "I know I've never been good at showing it, but I do. I knew I'd never be a fit parent myself, but you... you're going to be amazing at this."

Charlie's eyebrows shot up to his hairline. I tuned out. I only had eyes for Prue, still nestled in Ginny's arms. She was oblivious to the emotional minefield around her, content in her post-birth slumber.

I'd always prided myself on my independence, worn it like a badge of honour. But now, looking at my daughter, I saw the truth. I hadn't been independent — I'd been neglected.

Well, not this time. Between Lila, Charlie, and his family, we had all the support we needed. Our daughter would grow up surrounded by love, supported from all sides. She'd never doubt her place in the world or her worth.

As if sensing my thoughts, Lila appeared at my side. "Want her back?" she asked softly.

I nodded, desperate to hold my daughter again. Lila expertly extracted Prue from Ginny's arms and placed her in mine. That newborn smell hit me, and my entire body relaxed.

"Hey there, trouble," I whispered, nuzzling her soft cheek. "You certainly know how to make an entrance, don't you? Seven months of nausea, thirty-six hours of labour, and now you've got the whole room wrapped around your tiny finger. You're going to be a handful, aren't you?"

"Speaking of handfuls." Charlie slid himself onto the edge of my bed and lay down beside me, a mischievous glint in his eye. "Remember when you promised me two more of these?"

I shot him a glare that could have melted steel. "Oh, we are so renegotiating that deal, mister. The factory is closed for renovations after a giant baby destroyed it."

He laughed. "Alright, alright. We'll talk about it later."

But I caught the look in his eyes. The one that screamed 'challenge accepted'. Something told me he was already plotting to up the ante to four kids, probably googling whether twins ran in his family.

I shook my head, unable to keep the smile off my face. What had I gotten myself into? I stared down at Prue, and I knew the answer.

The best kind of trouble.

*L*oved **Charlie and Emma? Dying to spend a little more time with them?**

Then join them for their first time babysitting Jesse's demon triplets and read the bonus scene. Turn the page to read a bonus scene.

I usually reserve this for my mailing list but this is easier in print. Plus, it's just nice to have it all together, right?

BONUS SCENE

*C*harlie

"You look like you're about to face a firing squad."

Emma stopped beside me and eyed the driveway through the living room window. At thirty-two weeks pregnant, she looked radiant, even with the wrinkle of concern between her brows.

I forced a grin. "More like a tiny tornado of terror." My fingers found hers, intertwining. "You sure you're up for this? It's not too late to call Jesse and cancel."

She squeezed my hand. "And miss out on all the fun? Not a chance. Besides, it'll be good practice, right?"

Before I could respond, the roar of an engine cut through the air. A familiar SUV came barreling up the drive and screeched to a halt outside my door.

"Brace yourself," I muttered.

The car doors flew open. Excited squeals and incomprehensible babble filled the air as Jesse's little terrors spilled out before he could even get his door open. He'd helpfully forgotten to mention that they could undo their child seats. Great. Just great.

He corralled them with a look and a shout, ushering them towards the front door. Why had I thought this was a good idea?

The door burst open — why hadn't I thought to lock it? — and suddenly my pristine foyer was overrun by a swarm of tiny humans.

"Special delivery!" Jesse's voice rang out, filled with barely contained glee. "One trio of adorable terrors, as promised!"

"Wait, Jesse—"

But my so-called best friend was already backing away, hands raised in surrender, a manic grin plastered on his face.

"Gotta run! Important... uh, agent stuff. You know how it is. They've had lunch, but they'll probably want snacks soon. And maybe a nap. Or not. Who knows?" He laughed, the sound bordering on hysterical. "Good luck!"

Before I could even process what was happening, Jesse had vanished, leaving Emma and me standing in the foyer, mouths agape, as three tiny hurricanes disguised as children barrelled past me and chaos erupted around us. My pristine house transformed into a toddler warzone in seconds flat.

A blur that I assumed was Ezra zoom past, heading straight for my prized collection of signed scripts.

Emma, already waddling as fast as her thirty-two week pregnant belly would allow, called out, "I've got him!" She managed to intercept Ezra just before he could use "Pulp Fiction" as a colouring book.

I shook myself out of my stupor. Right. Three kids. We could handle this.

I turned to Emma, eyes wide. "Did he just—"

"Yep." She nodded, lips twitching with amusement.

"And we're—"

"Uh-huh."

"Shit."

"Language," she chided softly, gesturing to the kids still clinging to our legs.

Right. Tiny ears. I cleared my throat. "I mean, uh, shoot. Okay, team. Who wants to... watch Frozen?"

Three heads snapped up, eyes shining with an almost feral intensity.

"Fozen!" Luna shrieked, already making a beeline for the living room.

"Me first!" Ezra shouted, shoving past his sister.

Noah toddled after them, clutching a ratty stuffed elephant to his chest. "Ellie want Fozen too," he mumbled.

I exhaled slowly, my body tense like I'd just defused a bomb. "Well, that bought us five minutes of peace."

Emma laughed, the sound warming me from the inside out. "Oh, you sweet summer child. You think it'll be that easy?"

As if on cue, a crash echoed from the living room, followed by the distinct sound of something expensive shattering.

"Sparkle did it!" Luna's voice rang out.

I pinched the bridge of my nose, wondering if it was too late to call Jesse back. Or maybe hire a team of professional nannies. Hell, I'd settle for a small army at this point.

"Tell me again why we thought this was a good idea?"

Emma's arms snaked around my waist, her belly pressing against me. "Because we're going to be parents soon, and we need all the practice we can get?"

I leaned into her touch. "Right. Okay. We've got this. It's just three kids. How hard can it be?"

Another crash. This time, accompanied by Ezra's voice: "Oopsie!"

Emma patted my chest consolingly. "You were saying?"

I squared my shoulders, steeling myself for battle. "Alright, let's do this."

We marched into the living room, hand in hand, ready to face whatever chaos awaited. The scene that greeted us was... well, apocalyptic might be a bit dramatic, but it wasn't far off.

My pristine white couch was now decorated with what looked like grape juice stains.

Where had she found grape juice?

Luna stood proudly next to her artwork, marker in hand. Even better, where the hell had the markers come from?

"Sparkle says purple is pretty!" she declared.

A vein throbbed in my forehead. "Luna, sweetie, we don't draw on furniture. Or walls. Or anything that's not paper, okay?"

"But Sparkle said—"

"Sparkle needs to learn some manners," Emma cut in smoothly. "How about we find some paper for you and Sparkle to draw on instead?"

While Emma dealt with our budding artist, I turned my attention to Ezra, who was suspiciously quiet. I found him in the corner, my phone in his tiny hands.

"Hey buddy, whatcha got there?" I asked, trying to keep my voice calm.

"Phone!" he exclaimed, his little fingers already smearing the screen. "Why it no work?"

"It's sleeping." I gently pried it from his grasp. "How about we play with something else?"

"Why?"

Oh boy. Here we go. "Well, because phones are for grown ups?"

"Why?"

"Because they have important information—"

"Why?"

I looked to Emma for help, but she was busy trying to convince Noah to let go of the curtains he had wrapped himself in. I was on my own.

"You know what? Great question, buddy. How about we talk about it over some snacks?"

At the mention of food, all three kids perked up. "Snacks!" they shouted.

I led our little parade to the kitchen, feeling a small sense of victory. Food. I could handle food. Right?

Wrong.

"I want cookies!" Ezra demanded.

"No, ice cream!" Luna countered.

Noah just clutched his elephant tighter and echoed, "Ice cream!"

Emma waddled in, looking amused. "How about some apple slices and peanut butter?" she suggested.

You'd think we'd offered them Brussels sprouts dipped in cod liver oil. The chorus of "No!" was deafening.

"Okay, okay," I said, racking my brain. "How about... uh... monster toast?"

Three pairs of eyes stared at me blankly.

"Toast with silly faces." I said, hoping we had enough variety in the fridge to pull this off.

To my relief, this seemed to pique their interest. As I set about gathering supplies, Emma corralled the kids at the table.

"Why monster toast?" Ezra asked.

"Because monsters are fun," I said, pulling out bread, peanut butter, banana slices, and blueberries. "And who doesn't want to eat a silly monster?"

"What if a monster eat me?" Luna asked, eyes wide.

Emma jumped in, "Then you eat it first! That's the rule with monster toast."

I grinned at her quick thinking. We made a pretty good team.

As I assembled the faces — peanut butter spread, banana slice smiles, and blueberry eyes — the kids watched in fascination. Noah clutched Ellie close, whispering something about friendly monsters.

"There we go," I announced, presenting each child with their own monster toast. "Silly faces, ready to be devoured!"

Luna giggled, immediately biting off her toast monster's

"nose." Ezra studied his intently before asking, "Why monster have blue eyes?"

"Because... uh... blue-eyed monsters are the silliest," I improvised, catching Emma's amused smirk.

As the kids munched on their monster toast, I thought we might actually get a moment of peace. But then...

"Ellie wants to swim," Noah announced solemnly.

"Swim?" Emma repeated, confused.

Before we could stop him, Noah had toddled over to the sink and was attempting to hoist his stuffed elephant into it.

"Whoa there, buddy!" I scooped him up just in time. "How about we keep Ellie dry for now? Maybe she can take a pretend swim instead?"

Noah's lower lip trembled. Oh no. Please no.

"But... but... Ellie want real swim!" he wailed.

And just like that, the fragile peace shattered. Noah's cries set off a chain reaction. Luna decided she was no longer interested in her sandwich and instead wanted to "paint" the walls with peanut butter. Ezra, not to be outdone, made another grab for my phone.

As chaos reigned once more, I caught Emma's eye across the room.

Despite the madness, she smiled. "Still think we can handle this?"

I grinned back, feeling a surge of affection for this amazing woman. "With you? I can handle anything."

And you know what? I meant it. Sure, my house was being systematically destroyed by three tiny tornadoes. Yes, I was pretty sure I had peanut butter in my hair and marker on my shirt. But watching Emma navigate this chaos with grace and humour, I couldn't help but feel excited for our own little one to arrive.

\#

As the afternoon wore on, the kids started to get restless. Luna had run out of walls to decorate, Ezra had asked "why" approximately five hundred times, and Noah was still sulking about Ellie's missed swimming opportunity.

"Okay, troops." I clapped my hands, trying to sound more confident than I felt. "Who wants to see something really cool?"

Three little heads swivelled towards me, eyes wide with curiosity.

Emma raised an eyebrow. "What are you up to?"

I winked at her. "You'll see. Follow me, munchkins!"

I led our ragtag group to the guest room, feeling a mix of excitement and nerves. As I pushed open the door, I heard Emma gasp behind me.

"Charlie, what is all this?"

The room was filled with colourful baby toys — stacks of blocks, a mini ball pit, a play kitchen, and even a tiny slide. I'd gone a bit overboard during a late-night online shopping spree last week…

And add all of that to the stuff I'd bought before…

I have a problem, okay?

"Surprise?" I said, sheepishly rubbing the back of my neck.

The kids didn't wait for an explanation. They barrelled past us, squealing with delight as they dove into their new playground.

"Blocks!" Ezra shouted, immediately starting to build a wobbly tower.

Luna made a beeline for the play kitchen. "I make cake for Sparkle!"

Even Noah perked up, todding over to the ball pit with Ellie tucked under his arm.

Emma turned to me, her eyes shining. "When did you do all this?"

I shrugged, trying to play it cool. "Oh, you know, just thought it might come in handy. For practice."

She saw right through me, of course. "For practice, huh?" She placed a hand on her belly, smiling softly. "You big softie."

I wrapped an arm around her waist, pulling her close. "Don't tell the guys."

The first time she caught a large delivery, she'd teased me but didn't ask questions. She had a glint in her eyes now that warned me that the day was coming, but what did it matter? I had more than enough money to spare, and I wanted our son to have everything he could ever want.

Including Los Angeles Stingers signed skates…

For a while, we just stood there, watching the kids play. It was chaos, sure, but a joyful kind of chaos. Ezra's tower grew taller and more precarious by the second, Luna was having an animated conversation with Sparkle about proper cake-baking techniques, and Noah was contently buried in colourful plastic balls.

"Why tower fall?" Ezra asked as his creation toppled for the third time.

I knelt beside him, picking up a few blocks. "Well, buddy, it's all about balance. See, if we put the bigger blocks on the bottom, like this..."

As I helped Ezra rebuild his tower, explaining basic engineering concepts in toddler-friendly terms, I caught Emma watching us, a soft smile on her face.

"What?"

She shook her head, still smiling. "Nothing. You're just... really good with them."

My chest tightened, but in the best possible way. "Yeah?"

She nodded, then laughed as Luna tugged on her hand.

"Auntie Emma! Try my cake!"

I watched as Emma pretended to take a bite of the plastic pastry, making exaggerated "yum" noises that had Luna giggling uncontrollably.

The next hour flew by in a blur of imaginative play. We built cities out of blocks, cooked gourmet meals in the play kitchen, and went on daring rescue missions in the ball pit. I found myself getting more and more into it, putting on different voices for each character in our make-believe games.

The brave Sir Charlie scales the treacherous mountain!" I narrated dramatically as I pretended to climb an invisible peak, eliciting shrieks of laughter from the kids.

Emma leaned against the doorframe, shaking her head in amusement. "And they say I'm the dramatic one in this relationship."

I struck a heroic pose. "I'll have you know, this is Emmy-worthy material right here."

As I went to execute a daring leap, I miscalculated. My foot caught on a stray block, and suddenly I was on the floor, surrounded by the ruins of our block city.

For a moment, there was stunned silence.

Then, Noah's little voice piped up. "Uh-oh. Charlie go boom."

And just like that, the room erupted in laughter. The kids were in hysterics, Emma doubled over, tears streaming down her face, and even I couldn't help but join in.

As our laughter died down, Emma helped me to my feet, still chuckling. "My hero," she teased, pressing a kiss to my cheek.

I pulled her close, both of us a mess of dishevelled hair and clothes stained with who-knows-what. "I love you," I murmured against her hair.

She looked up at me, her eyes sparkling. "I love you too, you big goofball."

The moment was broken by a loud yawn from Noah. He rubbed his eyes sleepily, clutching Ellie to his chest.

"I think someone's ready for a nap," Emma said softly.

But as we tried to herd the kids towards the guest bedroom we'd set up for nap time, Noah dug in his heels.

"No nap!" he wailed. "No sleep without Ellie!"

I looked at the stuffed elephant in his arms, confused. "But Noah, Ellie's right there."

He shook his head vehemently. "Not real Ellie! Want other Ellie!"

Emma and I exchanged baffled glances. "Other Ellie?" she mouthed at me.

I shrugged helplessly. "Okay, Noah," I said, kneeling down to his level. "Can you show us where you last saw the, uh, other Ellie?"

What followed was a frantic search of the entire house. We looked under couches, in cabinets, and even in the washing machine. But "other Ellie" was nowhere to be found.

As Noah's cries grew more distressed, a knot formed in my stomach. How had we lost a stuffed animal in the span of a few hours? And more importantly, how were we going to get this kid to nap without it?

"I think I found Ellie," Emma called from the back door, her voice tight.

I rushed over, Noah in my arms. My heart sank. There, floating in the middle of my pool, was a bedraggled stuffed elephant.

"Oh no," I groaned. "How did she even get out here?"

Noah's lower lip trembled as he spotted his beloved toy. "Ellie swimming?"

I looked at the pool, then at Noah's tearful face, then back at the pool. There was only one thing to do.

"Ellie's just having a little spa day," I said, setting Noah down. "But I think she's done now. Watch this, buddy."

Before I could talk myself out of it, I kicked off my shoes and dove into the pool, designer clothes and all. The cold water shocked my system, but I pushed through, swimming towards the waterlogged elephant.

As I emerged from the pool, soaking wet but triumphant, Noah's face lit up like a Christmas tree. "Ellie!" he squealed, reaching for the dripping toy.

Emma wrapped a towel around my shoulders, her eyes

dancing with a mix of amusement and admiration. "My hero," she said, her voice warm.

I grinned, water dripping from my hair. "All in a day's work, ma'am."

With "other Ellie" rescued and properly dried, Noah finally agreed to nap. As we tucked the triplets in, I couldn't help but feel a sense of accomplishment. We'd done it. We'd survived a day of babysitting three toddlers.

As the last little head hit the pillow, Emma and I practically collapsed onto the couch, exhausted but exhilarated.

"I can't believe we did it," I said, running a hand through my still-damp hair.

Emma snuggled into my side, her baby bump pressing against me. "We make a pretty good team, don't we?"

I wrapped an arm around her, pulling her close. "The best. You know, I never thought I'd say this, but I can't wait for our own little chaos-maker to arrive."

She looked up at me, her eyes shining. "Me too. Seeing you with the triplets just makes me fall in love with you even more."

As we sat there, surrounded by the aftermath of our babysitting adventure — toys strewn about, a faint smell of dirty diapers in the air, and the quiet sound of three sleeping toddlers — I realised something. This chaos, this beautiful, messy, wonderful chaos, was exactly what I wanted for the rest of my life.

I pressed a kiss to Emma's forehead, my heart full to bursting. "I love you," I whispered.

She smiled, nestling closer. "I love you too, Charlie."

\#

The sound of the doorbell jolted us from our peaceful cocoon on the couch. Emma stirred, rubbing her eyes.

"Is it time already?" she mumbled.

I glanced at my watch and groaned. "Yep. The cavalry has arrived."

We dragged ourselves to the door.

"Well, well, well," Jesse said. He wore a grin that was far too cheerful for my liking. He peered past us into the suspiciously quiet house. "I half expected to find the place in flames. Where are my little monsters?"

"Asleep," Emma replied, stifling a yawn. "Finally."

Jesse's eyebrows shot up. "You got all three of them to nap at the same time? Impressive."

I shrugged, trying to play it cool. "What can I say? We're naturals."

As if on cue, a small voice called out from the guest room. "Daddy?"

Soon enough, three sleepy-eyed toddlers stumbled into the foyer, clutching various stuffed animals and dragging blankets behind them.

Jesse knelt down, opening his arms wide. "Hey, kiddos! Did you have fun with Uncle Charlie and Aunt Emma?"

The kids nodded enthusiastically, suddenly wide awake as they regaled their father with tales of monster toast, imaginary adventures, and Ellie's swimming expedition.

As Jesse gathered their belongings, he turned to us with a knowing smirk. "So, feeling ready for parenthood yet?"

Emma and I exchanged a glance, a silent conversation passing between us.

"As ready as we'll ever be," I said, wrapping an arm around Emma.

Jesse nodded approvingly. "You two are gonna be great parents. Thanks again for watching them."

After a flurry of goodbyes and last-minute hugs, the house was finally, blessedly quiet again.

Emma and I stood in the foyer for a moment, surveying the damage. Toys strewn everywhere, mysterious stains on the carpet, and I was pretty sure I could smell a lingering scent of dirty diapers.

"Well," I said, breaking the silence. "That was..."

"An adventure?" Emma supplied, a tired smile playing on her lips.

"I was going to say chaos, but adventure works too."

We made our way back to the couch, collapsing onto it in perfect sync. Emma curled into my side, her head resting on my chest.

We sat in comfortable silence for a while, both lost in our own thoughts.

"Hey, Em?" I whispered.

"Hmm?"

"I'm really glad Finn and Abi insisted on having that second wedding."

She shifted, looking up at me with curiosity in her eyes. "Yeah?"

I nodded. "If they hadn't, I might never have met you. And that expired condom? I'm grateful for it too. It brought you back into my life when I thought I'd lost my chance."

Emma's eyes glistened with unshed tears. "Charlie..."

"I mean it." I cupped her face gently. "I know this wasn't planned, and god knows we're in for a wild ride, but there's no one else I'd rather do this with. You're it for me, Emma Sullivan."

A tear slipped down her cheek, and I brushed it away with my thumb. "You're it for me too, Charlie Delacroix," she whispered.

As I leaned in to kiss her, our unborn child kicked, the movement vibrating against my side where Emma was pressed against me. I couldn't help but laugh.

"I think someone agrees," I said, placing my hand on her belly.

Emma covered my hand with hers, intertwining our fingers. "He takes after his daddy already. Always has to have the last word."

I pulled back, surprised. "He? What happened to being so sure it's a girl?"

Emma rolled her eyes, but there was a smile playing on her lips. "I've reconsidered. No self-respecting future debutante would host nightly raves on my bladder. This has to be your son, practising dance moves for whatever wild Hollywood parties he'll no doubt attend."

I couldn't help but laugh. "Oh, so now he's my son? I see how it is. When the baby does something cute, it's your daughter. But the moment there's a 3 AM dance party, suddenly it's my son?"

"Exactly!" Emma nodded, her face completely serious for a moment before breaking into a grin. "I'm glad you understand."

We sat in comfortable silence for a few moments, both of us gently caressing her belly. The peacefulness of the moment was a stark contrast to the chaos of the day, but somehow, it felt just as meaningful.

A year ago, I had no interest in anything outside of work. The next deal, the next client, that's all that had mattered to me. Now? So much had changed. Like the fact I was covered in marker stains, reeking of baby powder, but still grinning like an idiot.

I'd dreamed up some grand gesture — a weekend getaway, a private dinner on the beach. But those plans seemed... hollow now. This moment — us, exhausted and dishevelled, but so stupidly in love — this was us.

It had to be now.

I shifted, gently moving Emma as I stood. She grumbled, her face buried in the couch cushion.

"Where are you going?" she mumbled.

I bit my lip, staying silent as I crept to the bookshelf. My fingers found the small velvet box hidden behind my prized first editions. Palms sweaty, I gripped it tight and turned to face Emma.

Her eyes remained closed, a tiny frown creasing her forehead. "If you've found more toys, I swear I'll..."

Her voice trailed off as her eyes fluttered open, landing on me. One knee on the ground, box open in my trembling hands.

Emma's eyes widened, her mouth forming a perfect 'O'. She struggled to sit up, one hand on her belly, the other clutching the couch edge.

"Charlie?" Her voice quivered.

I gulped, willing my voice to steady. No turning back now, Delacroix.

"Emma Sullivan," I started, gazing into those eyes that had knocked me sideways from day one. "A year ago, I couldn't have imagined this moment. Me, on one knee, covered in god-knows-what, proposing in a living room that looks like a toy store exploded in it."

Emma laughed, tears already welling in her eyes.

"But here's the thing — I wouldn't change a single second of it. You've turned my world upside down in the best possible way. You've made me laugh, challenged me, and shown me what real partnership looks like." I took a deep breath. "I love you more than I ever thought possible, and I want to spend the rest of my life making you as happy as you make me. Will you marry me?"

Emma's hands flew to her mouth, tears now streaming down her face. For a heart-stopping moment, she stared at me.

Then, she nodded. "Yes," she whispered. Louder, "Yes! Of course I'll marry you, you big goof!"

My hands shook as I slid the ring onto her finger. I pulled her into a kiss, pouring every ounce of love and joy I had into it.

When we finally broke apart, both laughing and crying, Emma looked down at the ring, then back at me.

"You know," she said, a mischievous glint in her eye, "if this is how you propose, I can't wait to see what you do for the wedding. Should I expect skywriters? A marching band?"

I grinned, pulling her close. "For you, my love? Nothing but the best. Although maybe we should wait until after the baby comes. I have a feeling our little dancer might steal the show."

Emma laughed, resting her forehead against mine. "I love you, Charlie Delacroix."

"And I love you, soon-to-be Emma Delacroix."

As if on cue, a tiny foot (or elbow, who could tell?) pushed against her belly where it pressed between us. We both laughed, our hands meeting over the spot.

"Well?" she asked, raising an eyebrow. "Any thoughts on the wedding, daddy-to-be?"

I pretended to consider it seriously. "How about monster toast for the reception? I hear it's all the rage with the under-five crowd."

Emma swatted my arm playfully. "Don't you dare. Although..." She paused, a soft smile spreading across her face. "Maybe we could ask Jesse's kids to be in the wedding party. After all, if it weren't for them, who knows how long you would've waited to pop the question."

I clutched my chest in mock offence. "I'll have you know I had a very elaborate plan involving skywriters, a flash mob, and possibly a trained dolphin."

"Of course you did." She nodded solemnly.

I pulled her closer, marvelling at how perfectly she fit in my arms. "In all seriousness, though," I murmured into her hair, "as long as I'm marrying you, I don't care if we do it in a palace or a drive-through chapel in Vegas."

Emma tilted her head up, her eyes shining. "Sweet talker. But let's maybe aim for something in between, yeah? I do have a reputation as a wedding planner to maintain, after all."

"Whatever you want, future Mrs Delacroix," I said, leaning in for another kiss. "Whatever you want."

This is the end of the Kings of Screen series, but don't worry I've got plenty of celebrities to keep you entertained.

❆

*W*elcome to Wales, the birth place of some of the best rock bands in history.

Over 9 steamy books, join Rhiannon and The Brightside as their bands climb to music fame — and wrestle with their personal lives along the way.

✔ Bassist Dan grapples with a surprise toddler in Enticing Mel.

✔ Persistent frontman Ryan pursues love-resistant Alys in Chasing Alys.

✔ Trapped in an elevator, Daphne clashes with her sabotaging ex-Matt in Charming Daphne

✔ Guitarist James fights for a second chance with ex-Nia in Winning Nia.

✔ Bad boy drummer Jared met his match in Defying Ella.

✔ After a drunken night in Las Vegas, Emily wakes up wearing a ring from hot rocker Owen in Needing Emily

✔ A charity date goes awry for Lily and Rhys in Braving Lily.

✔ The fallout of a drunken fling forces Alex and Ceri back together after eight years apart in Daring Ceri.

✔ And Olivia's childhood celebrity crush on Lewis turns to instalove and an impromptu Vegas wedding in Marrying Olivia.

Find all the on my website.

ALSO BY MORGANA BEVAN

True Platinum Series (Rock Star Romance)

(Rhiannon)

Chasing Alys–Ryan (Resistant to Love)

Charming Daphne–Matt (Force Proximity)

Winning Nia–James (Second Chance)

Enticing Mel–Dan (Secret Baby)

Needing Emily–Emily (Accidental Marriage/Runaway Bride)

Defying Ella - Jared (Close Proximity / Snowed-in)

(The Brightside)

Braving Lily - Lily (Opposites Attract)

Daring Ceri - Alex (Second Chance)

Marrying Olivia - Lewis (Accidental Marriage)

Craving Leah - Andy (Best Friend's Sister)

Kings of Screen Series (Hollywood Romance)

Between Takes (Enemies to Lovers)

Married Blind (Marriage of Convenience)

Acting Counsel (Close Proximity, Forbidden)

Fashionably Fake (Fake Dating)

Lights, Camera, Baby! (Accidental Pregnancy)

Sign up for Morgana Bevan's mailing list: https://morganabevan.com/mailing-list/

ABOUT MORGANA

Morgana Bevan is a sucker for a rock star romance, particularly if it involves a soul-destroying breakup or strangers waking up in Vegas. She's a contemporary romance author based in Wales. When Morgana's not writing steamy celebrity romances with gorgeous British rock stars and movie stars, she's travelling the world, searching for inspiration.

She enjoys travelling, attending gigs, and trying out the extreme activities she forces on her characters.

Find Morgana online at morganabevan.com.

Morgana's Facebook Reader Group: facebook.com/groups/498919364708263

www.ingramcontent.com/pod-product-compliance
Lightning Source LLC
Chambersburg PA
CBHW031323210726
48287CB00005B/1668